CRYING SHAME

REBEL SHAW

All Rights Reserved.

© 2022 Rebel Shaw

This book may not be reproduced in any manner whatsoever without the written permission of Rebel Shaw except for the use of brief quotations in articles and or reviews.

This book is a work of fiction. Names, characters, events, locations, businesses and plot are products of the author's imagination and meant to be used in a fictitious manner. Any resemblance to actual persons, living or dead, or actual events throughout the story are purely coincidental. The author acknowledges trademark owners and trademarked status of various products referenced in this work of fiction, which have been used without permission. The publication and use of these trademarks are not authorized, sponsored or associated by or with the trademark owners.

The following story contains sexual situations and strong language.

It is intended for adult readers.

Cover Design: Book Cover Boutique

Editing: Hot Tree Editing

Proofreading: Kara Hildebrand, Deaton Author Services, Sandra Shipman & Joanne Thompson

One

Graham

The moment I step through my front door, I feel the change. "Bri?" I holler as soon as the door closes behind me.

When she steps into the hallway from my bedroom carrying a duffle bag, I know she's leaving. "You're home early."

Tossing my keys on the entry table, I cross my arms and lean against the wall. "Going somewhere?"

The woman I've been seeing for about nine months sighs dramatically before walking over to the couch and retrieving her purse. "Yes. To my place."

Nodding, I watch as she grabs her keys and heads my way. My heart pounds, but not for the reason I expected when this moment came. She's leaving me, and while that sucks, I don't have the urge to fight for her to stay.

As if reading my mind, she declares, "That's exactly why I'm going,

Graham. This thing between us has run its course. You're so closed off and refuse to let me in any further than on the surface."

"You stay with me a couple nights a week," I argue lamely.

"No, we have sex a couple nights a week, and not even that in the last few weeks. Not the same thing. You want me here because it's comfortable, not because you need me. You don't need anyone, Graham Morgan," she counters, adjusting the strap of her bag over her shoulder. "You only need yourself."

I don't argue.

I can't.

She's not wrong.

My relationship with Brianne started off casual. She had just come out of a long-term relationship and wasn't looking for anything serious, which worked perfectly for me. I've always been into a more casual arrangement, and I thought she felt the same.

"I thought we were on the same page," I comment.

Brianne throws her hands in the air, her keys falling to the floor with a clang and her bag slipping from her arm and dropping. "We were. *Were*, being the key word there. I've been trying to take our relationship to the next level for months, and you, you've been dragging your feet ever since I brought it up. You won't even cuddle with me when we're falling asleep, Graham."

I stand up straight, hands on my hips, as I take in the woman before me. "You know I hate that shit. It's too hot, and I choke on your damn hair."

Brianne rolls her eyes. "And let's talk about you working."

I growl in frustration. "You know I'm committed to my family business. I work four days a week, open to close."

"But you wouldn't even take last Saturday off to go with me to that party at work. Do you know what it was like to be the only person in a relationship who showed up *without* a date?"

I close my eyes and rub my forehead, specifically to the spot a headache is forming. "You know my dad was out of town last weekend and I had to cover. What should I have done? Closed down the pharmacy so you didn't have to show up alone to a work function?"

"Yes!"

My eyes open and zero in on the woman I've spent the last nine months with. "Bri, you know I couldn't do that," I argue, shaking my head and trying to wrap it around what the hell is going on here.

"Listen, Graham, I like you. I *really* like you. I was fine with casually seeing each other when it was convenient for us, but not anymore. I want more, but if you're not interested in taking this to the next level, then I'm out of here. Choose." She annoyingly taps her foot on the floor as she waits. The sound of her shoe hitting the hardwood resembles the pounding in my head.

As much as I like spending time with her, I don't see it progressing past this. She's a great woman, but she's not for me. At least not in the way she's wanting. I can't offer her the ring and the family she's apparently after now.

"Bri, I'm sorry," I start, but don't get a chance to finish.

She lets out a very unladylike roar and grabs her stuff off the floor. "I'm sorry too. We had fun, but I want more. You're unable to offer me that, so I'm done," she declares, stepping past me and pulling open the front door. She whips around, meeting my gaze one last time. "Last chance, Graham."

"You're a great woman, Bri," I start again.

"Goodbye, Graham. Don't call me for a booty call," she announces, slamming the door behind her as she storms out.

I sigh deeply, lean my back against the wall, and close my eyes. I can hear her shut her car door with a little excessive force before her engine fires to life, and she peels out of the driveway like her ass was on fire. As bad as I feel, because the last thing I want to do is hurt her, I'm overwhelmed with relief. At the end of the day, she wanted to get serious, and I didn't.

I tug at the tie around my neck and pop the top button of my shirt open. It's a tradition established by my grandfather decades ago when he opened his own pharmacy in the small town of Cedar Hills, Kentucky. He always said the definition of a professional was a well-dressed man. Therefore, he wore dress slacks, a button-down, and tie to work every day. When my father followed in his footsteps, he was expected to dress professionally, as am I now.

Three generations of Morgan men, serving Cedar Hills and the surrounding communities with their pharmaceutical needs.

I head to my bedroom, noticing instantly the absence of what little personal items she usually kept here. Brianne only stayed a few nights a week, but when she did, she wanted to make sure she had her own toiletries. I never really told her to bring stuff over. She just sort of showed up one night with her own shampoo, conditioner, and body wash. From there, a few more things appeared over time, including some wax warmer thing on my dresser and a decorative towel with lace trim at the bottom.

All those items are gone now.

I strip out of my work clothes and grab a T-shirt and khaki shorts. It's mid-August, the heat and humidity slowly suffocating the life out of the Midwest, and even though it's almost eight o'clock, there's still a bit more sunlight at the end of the day. Usually, when I'm needing to burn off excessive energy or stress, I'd throw on a pair of running shorts and my favorite trainers and go for a run, but not when there's sixty-eight percent humidity outside. I wouldn't even make it to the end of the block before I was soaked with sweat and struggling to breathe.

That's part of the reason I have a full gym set up in my basement. In high school, I discovered a love for running and working out, so when I bought this house a couple of years back, my first remodel was the finished basement. Over the years, I've purchased pieces of equipment and now have it set up exactly as I want it.

But tonight, I'm not feeling it.

Instead, I grab my cell phone and fire off a text to my friend Adam.

Me: Busy tonight?

Adam: Not really. Joy is working and it's too damn hot to do anything.

I can't help but shake my head at the mention of his wife. Adam and Joy have been married three months now and are definitely still firmly in the honeymoon phase. They don't do much without the other, so the fact I might be able to steal him away for a bit is a plus.

Me: Wanna meet at Hank's for a beer?

Adam: Fuck yes. This week has blown balls. I need a drink. Or five.

Me: Hey, what you do with balls is on you, man.

Adam: Funny. *insert middle finger emoji*

Me: I thought so. Meet me in thirty?

Adam: See ya soon.

I put my phone in my pocket and head for my bathroom. I throw on an extra layer of deodorant before moving to the kitchen. As I drink a bottle of water, my stomach growls, reminding me I haven't eaten since lunch, but none of the leftovers I have in the fridge sound appealing. Instead, I'm craving some honey barbecue wings and greasy fries from the bar.

As I throw my bottle in the recycling, it's then I find my house key on the counter. I had only recently given Brianne a copy, mostly because she promised to be naked in my bed one night when I got home from work. Since, she used it to let herself in, and yes, often would fulfill her promise of being naked in bed when I arrived.

I grab the key and toss it in the drawer where I keep pens and notepads before heading out. With one quick glance at my house, I realize I'm a little disappointed to have things end with Bri, but I'm not torn up about it.

She knew the deal.

She chose to try to change it.

I drive across town to Hank's Bar and Billiards. I've been coming here since I was in high school, back when Hank would let a few of us boys come in and shoot pool after school. Even though there are a few other bars in town with more modern décor and a fancier drink menu, I choose to spend my money at Hank's.

Pulling into the lot beside the building, I make sure I have my wallet, phone and keys and head inside. Classic country pipes through the speakers, and I instantly feel a sense of calm as I breach the threshold. Ever since I turned twenty-one, I'd meet my friends here every chance we'd get. Over the years, some have moved away, and even though Adam bought a house one town over, he still meets me here whenever he can.

"Graham," Hank greets, stepping over to the barstool I slide onto and dropping a cardboard coaster in front of me. "Whatcha drinkin'?"

"Bud Light, please."

He pulls a bottle from the cooler beneath the bar, pops the top, and sets it in front of me. "Dinner?"

"A dozen wings with honey barbecue and fries," I reply, reaching for my beer and taking a big drink.

"Coming right up," he states, turning to place my order with Donna in the small kitchen.

Hank's offers burgers and fries for lunch, as well as a small bar food menu for dinner, including wings, burgers, and the occasional daily special. I spot the older woman through the small window, and she offers me a big wave. Donna's been cooking for Hank for more than two decades, working through the lunch hour, and then coming back for the three hours he offers food in the evening. She's a staple here, just as much as the old bar owner himself. In fact, for years, we assumed they were involved in a relationship, but both have assured us they're merely friends.

"Hey," Adam says, taking the stool beside mine. "You order?"

"Just did. How's Joy?"

He instantly smiles. "She's great. Filling in for someone at the hospital this evening. She should get off around nine."

Hank appears seconds later and pulls a second bottle of Bud Light from the cooler. Before he opens it, he holds it up, seeking confirmation from Adam. When my friend nods, he slides it across the bar. "Dinner?"

"Yeah. A dozen garlic parmesan with fries, please," Adam replies before reaching for his beer. "What's up with you?"

"Bri left," I announce, ripping off the proverbial Band-Aid.

"Really? Why?"

I lean against the bar, my eyes following a basketball game on the television screen. "I'm apparently emotionally unavailable."

Adam snorts a laugh. "Well, no shit. I thought you guys were okay doing the casual thing."

"Me too," I reply, taking another drink of my beer. "Bri decided she wants more. Plus, she was pretty pissed off at me last weekend when I didn't close down the pharmacy to go with her to a work thing."

Adam pulls a confused face. "That's dumb. Of course you can't just close down for that. I mean, what if some kid needed medicine or an elderly person? When you're the only pharmacy in town, you can't just lock the doors when you feel like it."

"Exactly," I state, just as Hank delivers our food.

He grabs a bottle of ketchup from another cooler and sets it between us. "Anything else? Another beer?"

"No, I'm driving. Just this one, Hank," I say, squirting a blob of ketchup on my plate.

"I'm good too," Adam adds, taking the bottle when I'm finished.

"Holler if you need anything else," Hank announces before disappearing to the opposite end of the bar.

"So now what?" my friend asks after swallowing a few fries.

"Now I just focus on work. Eight years of schooling was intense as fuck. I don't need to date." Obtaining my Doctor of Pharmacy degree was the hardest thing I've ever done, and there's no way I'm going to let my father or grandfather down.

Adam chuckles and grabs a napkin to wipe the sauce off his fingers. "No, but sex is pretty fucking nice. Usually you have to date for that."

"Not necessarily," I counter between bites of my chicken. "But the older I get, the less I'm into one-night stands or bar hookups."

"But you don't want to get serious," he states.

"I don't mind monogamy. In fact, I prefer it, but I don't understand why you have to make declarations and promises after a specific amount of time. Why not just have fun until it's not fun anymore?" I think back to how Brianne said she wasn't looking for anything serious, but over the course of our time together, changed her mind. She went from fun and casual to wanting labels and assurances.

Maybe all women are like that.

"Want me to set you up with Mindy from the city office?" Adam offers, referring to a woman a few years younger than us in school, who was just hired on as the clerk for the city. Adam is the city manager, overseeing the maintenance department in town, and shares an office with a few city officials, including the new clerk.

"Naw, I'm good. It's been like an hour since Bri left. I think I'm just gonna ride some solo time for a while."

Adam snorts, bringing his beer to his mouth. "I'll pick you up some lotion for your hand."

We eat in comfortable silence for a bit, both watching the basketball game on television. Just as he pushes his plate away, his phone rings.

"Hello?"

There's a brief pause, and then a loud voice on the other end of the line catches my attention. "Hey, hey, slow down. What do you mean?" Pause. "The ceiling fell in?" Another long pause, and before I realize it, I'm pushing away my own plate and reaching for my wallet. "Shit, okay. I'm on my way," Adam says into the phone before setting it on the bar and standing. "I gotta go."

"Joy? Is everything all right?"

Adam pulls out his own wallet and tosses a few bills on the bar. "Not Joy. Addyson."

Addyson.

His sister.

She's four years younger than him and lives not too far away in an apartment with her son, Noah. I've been around the kid a lot, thanks to my friendship with Adam, and the thought of something happening to him makes my heart stop beating. "What's wrong?" I ask, throwing too much money on the bar for my bill, but not caring to get change.

"She just got home and evidently there was some water leak in the apartment above her. Her place is trashed. Said the ceiling just caved in," he informs me, panic lacing his words. "I gotta go, man. Sorry."

"I'm going with you."

If Addyson needs help, I'm there.

Two

ddyson

My hand holding my cell phone falls to my side while the other grips my five-year-old son's tight. We're standing in the doorway of our apartment, looking at the destruction of our cozy home. Sure, our place isn't much, but it's a nice two-bedroom with good air conditioning and heat. It's in a decent neighborhood, and it's within my price range as a single mom. Right now, however, it's not livable.

"That's a big old mess," Noah says from his place beside me.

"Yeah, buddy, it is," I agree with him.

"Is Uncle Adam going to fix it?"

I peer down at him and force a smile to my lips. "No, but he is coming over." What I don't tell him is that we need a new place to live until the landlord can get this taken care of. This is the worst possible time for this to happen. School starts in two days for Noah and for me. He's starting kindergarten, and I'm teaching my first graders.

I'm glad we weren't home when this happened. It would have

freaked us both out. I was working late putting the final touches on my classroom. Then I had to drive to my parents' house, which is about fifteen miles away. They live just outside Oak Valley. Noah had to tell me all about his day with Grandma and Grandpa before we could leave, which prompted Mom into heating up leftovers to feed me dinner.

All I wanted to do was come home, give Noah a bath, get him in bed, and unwind before I did the same. Now, I have to deal with this. The entire ceiling of our apartment is now laying on the floor, along with some of my upstairs neighbors' belongings, such as their couch. It's a mess, and I'm overwhelmed.

"Oh, shit." I hear from behind me. Noah gasps, not because of the language but because of the voice.

"Uncle Adam!" He pulls away from me and rushes to the door, launching himself at my older brother.

"Hey, bud." Adam settles my son on his hip. Something he's getting way too big for me to do. "Ads, what happened?"

I sigh. "Water leak from the apartment above. I don't know for sure what happened, but something about falling asleep and the tub running over. I'm not sure."

"It would take a lot of bath water for this kind of damage," my brother's best friend, Graham, says. He steps around Adam and Noah and walks farther into the room, surveying the damage.

"Apparently, this isn't the first time this has happened. I didn't ask for more details than that. It doesn't really matter at this point. The damage is done." I take a step toward Graham, but he holds up his hand to stop me. "You shouldn't come in here," he says, looking up at the ceiling.

"None of you should be in here," a deep voice says from behind me. I turn to see my landlord, Mr. Garcia, standing just inside the door next to Adam.

"Hi, Mr. Garcia." I give him a tight smile.

"Sorry about this, Addyson. It's going to be a few weeks, maybe longer, before we can get this repaired."

I nod. I didn't need him to tell me for me to know. Any fool who sees the damage would be able to figure that out. "I figured."

"We will waive your renter's fee until you are back in your home. And you have renters insurance, correct?" he asks.

"I do." Even as a single mom, that's not an expense I was willing to skimp on. I've worked hard to provide for Noah and me. The thought of losing it all was great motivation for sending in that monthly payment for our renters insurance.

"Hopefully, that will cover a place for you to stay until then." Mr. Garcia waves, backs out of the doorway, and walks away.

"That's it?" Adam asks. "Does he not care about where you're going to stay?" He doesn't bother to hide the annoyance in his tone.

"It's not his fault, Adam. He's losing in this too. It's just a bad situation."

"Oh, no!" Noah wiggles and tries to slide out of Adam's arms, but my brother holds tight.

"What's up, little man?" he asks him.

"My backpack. It's smashed." Noah points to the living room where his brand-new backpack and matching lunch box in dinosaur print which we went to three stores to find, are now covered in ceiling plaster and flooring. "Mom!" he cries.

"I'm sorry, bud. I'll get you a new one."

"But we looked forever for that one." Big tears well in his eyes, and I hate that I can't promise him that I'll get him the exact same bag and lunch box. School starts in two days, and I'm not sure I'll be able to find them, let alone have the time to shop for them with the mess that is our living situation.

"I know. I'm sorry. I'll try my best to get you the same set. We might have to settle for something else just to get us started, and then I can try and find them for you."

"Stupid ceiling." Noah tilts his head back and glares at the ceiling that's no longer there.

My son, an only child, is very bright for his age. I'm not just saying that because I'm biased. He's my best friend, my sidekick, and there are often times he talks well beyond his five years of age.

"Hey, bud, your mom's doing the best she can," Adam tells him.

"I know. She loves me a whole bunch," Noah replies, and my heart swells in my chest.

"What do you need from me?" Adam asks.

"Can you watch him while I sift through the rubble and pack us a bag? I need to call Mom and Dad and see if we can stay with them, I guess."

"I wish you could stay with me, but our place is a Cracker Jack box. I don't know why I let Joy talk me into moving into her place while we search for a house," Adam grumbles. "At least my apartment was a two-bedroom."

"I know why," Graham mumbles under his breath, and I grin.

I know why too. My brother is head over heels in love with his new wife. There isn't anything that Joy could ask for that Adam wouldn't try like hell to give her.

"Can I still ride the bus like a big boy?" Noah asks.

I wince. Even though I work at the school, all Noah has talked about is riding that damn school bus. When he begged me to let him ride the cheese wagon instead of riding to school with me, I agreed. The smile on his face and his little victory dance around our small living room were well worth the concession. However, living with my parents that's not going to be possible since they live outside the district. Just more bad news I get to deliver.

"Hey, why don't you get Uncle Adam to take you down to the swing set. I'll pack us some clothes, and we'll go back to Grandma and Grandpa's and have a sleepover."

"Am I going to get to ride the bus?" Noah asks.

I exhale a deep breath. "I'm sorry, Noah. The bus that goes to your school doesn't come to Grandma and Grandpa's house."

He turns to look at my brother, who is still holding him on his hip. "Does my bus come to you, Uncle Adam?"

Adam's eyes widen as they seek mine for help. "Noah, Uncle Adam and Aunt Joy don't have the place for us to stay with them. We wouldn't have anywhere to sleep."

"We can sleep with them like I do when I spend the night. Right, Uncle Adam?" Noah asks.

"Sorry, bud. I think my queen-size bed is a little small for four people."

"Graham, does my bus come by your house?" Noah asks.

"Yeah, bud, I think so." Graham looks to me for guidance, and I nod. Graham lives close, so yeah, he's in the same district.

"Do you have a bed big enough that me and my mom can sleep at your house? I'm real tiny. I could sleep on the couch."

My heart cracks wide open for my sweet boy. He's been looking forward to this day since I signed him up for kindergarten in the spring. I hate that he's missing out on this. I know in the grand scheme of life, this is small, but I still hate to disappoint him. I'm busting my ass to provide for him, to give him all the love a mom and dad could give him. My parents as well as my brother and new sister-in-law are incredible, and they help me so much. Some days are still harder than others, knowing that I'm the sole hug giver as well as a disciplinarian to my sweet boy. Sometimes I wish I had someone outside my parents and my brother and his new wife to lean on. A partner who will always be by my side in this journey of life.

"I can do one better," Graham tells him. "I have extra bedrooms that both have beds. One for you and one for your mom."

"Really? 'Cause Mom can sleep with you, and I can sleep on the couch," he reminds him.

Graham's eyes, blue like a summer sky, find mine. A shiver races through me, but I work hard not to let it show. Graham has been my brother's best friend since they were kids. Probably Noah's age. I was too young to remember—being four years younger than the two of them. What I do remember is that Graham has always been there.

I went through my stage of having a crush on him, but I never told a soul. Well, my best friend, Tosha. She's my Graham in the sense that I can't ever remember a time in my life when Tosha wasn't by my side. When I found out I was pregnant, I knew I needed to leave my schoolgirl crush behind. I was twenty-four years old, holding on to a fantasy, when my world tipped on its axis. I was suddenly going to be a single mom. I didn't have time for crushes on my brother's best friend, especially one that sees me as a little sister. I was going to be a mom.

However, there are still times, like this one, where those blue eyes of his hold me captive and those feelings I harbored for him all those years come rushing back with a vengeance.

"Yeah, bud, I'm sure. I have plenty of room for both of you."

"Graham, I can't let you do that." Not only can I not inconvenience him, but I'm also not sure my libido can handle living with him, no matter how temporary it is. The last man I was with was Noah's sperm donor, and yeah, not sure I could handle it.

"It's a great idea," Adam chimes in. "He has that big-ass house."

"Uncle Adam, that's a bad word," Noah reminds his uncle helpfully.

"Remind me to put a dollar in the swear jar," Adam says, turning his attention back to me. "You would save on gas, and Noah can ride the bus."

"Yes!" Noah throws his little fist into the air.

"Adam," I hiss.

"He's right," Graham tells me. "I have the space, and Noah could ride the bus."

"I don't want to impose."

"It's not an imposition if you're invited."

"You're a guy. I'm sure that the last thing you want is for a single mom and her kid to move into your house. You heard Mr. Garcia. He doesn't really know how long it's going to take to repair all of this. I'm sure there are insurance hoops to jump through, then finding a contractor. It could be more than just a couple of weeks."

"Addyson."

The way he says my name in his deep voice, all commanding like, sends a rush of heat between my thighs. "Graham." I place my hands on my hips and give him my perfected mom glare, but all he does is smile.

"You and Noah are staying with me. Tell me what you need, and I'll get it for you." He motions to the disaster that is my apartment.

"The swear jar, my backpack, and lunch box, 'cause my mom can fix things, and my dinosaur blanket, and jammies, and clothes, and…" Noah taps his chin. "Oh, my dinosaur book. Mommy reads it to me every night."

Graham smiles at Noah. "Sure thing, little man."

"I'm going to take him down to the swings." Adam nods to Noah. "We'll meet you two down there." With that, he turns, leaving me alone with Graham.

"Are you sure about this?" I ask Graham.

"Addyson, the decision is made. Now, tell me where I can find the list of things that Noah asked for, and be thinking of what you need."

"I can get it." I take a step, and Graham, with his quick reflexes, steps in front of me, his chest bumping into mine. He stares down at me, his blue eyes filled with an emotion I can't name.

"It's not safe," he says, tucking my hair behind my ear. "Just tell me what you need and where I can find it."

"I'm going to need clothes. I don't really want you going through my underwear drawer."

"You don't have a choice," he says, not bothering to step back. "Not like it's something I've never seen."

I hate that I want to kiss the smirk off his too handsome face. "Fine."

"Good girl," he rumbles in that deep sexy voice of his.

I spend the next ten minutes directing him to the supplies Noah asked for, even the stupid swear jar. I swear that kid has more cash than any of us because of that jar.

"That should be good for Noah."

"I grabbed extra clothes, just in case."

"Thank you."

"Now you."

"Right. I'm going to need something to sleep in, a bra, panties, clothes for tomorrow. I can come back and get more later."

"No."

"What do you mean no?" I ask, my eyes trailing him as he sets down the trash bag he grabbed from under the kitchen sink that's now full of the items Noah asked for.

"It's too dangerous, Addyson."

"Because I'm a woman?"

"No. Because you're you."

"What's that supposed to mean?"

He blows out a breath. "Nothing. Just tell me what you need."

"Stubborn," I mutter.

He grins. "List, Addyson."

"Fine."

I watch as he pulls another trash bag from his back pocket. "I'm ready."

"Top two dresser drawers are bras and panties. The third drawer down is pajamas. I need something to wear tomorrow. The dresser on the left of the room has shorts and T-shirts. Just grab me whatever."

"What about work?"

"I'm going to have to come back. I'll have my dad or Adam come back tomorrow. I need to get Noah more clothes for school too."

"I can bring you back."

Instead of arguing with him, I continue with my list. "I have a cell phone charger plugged in beside the bed, and my Kindle charger should be plugged into the same outlet. In the bathroom, I need... everything. Just grab everything out of the shower, and as far as makeup goes, I'll just pick up new." I'm already mentally going through my finances. It helps that I'm not going to have to pay rent, but I'm essentially homeless.

Fifteen minutes later, Graham walks out of my room with two stuffed trash bags. He picks up the bag for Noah and nods toward the door. "We can come back tomorrow. Let's get you home. I'm sure it's past Noah's bedtime."

"Thank you, Graham." His reply is another nod as he steps outside and waits for me to lock up, then follows me down the hall. "I can take one of those."

"I'm fine, Addyson. Go get your boy. I'll put them in my truck."

With a nod, I head to where Adam and Noah are hanging out by the small swing set. "We're good to go," I tell Adam. "Noah, come on, we need to get going." To my surprise, he doesn't complain.

"Uncle Adam, can I have a piggyback ride?" Noah asks.

"Sure, bud." Adam bends down. "Hop on."

Five minutes later, with a wave to my brother, I'm pulling out of the lot, with Graham right behind me. I don't know if he thinks I forgot how to get to his place or what, but I'm too exhausted mentally to worry about it.

"Night, sweetie." I lean over and kiss Noah on the forehead. "Sweet dreams."

"Sweet dreams," he says as he snuggles under the covers. "This bed is huge."

I smile at my sweet boy. "Then you should sleep like a king." I bop his nose with my index finger. "I'm just across the hall if you need me," I remind him.

"I know, Mom. I'm a big boy in a big-boy bed, and I get to ride the bus like a big boy. I'm five, remember?" he rambles.

"I remember. I love you."

"Love you too." I pull the door closed, just leaving a gap in case he needs me.

"He good?" Graham asks. He's standing in the hallway. Arms crossed over his chest, legs crossed at his ankles, he's leaning against the wall.

"He is. Thank you for this, and grabbing the nightlight. That was genius. I should have thought about that."

He nods. "I remember you mentioning he likes to sleep with it."

I'm surprised, but I shouldn't be. Graham is always around. "I'm going to unpack and go to bed myself. Noah is an early riser. We'll try not to wake you."

"It's fine." He waves off my concern. "I'm taking tomorrow off."

"You are?"

"Yeah. I called Dad on the way here. It's fine. I want to help you get whatever it is that you and Noah are going to need while you're here."

"I can't ask you to do that."

"You didn't." He holds my gaze for what feels like hours when in reality, it's a few seconds at best. "This is my room." He points to the door behind him. "You come to me if you need me."

"Thank you."

He stands to his full height and walks toward me. I'm shocked when he leans down and presses his lips to my temple. "Night, Addy."

My breath stalls in my lungs as I watch him walk away and disappear behind his door. Finally, pulling oxygen into my lungs, I do the same. Grabbing both trash bags, I dump them out on the floor to start sifting through my options. To my surprise, Graham did a great job. He even grabbed my makeup, my hair dryer, and my flat iron, and my shower stuff is in another trash bag. I pick up a pair of sleep shorts and gasp. Underneath lies my purple vibrator. This is definitely not something I asked for, and it was in my nightstand drawer.

I don't know how I feel about Graham packing my vibrator for me, but I can't dwell on what's done. Besides, it's waterproof, and after the day I've had, I could use the release. Grabbing my pajamas and my purple friend, I head to the en suite bathroom.

Three

Graham

I'm so damn hard, it hurts to think.

I've been that way since the moment I opened her nightstand, looking for anything else she may need, like glasses, a paperback, medication, anything, only to discover that fucking purple vibrator.

Fucking. Purple. Vibrator.

Now that Noah is sleeping in the second guest room and Addy is getting settled in the other, I'm able to lock myself in my room and take my first real breath since we arrived at the scene of her trashed apartment.

I know this isn't the first water leak, not by the state of the rotten floorboards and beams that used to hold drywall and insulation between the two floors. Clearly, the resident above Addy has had trouble with falling asleep and leaving the water running before.

With a sigh, I strip off my T-shirt, shorts, and boxers, leaving them in a pile on my floor, and head for the bathroom. I step into the shower, not even bothering to let the temperature adjust as I crank on the water. It's freezing cold, but I don't move. I stand under the spray and let the frigid water seep into my bones, praying it works its magic on one particular *bone*.

It doesn't, of course.

My dick is unable to forget the sight of her vibrator laying in the drawer. He's unable to stop picturing her using it late at night when the rest of the world around her sleeps. He's unable to stop picturing her using it *in our presence*.

That's not going to happen.

I've never thought of Addy that way.

I mean, sure, she's always been pretty—gorgeous, even, with her big brown eyes and curves that could make a grown man drop to his knees and beg—but I've never looked at her any other way than as Addyson, my closest friend's little sister. She was always there, in the background. Wherever Adam went, she was usually not too far off.

But now...now that I've seen that fucking purple vibrator, which had some settings on it I'd love to help her explore, I'm thinking about her differently. I see the stunning woman she's become with full, kissable lips and an ass made for the palm of my hands.

"Fuck," I growl, hating myself a little for the thoughts and images in my mind. Adam would kick my ass if he knew I was hard as stone, standing under the cold water, and thinking about using a vibrator on his sister.

I turn the knob, grateful for the warmth that rushes from the showerhead. The water washes over me and slides down my body as I reach down and grip my cock. Pleasure courses through my veins, my balls heavy with desire. I close my eyes, slowly stroking myself from root to tip, all while picturing that damn purple vibrator.

Seeing it sliding inside Addy's pussy.

Watching as she buries it so deep in her, she shakes and cries out when her orgasm rips through her limbs.

I cry out myself, my balls drawing up tightly against my body. My spine tingles as I come hard, shooting my release all over my shower wall. The air is heavy as I greedily suck it into my lungs, trying to get my heart rate under control again.

It isn't until I sag against the cold tile walls that guilt sweeps in. I can't believe I just did that to images of Addy, but fuck. What man would be able to *not* think about her using her vibrator?

Not me, apparently.

I'm too weak.

I grab my shampoo and roughly lather my hair. When it's rinsed clean, I do the same with body wash, scrubbing myself from head to toe, as if I can somehow wash the images and guilt associated with seeing them from my head. It doesn't work, of course.

"She's here because she needed help, dumbass," I grumble, finishing my shower.

Grabbing a towel, I dry off and vow to forget this entire jerk session ever happened. The last thing she needs is for me to be lusting after her. She's here because I'm her friend, and she and her son need help.

Period.

That's what I keep repeating, over and over, as I slip into my bed and pray sleep finds me.

Something wakes me from restless sleep. I lie still, surrounded by silence and listening. It takes almost another minute, but I hear it again. The sound is distant, like it's coming from my kitchen, and before I can stop myself, I'm up and moving. I toss on a pair of boxers and pull open my bedroom door.

The hallway is silent as I slowly step out and tiptoe toward the front of the house. I can see the lock still engaged on the front door, but I head that way to double-check. That's when I hear the noise again, followed by a whispered, "Shit."

I move in the direction of the noise and flip on the light, only to find Addy standing by the counter, doing what can only be described as wrestling with a jar of pickles. She startles the moment the lights flip on and nearly drops the jar in her hand. "Jesus, Graham. You scared the shit out of me," she whisper-yells, placing one hand over her heart.

"What are you doing, Addy?" I ask, joining her at the counter and reaching for the jar in her hand.

"Oh, I, uh, couldn't sleep and thought I'd raid your pantry for a snack. You keep horrible midnight snacks, by the way."

I snort a laugh and open the pickle jar with a twist.

"Figures. I've been trying to get that open for about five minutes. I tried running it under water, tapping the rim of the lid on the counter, which was probably a little louder than intended. I'm sorry if I woke you," she says, offering me a smile that lights up her makeup-free face.

I open my mouth to respond, to tell her it's all right, but I notice her outfit, and suddenly my brain processes the vision in front of me. Addy is standing there in the skimpiest pair of satin shorts and something that should probably be classified as a tank top but looks more like lingerie to me.

And no bra.

She's not wearing a damn bra.

Can't be with the way her nipples are suddenly pebbled against the flimsy material.

My mouth salivates with anticipation of one little taste.

"Thank you," she whispers, drawing my eyes up to meet her own gaze. There's a fire dancing within those brown orbs, one that seems to ignite the desire swirling deep in my gut.

I step forward until I'm directly in front of her, invading her personal space and breathing in her intoxicating sweet scent. She gazes up at me and reaches for the jar. Our fingers brush as she grips the pickles and finishes removing the lid, tossing it onto the counter. With her eyes locked on mine, she reaches in and pulls out a single spear, bringing it to her lips. Juice pools on her lips, a single drip sliding down her chin. My hands flex to keep from touching her, my tongue tingling to swipe that moisture from her skin.

And I hate pickles.

Our slightly labored breathing mixes with the audible crunch of her biting down on the pickle spear. Addy's little tongue snakes out, licking the wetness off her lip before she chews her snack. The moment she swallows, I ask, "Good?"

The corner of her mouth turns upward. "Delicious. Want some?"

Fuck yes.

Except it's not exactly what I was referring to when she holds up the pickle to my mouth. I take a small bite, the bitter vinegar taste sitting heavily on my tongue as I chew and swallow.

"I thought you hated pickles," she states, her eyes dancing with laughter.

"I do."

"Then why are you eating one?"

I lift a single shoulder and take the jar, setting it on the counter beside her. "Just trying to see what the big deal was. You seemed very... *delighted* with your bite."

"I was delighted. It was very... refreshing." Addy looks up, daring me to make a move. I can see it in her eyes—the desire mixed with challenge.

My hands move to her hips, lifting and gently setting her on top of the counter. As I step between her open legs, I spy the creamy flesh of her thighs dangerously close to her panty line, and I have to bite back my groan. When I place my hands on the counter beside her hips, it brings my face closer to her own. She smells like vanilla and pickles, something I never would have thought I'd be attracted to, but here I am, sporting a hard-on no pair of boxers could conceal.

I lean forward, our lips so fucking close. "Addy," I whisper, closing my eyes.

"Graham," she responds, her warm breath tickling my lips.

Fuck, I'm going to kiss her.

I'm going to kiss Adam's sister, and she wants it.

I can *feel* it.

"Mom?"

Like a bucket of ice water, Noah's voice slices through the thick sex-infused air. I jump back like I've been burned and turn, wincing when I realize I'm sporting a massive woody and probably flashing it to a child. Fortunately, Noah's not there.

Addy jumps off the counter and practically sprints to the doorway. "I'll be right there, Noah!" she hollers before spinning around to face me. She's wearing her nerves and embarrassment on her face as she adds, "I'm sorry. I—"

"No, I'm sorry, Addy. I'll put the pickles away. Go take care of Noah," I insist, turning away and reaching for the jar.

She doesn't leave, at least not right away, and I wonder if she's going to say something. What do you say? I shouldn't have practically mauled her the way I did. I shouldn't want to kiss her. I shouldn't be so fucking turned on right now, I can barely see straight.

I shouldn't want her.

But I do.

I place the jar in the fridge and flip off the light, slowly making my way back to my room. I can hear Addy's soft voice through the crack of the bedroom Noah's staying in, and even though I want to knock, want to go in and make sure they're okay, I don't. She knows where to find me if she needs something.

Closing my door, I climb back into bed and sigh. My erection has subsided, thanks to Noah, but I can still feel a crazy amount of desire coursing through my veins. All I can do is hope I wake up tomorrow and this feeling will be completely gone. The last thing I need is to pop a boner every time she gets near because I can't stop picturing her in those damn pajamas.

If you can even call them that.

I roll over, punch my pillow a few times in an attempt to get comfortable, and try to relax. Problem is, I'm not sure I'll ever truly relax again. Not with Addy under the same roof.

One thing's for certain, I'll never be able to look at a jar of pickles the same again.

"Graham!"

My face breaks out into a big grin the moment I step into the kitchen. "Hey, No," I reply, ruffling his shaggy sandy-blond hair.

"Mom made cheesy eggs," he proclaims, holding up his fork and dropping the yellow eggs back onto his plate.

"I see that. Are they good?"

He nods emphatically, scooping the eggs once again with his fork and shoving them in his mouth.

Glancing over at Addyson, I find her looking everywhere but at me. In fact, she seems very interested in her cup of coffee. "Good morning."

Over her cup, her brown eyes meet mine, a light pink coloring her cheeks. "Morning." She holds my gaze for several seconds before clearing her throat. "Uhh, I hope you don't mind. I made some eggs for Noah. There's some left in the skillet on the stove."

Pouring myself a cup of coffee, I reply, "I don't mind at all, Addy. Anything here is yours."

"I'm going to go grocery shopping after work today, so I'll replenish what we've used."

Turning to face her, I lean back against the counter and study her. She's wearing black capris and a light blue top. She's wearing sensible flats and her sandy-blonde hair is hanging loosely around her face. "Why don't I go shopping for you today? It's one less thing you have to worry about when you get off?"

She seems startled by the offer. "Oh, that's not necessary, Graham."

Coffee in hand, I head over and take the seat across from her at the kitchen table. "It is. I took today off, so I'm available to help. Let me help, Addy."

Once again, she seems completely off kilter by my offer. I know she receives help every now and again. I've been friends with her brother long enough to know being a single mom is incredibly difficult. She relies on her parents, brother, and sister-in-law every so often to watch Noah. "I can give you money."

Taking a drink of my coffee, I relish the burn sliding down my throat from the too-big gulp. "Just a list of some of the things you'd like."

Her gorgeous eyes narrow. "You're not buying our groceries."

"Why not?"

She scoffs. "Because!"

"What's the plan for today?" I ask, changing the subject.

"I'm going to Grandma's," Noah informs me, his mouth full of eggs.

"Don't talk with your mouth full," Addy reminds her son before turning her attention back to me. "I have Teachers' Institute to prep for the first day of school tomorrow." She glances at the watch on her delicate wrist. "Shoot, we gotta get going, Noah. I have to run you all the way to Grandma's," she adds, jumping up and taking her dirty dishes to the sink.

"Leave them. I can clean up." And then another idea hits me. "Why don't you leave Noah here with me today?"

"What?" she asks, spinning around to face me. "I can't ask you to do that."

"You're not. I offered."

"But—"

"No, buts. It'll save you time from running all the way to your parents' house." When she seems hesitant, I go for the kill. "Hey, No? You wanna stay with me today? We can go do some shopping for your mom, and maybe stop by Adam's office and bother him."

"Yes! Can I, Mom?" His wide, hopeful eyes turn toward Addy.

I can tell she's caving as she smiles down at him. Then, those soulful brown eyes turn to me. "Are you sure?"

"Absolutely. I wouldn't have offered if I wasn't sure, Addy. I promise we'll be fine."

She glances down at her watch before hesitantly replying, "Okay, but only if you let me take care of dinner tonight."

"Deal," I state, a bubble of excitement spreading through my chest. The anticipation of coming home and having dinner with her and her son is surprisingly welcoming.

Addy looks down one last time at her watch. "I guess I should get going."

"Text me a grocery list."

"I really can stop after work."

"And I really can take care of it this afternoon for you. Text me, Addy."

She gives a hesitant nod and turns to Noah. "You're okay with staying with Graham today?" she asks quietly, searching her son's face for any hint of hesitancy.

The little boy nods insistently. "I'll be good, Mom. Promise."

She gives him a small smile and kisses his forehead. "I'm sure you will be. Make sure you listen and use your manners."

Noah agrees readily and dives back into his eggs.

"If you need anything, just text me. Since there are no students in the classrooms, I'm able to check my phone more often, and if you have any problems, I can have my mom come over and get him."

"We'll be fine, Addy. Go."

She nods. "I'll go grab my purse and leave his booster seat in the garage. I should be home around three."

"Sounds good." My eyes automatically go her ass as she bends down to give Noah another kiss before hurrying off to gather her things. A few minutes later, I hear the front door close, and I'm left looking after a five-year-old for the day.

"Hey, Graham?" Noah asks, looking up at me from his seat.

"Yeah, buddy?"

He looks nervous as he shifts in his chair. "Do you think we can look for a new backpack and lunch box?"

Crouching down next to his chair, I ruffle his hair and give him a small smile. "Absolutely. Let's go find you a dinosaur backpack."

He gives me a big, toothy grin as he jumps down, takes his dirty plate over to the sink, and races off to find his shoes. Suddenly I find myself smiling as well. Spending the day with Noah wasn't how I planned to spend my impromptu day off, but it might be better. The thought of seeing excitement and happiness on his face puts a little extra spring in my step and an eagerness to find him exactly what he's looking for, despite how hard a task that might be.

We have a backpack to find.

Four

ddyson

It's nearly noon, and I've not been as productive today as I had hoped. The first few hours of the morning were occupied by a Teachers' Institute meeting. When that ended, I came to my classroom to finish setting up for tomorrow, but my mind has been wandering. I'm starting to act like my first graders staring off into space.

Shaking out of my thoughts, I get busy taping each of my students' names on their desks. We can move them around later if needed, and that's always needed. I'm just taping on the last name when I hear Noah's voice entering my classroom.

"Mom!" He runs into my arms while I'm still crouched down and almost knocks me over.

"Hey, bud. What are you doing here?"

"We're running errands, and I showed Graham my school and your work and we bought lunch."

"You mean I bought lunch." Graham chuckles. "Let your mom up, No." He ambles toward us with a lazy grin tilting his lips.

He looks hot as hell today in a pair of faded blue jeans and a T-shirt that does nothing but show off what he's hiding underneath. Trust me on this, I got up close and personal with all that is Graham Morgan last night, and that T-shirt of his and those faded blue jeans do not do the man justice.

Noah steps back, allowing me room to stand, but I stumble over the chair behind me. Graham reaches out and wraps his arm around my waist, saving me from falling on my ass. A fresh woodsy scent wraps around me, and involuntarily, I lean in a little closer. Tilting my head back, I peer up at him. "Thank you."

"You're welcome." His voice is deep and husky and reminds me of last night when he gripped my hips and sat me on the counter. It's sad that our late-night interlude is one of the hottest moments of my life.

"What are you two doing here?" I ask Graham.

"We went to the apartment and grabbed a few bags of things for you two, then we went grocery shopping and dropped it all off at my place. We were starving, and when we drove past the school, my man Noah and I decided that bringing you lunch was a solid plan, so here we are."

"Thank you. You didn't have to do that," I tell Graham as Noah hands me a small bag with the logo of a local fast-food joint on the side, making my stomach growl and Noah howl with laughter.

"Your belly is angry." He giggles.

"It's a good thing you brought food then, huh?" I ask, running my fingers through his hair. "Did the two of you already eat?"

"We did," Graham answers. "We still have a lot of errands to run, so we can't stay."

"Yeah. We gots jobs to do." Noah pushes his chest out and stands just a little taller. Tears well in my eyes. He's having the best day, and I have Graham to thank for that.

"It's have jobs to do, not gots. Why don't you go write your name on the board while I talk to Graham for a minute?"

"Okay, but don't forget we have jobs to do," he says, skipping off to the dry erase board in my office.

"Thank you for taking such great care of him today, and for lunch, and groceries, and my apartment. I don't know how I will ever repay you."

Graham steps in close and tucks my hair behind my ear. "He's a great kid, Addy. That's all because of you. As for repaying me, that's already been done."

"What? What are you talking about?"

"I get to see you every day. I get to hang out with Noah, and if I'm lucky, maybe you'll reward me with the task of opening more pickle jars." He winks.

My face flames. "I'm sorry about that," I say, looking down, trying to hide my embarrassment.

I feel the slight pressure of his index finger beneath my chin. Lifting my head, I peer into his deep blue eyes. "You have nothing to be sorry for, Addy. And before you get into your own head, let me just say that I want you and Noah to stay with me. You're not a burden or an inconvenience, and anytime you need me to... open your pickles, you know where to find me." He drops his hand and takes a step back. It's probably because the beating of my heart is too loud, and he needs to get away from the deafening sound.

"Noah, we've got more errands to do. Come give your mom a kiss."

Noah happily skips over, and I bend to give him a hug and a kiss. "Bye, Mommy."

"Bye, sweetie." I stand and once again focus on Graham. "Thank you for today."

He nods. "What's that?" He nods toward a plastic grocery store bag sitting on my desk.

"Oh, well, my bag that I carry back and forth was covered in water, and plaster from the ceiling, so, grocery bag it is." I laugh it off because what else can you do in this impossible situation.

"We're going to grab more of your things from the apartment. Anything specific you need us to get?"

My face flames and there is no hiding it from him. "Just clothes." I shrug.

"Is purple your favorite color?" he asks, licking his lips.

"W-What?" I ask, stumbling over my words.

Instead of replying, he smirks. "I'll see you at home later." With a wave, he scoops Noah up, tossing him over his shoulder. Their combined laughter follows them out of my classroom and down the hall.

As for me? I drop into one of the way-too-small chairs and bury my face in my hands. I don't know what's gotten into me or into him, but I think I like it.

Walking into Graham's house just after four, I'm greeted by the smell of something delicious filling the air. It's on the tip of my tongue to yell out "Honey, I'm home," but that would make things even more awkward between us. At least, that's how I think it would go. The last twenty-four hours have proven that I truly have no clue. And apparently my new roommate doesn't know how to make a deal. I was supposed to handle dinner tonight.

"Mommy!" Noah cheers as I step into the kitchen. "We made sketti." He holds up a fork full of spaghetti noodles before shoving a messy bite into his mouth.

"I see that. It looks delicious."

"Sit." A deep, commanding voice that fills my dreams speaks out.

"What can I do to help?" I ask, moving to the sink to wash my hands and ignoring his command to sit.

"You can get off your feet after working all day and eat something."

I open my mouth to argue and find that I don't want to. Not with Graham. Instead, I take a risk. It takes me four steps to reach him, where he's standing near the stove. I stop next to him, place my hand on his arm, and rise on my toes to kiss his cheek. "Thank you for today and for dinner."

As I drop back to my heels, he clears his throat and gives me a stiff nod. "I'll make you a plate."

I walk to the table, take a seat next to Noah, and offer him a napkin for his sauce-covered face. Although I know it's no use. He's going to be a mess by the time he's done. "How was the rest of your day?" I ask him, just as Graham sets a place of spaghetti and garlic bread in front of me. I look up to say thank you just as he leans in, and his lips land on the corner of my mouth. I suck in a shocked breath, but it doesn't seem to faze him.

"Eat." The single word is whispered huskily and causes a rush of heat to pool between my thighs.

I don't understand what's going on here. I've managed to spend time with Graham over the years for long periods of time, and nothing like this has ever happened. Hell, we vacationed together with my brother before I had Noah. I'm a mom now. I can't go around flirting with my crush from when I was a damn teenager, and I most definitely should not be doing it in front of my son.

"We have lots of our stuff," Noah says, pulling my eyes from Graham to him.

He doesn't seem the least bit concerned that Graham's lips were just so close to mine. Me on the other hand, my lips are tingling, and even though I know I shouldn't, I can't help but wonder what the full press of his lips on mine would feel like.

"What kind of stuff?" I manage to ask with a steady voice.

"We have food, and lots of bags from home, and—" he says, but Graham cuts him off.

"No, eat your dinner, and then we can show and tell your mom about our day." To my surprise, Noah gives him a wide grin and goes back to shoveling food into his mouth.

I turn to look at Graham, who is sitting at the table with his own plate of food. "I don't know how you managed that. Some nights I can hardly get him to stop talking to eat before his food gets cold."

A slow smile spreads across his face, and this time it's not pointed at me but at my son. "Noah knows he has to eat all his meals to grow big and strong, right, bud?"

"Yep." Noah bobs his little head up and down. "I'm going to be big like Graham and Uncle Adam. But I have to eat all my food."

"I've been telling you that for your entire life." I laugh. I glance over at Graham and mouth, "Thank you," and he nods. This time the smile is mine, and I wish I had my phone close to take a picture to remember it. To remember this moment. I'm letting my mind get ahead of me, but it's hard not to. Graham has always been a... craving. Now here I am with my son, having dinner that Graham made, and he's teaching my son life lessons, and I can't help but wonder what it would have been like had Graham been Noah's father. I know that's not what this is, and I would never change my son for a single second, but this is... nice.

"All done," Noah announces proudly.

"Great job," I praise him when I see his plate is empty. "Let's get you cleaned up, and then I'll do the dishes while you and Graham relax."

"I'll do the dishes." Graham stands and begins to gather them. "You go take care of my man, Noah, and then we're all three going to relax."

I want to argue with him, but the sound of "relaxing" with Graham has me nodding instead. "Thank you for dinner and for watching Noah today. I appreciate it very much."

"You're welcome, Addy."

He walks to the sink and begins to rinse and load the dishes into the dishwasher. "Come on, you, it's bath time."

"Ah, man, do I have to? I wanted to show you all the stuff."

"Noah." I hear Graham's deep voice. We both turn to face him. "We can't show your mom until you're clean. You have spaghetti all over you. We don't want to dirty anything up."

"Oh." Noah's mouth forms the perfect O, and he nods. "Let's go, Mommy." He grabs my hand and pulls me down the hall to the bathroom.

Twenty minutes later, Noah is clean and in his pajamas. He races down the hall to the living room and jumps on the couch next to Graham, who just smiles at him.

"No jumping on furniture," I remind him.

"Oops." Noah places his hand over his mouth.

"So, tell me all about your day," I prompt Noah, trying to give him all my attention.

"We went shopping and bought lots of food, and we went home, and Graham made me deputy, and I got to sit by the door and make sure no one came in while he put our stuff in bags."

"Thank you for doing that. I had planned on going over this weekend."

"It was better we did it. I made sure Noah stayed by the door and was safe the entire time," he assures me.

"I trust you." Three words that I feel in my soul. I know without a shadow of a doubt that Graham would never allow anything to happen to Noah.

"Then, we went to see you, and our old house, and then we went shopping." Noah bounces on his knees, where he sits on the couch next to Graham, and it's on the tip of my tongue to tell him to sit still, but it's the matching smile on their faces that has me clamping my mouth shut.

"Can I show her now?" Noah asks.

"Yeah, bud. It's in my bedroom." Like a bolt of lightning, Noah darts off the couch and down the hall. The pitter-patter of his little feet fade and reappear before I can think of what to say to Graham.

"Mommy, you have to close your eyes," Noah says, standing just at the edge of the hallway with both arms behind his back. He's dancing on the balls of his feet, his little body radiating with excitement.

"They're closed," I assure him as my eyes fall shut.

"Open!" Noah cheers, not seconds later.

Feeding off his excitement, I open my eyes and stare at what he's holding. Instantly my eyes well with tears as I glance over at Graham. He's watching Noah with a smile on his face. He must feel my stare because his eyes slide to mine, and his expression changes from one of happiness to hesitant.

"See, Mommy. It's just like my other one. And the matching lunch box too!" Noah is still bouncing, and I'm on the verge of tears.

"I see that," I say, swallowing thickly. My gaze goes back to Graham. "I don't know where you found it, but thank you. I'll pay you back. I—Thank you, Graham."

"Took us a few tries, but we came out victorious, right, No?"

"Yep," Noah says proudly.

"Hey, Noah, it's time for the other bag. Can you go get it from my room?"

"Oh! Mommy, hold these. I'll be right back." He thrusts his backpack and lunch box at me and races back down the hall to Graham's room.

"Graham, I can't tell you what this means to him. To both of us. He was so excited to start school, and he loved this backpack and lunch box, and when it was ruined, well, I knew I wouldn't have time to find another before school starts tomorrow. My plan was to look online tonight. I actually stopped after work and bought him a plain one he could use to start this week, but this is so much better. Thank you."

"You're welcome. It wasn't a hardship. It was actually really gratifying to see his eyes light up when we found it. He thanked me so many times, and his smile, well, that was thanks enough."

I nod. I know the smile and the feeling I get when it's directed at me. "I still want to pay you back."

"It was a gift, Addy."

"Mommy, close your eyes," Noah calls.

"They're closed," I call back. I hear the rustling of another bag.

"Open."

I do as I'm told, and I have to blink hard once, twice, three times to battle with my tears, and I still end up losing, and one slides over my cheek. "What is this?" I ask, my voice cracking. I know what it is, but that's all I can think to say. Noah is holding a Vera Bradley tote bag. Not just any tote bag, but the very same one that was nasty and covered in debris and plaster from the ceiling.

"This is for you. We have it for you." Noah thrusts the tote bag at me and turns to smile at Graham. "She likes it, I can tell. She does that" —he points over his shoulder—"when I give her my art too."

"I love it. Thank you." I reach out and pull Noah into a hug and kiss his cheek. "Moommm," he whines.

I let him go and hug the bag to my chest, my eyes finding Graham's. He nods, but that's not good enough for me. I stand. My knees are wobbly as they carry me the few steps to the couch. Bending over, I wrap my arms around him in what I fear is an awkward hug. "Thank you," I whisper. When his arms wrap around me, there is nothing awkward about it.

No. Instead, it's safety, and security, and warmth, and desire. His touch lights my body on fire, and I let the hug linger for way longer than what's appropriate, because I crave the feeling it gives me. All the feelings it gives me. Who knew one simple embrace could hold so much?

"Oh, and guess what? All my books were wet, so Graham bought a new one for you to read to me at bedtime."

"That was very nice of him." I turn to look at Noah. "Tomorrow is a big day. Your first day of kindergarten, so we need to get you to bed."

When he doesn't argue, I know he's exhausted. "Tell Graham goodnight."

"Will you read to me?" Noah asks Graham.

Graham's gaze finds mine, and I nod, once again fighting back the tears. "Sure, No. Go brush your teeth and get the book ready. I'll be right there."

"You're coming too, right, Mommy?" Noah asks.

"Always," I assure him with a nod.

He races down the hall. I hear the water turn on and know I'm probably going to have a mess to clean up. He's untidy with his stepstool to reach the faucet and sink. I can only imagine the state he's going to make without it.

I'm staring after Noah when I feel strong arms wrap around me from behind. "He's a good kid, Addy. You should be proud."

"I am." All I want to do is melt into his embrace, but that thought alone scares the hell out of me. "Graham—" I start, but his lips connect with my cheek, and my words disappear.

"They're gifts, Addyson. I wanted to give them to both of you." His grip tightens. "Let's go read him a story." He pulls away far too soon and laces his fingers with mine, leading me down the hall to the room that is Noah's during our stay.

Noah is sitting in the middle of the queen-size bed that seems to almost swallow him whole. "Mommy here." He pats one side, and I lie next to him. "Graham here." He pats the other side.

It's on the tip of my tongue to tell Graham he doesn't have to do this, but before I can, he claims the spot Noah declared as his, opens the book, and begins to read.

Five

Graham

I can tell the moment Noah falls asleep beside me. His head hangs heavily against my arm, his breathing evening out into a steady rhythm. But I keep going. I know there's only a page or two left in the book, and the last thing I want to do is not finish in case he wakes.

"The end," I mutter, gently closing the book before glancing over. First, I take in the sleeping child resting his head on my arm, but then I take in his mother. Addy's curled up beside him, her head resting on the pillow and her hand protectively touching his arm.

Even in slumber, she's stunning.

I have no clue how long I sit here, watching, but it's longer than what would be deemed appropriate. After a few minutes, her eyelids flutter and slowly open, revealing the most stunning brown eyes I've ever seen. In fact, they make my heart rate kick up a few extra beats and my breath stills in my lungs.

Addy glances over and notices her son is sleeping. An instant smile plays on her lips. "Sorry. I can't believe I fell asleep too," she whispers, moving her hand from his arm to his forehead, where she gently brushes the hair back.

"You had a lot on your mind last night and didn't sleep as soundly." I leave off the part about our almost-kiss in the kitchen.

"True," she whispers, leaning over and kissing Noah on the forehead.

I follow her lead and gingerly get up, setting the book on the nightstand, while Addy covers her son with a thin blanket. I flip on the nightlight, even though it's still light out, thanks to the late sunsets in August, but I know if he wakes again in the middle of the night, he'll appreciate having it.

Once we slip into the hall, I quietly close the door and turn to face Addy. "Do you want to have a drink, or would you prefer to turn in early? I know you have a big day tomorrow."

She seems slightly surprised by the offer but quickly recovers with a nod. "Sure, I'd love a drink."

We walk toward the kitchen, my hand resting on her lower back. I open the fridge, knowing I only have two choices for her. "I have Bud Light bottles or there's a sweet white wine," I state, leaving off the part about it being in there because it's Brianne's favorite kind.

"Beer, please," she replies, silently pleasing me with her choice.

When was the last time I hung out with a woman who liked beer?

College, maybe?

I twist the top off the first one and hand it over, followed by the second. "Wanna take these to the back deck? We'll leave the door open in case Noah wakes up."

"That sounds good."

We step into the warm air, and I'm instantly grateful it isn't as humid as it was yesterday. Hot I can deal with, but when it's humid as hell, it makes everyone miserable.

Addy looks at the patio furniture but doesn't sit down. Instead, her eyes go to the double swing sitting under the big oak tree in the backyard. "Mind if we swing?"

"Nope. I prefer it, actually."

When we sit, I can't help but notice how close my leg is to hers.

While I'm wearing khaki shorts, she's still wearing the capris she wore to work earlier, yet she looks comfortable and casual as she leans back in the swing and gazes up at the sky.

"Why?" she finally asks, glancing over and catching my gaze.

"Why, what?"

"Why do you prefer it?"

I shift in my seat, using my long legs to keep us slowly moving back and forth. "When I was in third grade, my teacher told my parents to get me tested for ADD or ADHD. I was always moving. Always. They did, but my scores were fairly low on the scale, so I've never been medicated. When I got into junior high, I found outlets to help me release all my extra energy, like baseball and basketball, and in high school, I added football and weightlifting. Since then, I've continued to use lifting weights and running as my release. So for me to just sit in a chair and watch the stars or something, well, I struggle with it, but on a swing, I can keep my legs moving and still sit back and look at the stars."

Even though I'm looking up, I feel her eyes on me. "I didn't know that."

I shrug and look her way. "I don't really talk about it. Adam knows, of course, because he used to have to reel me back in sometimes when we were studying, especially in college. When he was finished and I still had four more years of pharmacy school, I thought I'd go crazy without him telling me to calm the hell down and focus, but I managed. I learned ways to cope and still get my work done."

She reaches over with the hand not holding her beer and squeezes my hand. "That's pretty admirable, Graham. You've accomplished so much, despite the ADD."

"Thanks," I reply, my throat thick with emotion.

Addy doesn't move her hand, just sits back and lets me move the swing. We both drink our beer and enjoy the calm of the evening. The crickets and birds in the background, the faint road traffic out front, and the neighbor's dog barking, probably at a squirrel in the tree.

She yawns just as I finish my beer. "I should probably go to bed early. Tomorrow's a big day," she says.

Stopping the swing, I stand up, still holding her hand. Her small, delicate fingers lay across mine, our palms grazing with only the faintest touch. Yet that one little trace is like adding an accelerant to a brush fire.

"What time does the bus get here?" I ask, oddly excited to experience this big moment with both of them.

"Around seven forty-five. It picks up and drops off just down the block at the corner. There's seven other kids who will get on at that stop."

I'm supposed to be to work at seven forty-five to open the pharmacy at eight, but I make a mental note to text the pharmacy tech on duty tomorrow, to let her know I'll be a few minutes late. There's no way I'm missing Noah's big moment. "I'll walk down with you."

Together, we move up the steps and head for the back door. "You don't have to do that, but I'm sure Noah will be excited. Adam is coming over too as a surprise."

"I wouldn't miss it." Then something else hits me. "Does Noah need to get picked up from the bus after school?"

Addy stops and faces me. "No, we agreed he'd ride the bus to school, but after, he'll go to my classroom and sit with me until I'm finished."

"I'd be happy to help on my days off," I offer.

She gives me a warm smile. "You've already done so much, Graham," she replies, her voice a hushed whisper.

"It doesn't feel like enough," I confess. I don't know why I have this crazy desire to be there for her and Noah. It's not because she's not able to do it on her own—hell, she's proven just how capable she is—but it's more of my want to help share the burden.

She goes up on her tiptoes and leans in. "Thank you. For everything," she mutters as she brushes her soft lips across my scruffy cheek.

Before I can move my head to claim her lips with my own the way I'm craving, she pulls away and releases my hand. Addy opens the door and slips inside, leaving me standing on the deck, a new wave of heat coursing through my body that has nothing to do with the temperature outside.

It has everything to do with the woman staying in my guest room.

How in the hell am I going to keep my hands to myself while she's here?

The bigger question is: Do I want to?

I'm careful as I set the weights down and suck in a deep, greedy breath of air.

I've been awake ever since Addy went to bed, unable to stop thinking about her. Her mouth, her sweet vanilla scent, her sexy little body in those fucking satin pajamas. It was enough to ensure I had a raging hard-on with no hope of subsiding without taking matters into my own hand.

Instead of another jerk session starring my best friend's beautiful sister, I opted to come downstairs to get an extra workout in. It's worked, to an extent. At least I'm not sporting wood while physically abusing my muscles with this extra workout.

The music is low—much quieter than usual, trying not to wake my houseguests—even though the basement is well insulated. When I turned this large space into my private gym, I spent extra time and money to soundproof the room. This way, I could be down here at any time and not disturb anyone else in the house.

My mind flashes to the extra pickles I bought during our shopping trip today. Noah asked me if I liked them as much as his mom did, and even though I told him no, I explained I was buying them because they made her happy. The five-year-old proceeded to pull a face, telling me how he doesn't like them on his cheeseburgers like her.

Only ketchup for the little guy.

I can't help but smile when I think back to our conversation in the middle of the grocery store. I've never really bothered to pay this close attention to Noah's likes and dislikes. Or Addy's for that matter. I've always let Adam take the lead when we're all together, to make sure the boy has what he wants.

But now?

Now, after spending the day with him, I find myself wanting to step into that role, which is a little startling, if I'm being honest. How can I feel so connected to Noah after just one day? I've been around him countless times since he was born, but today was different. Today was him relying on me for everything and me really enjoying our time together.

I also realize I haven't once thought about Brianne. That's pretty damn telling. While I hope she's okay and not too upset over our breakup, I knew her leaving was the right thing to do. I didn't see a future with her, at least not the way she did. My only hope is she meets someone who gives her exactly what she wants.

That person is not me.

When I have a punishing amount of weight on the bar, I lie back to bench press. I get through a rep of ten, my arms a little shaky as I slide the bar back onto the rack. Movement catches out of the corner of my eye, and I turn to see Addy sitting on the stairs, watching.

"Hey," I gasp, breathing heavily from exertion. "Everything all right?" I ask, sitting up and facing her.

"Fine," she quickly insists, the apples of her cheeks turning a lovely shade of pink. "Sorry to barge in on you when you're..." She waves her hand toward the equipment to finish her sentence.

"I hope I didn't wake you." I jump up and turn off the music, grabbing a bottle of water from the mini fridge and chugging most of the contents.

"You didn't. I was already awake. First day nerves, I guess," she confesses with a chuckle. "I could hear something, like a soft clanking noise, and guessed you were down here." She stands up and walks the rest of the way down, her eyes taking in the room and all the equipment. "It's nice."

"Thanks." I take a few long seconds to enjoy the view as she looks around. She's wearing another skimpy pajama set, but this one's cotton with pink elephants on it. While I'm sure she chose it for comfort and coolness during the hot August nights, I still find it sexy as fuck.

No.

I find *her* sexy as fuck.

"How often do you work out?" she asks, finally bringing those intoxicating brown eyes back to me.

"I do weights three days a week and cardio four or five. I prefer to run outside but hate it during high humidity."

She wrinkles her nose. "You lost me at running."

Propping my backside against the cabinet, I watch as her lithe fingers slide across the bar I just lifted. "What do you do to blow off steam?"

She glances my way, another blush creeping up her neck and staining her cheeks. I can't help but wonder what she's thinking about. Something tells me it's dirty as hell, which goes straight to my groin, my balls aching with need. "I read."

I fight a smile, mostly because that was the answer I was expecting. Ever since we were little, I remember seeing Addy with a book in her hand. When Adam and I were in high school, we used to roll our eyes every time we'd find her sitting on the couch after school, reading one of those books about babysitters. Those were always her favorite.

"Graham?"

"Yeah?" I ask, trying to keep my feet planted where they are. Mostly because I'm sure I'm a sweaty, smelly mess, but also because I'm afraid if I get close, I'll cave to the desire to touch her.

"Can I ask you something? Something personal?"

"Of course," I reply, finishing off the rest of the water bottle.

She doesn't ask right away, just seems to be working up the courage to say the words. After a solid minute, she finally turns, squares her shoulders, and asks, "Are you still dating Brianne?"

Her question completely catches me off guard, and I find myself a little stumped.

When I don't reply right away, she jumps in and says, "I'm just wondering if she's going to be okay with Noah and I being here. I mean, if my boyfriend moved a woman and her child in with him temporarily, I'd probably be a little upset. I don't want her to feel threatened or anything by my presence."

This time, I do move. I walk right over to where she stands, not caring that I probably smell nasty. "Addy? If I was still with Bri, I wouldn't have thought about kissing you last night."

She seems startled by my words, her eyes flaring wide with shock.

Again, I take a step forward, this time invading her personal space. "Brianne and I broke up. I'd never be the guy who'd touch you, who'd step between your thighs and think about nothing else but taking your lips with my own and making you moan with my hands, with my mouth."

Addy swallows hard, but her stare never wavers. "Can I confess something?" she whispers, moving forward and pressing her chest against mine.

"Of course." It's so hard to breathe right now, especially with her body against mine.

"I realized it was a possibility, but I wouldn't have cared. I really wanted you to kiss me, even if you had a girlfriend." Guilt fills those beautiful brown orbs. "Does that make me a bad person?"

Clearing my throat, I quickly insist, "No. It makes you human. But, Addy? I never would have put you in that position if I had a girlfriend. It never would have gotten that far."

She relaxes and nods.

"Can I confess something?" I ask, repeating her question.

"Yes."

My hands flex and tighten into fists to keep from wrapping my arms around her. "I came down here to try to work you out of my thoughts."

If she's surprised by my statement, she doesn't let on. "Did it work?"

With my eyes locked on hers, I slowly shake my head. "No."

"Good."

And then she goes up on her tiptoes and leans in, plastering her full, sexy lips to mine. That's the moment my brain short-circuits. The moment I forget about Adam and worrying about Addy being his little sister. The moment I give in to this burning urge smoldering inside me.

It's the moment I let it all go and focus solely on this kiss.

On kissing Addyson.

It's in this moment, I know I'll never be the same.

Six

I'm kissing Graham!

When I climbed out of bed, I didn't have a plan or a destination. I knew that tossing and turning wasn't cutting it. I needed something to clear my mind. On my way to the kitchen for a snack, I heard a slight clanking noise, and all thoughts of a late-night snack were forgotten. Instead, my mind ran wild with what Graham was doing down in the basement. Curiosity got the best of me, and I quietly crept down the stairs.

I watched him. Like the creeper that I apparently am, I watched him. His body truly is a work of art, and I wanted to commit every move, every muscle to memory. I already have the image of him pressed up against me as I sat on the counter in my Graham bank, and now this... he's magnificent.

I don't know what it is, but being here, living under his roof, knowing that he's sleeping just down the hall. Having dinner with him, seeing him with Noah, all of it is working on my emotions. It's not just my emotions he's wreaking havoc on. It's my hormones too. Sure, the two go hand in hand, but I can honestly admit I've never gotten wet just by watching a guy lift weights.

Not until tonight.

Not until Graham.

I never in my wildest dreams thought I would ever be brave enough to make the first move on my brother's best friend. I've imagined myself doing this very thing multiple times over the years, but I never allowed myself to act on it. The tension between us tonight was too strong, the desire roaring through my veins too heavy to just walk away. After all these years, my feelings for him have come rushing back to the surface, telling me they never really went away.

And now, for the first time, he's giving me the impression that he feels this too. This deep-rooted connection that tethers us together.

That's why I made the first move.

That's why I kissed him.

And now... he's kissing me back.

His lips are soft yet firm, and I can taste mint on his breath. He's hesitant for maybe five seconds before his tongue glides over my lips and seeks entrance into my mouth. I open for him, because not only do I want to, but this is Graham. My childhood crush, the man who I've dreamt about and fantasized about since I was old enough to know the true details of the birds and the bees.

"So damn sweet," he murmurs as his hands slide over my ass cheeks. He squeezes, and I moan into his mouth.

His hands are everywhere while mine dig into the bare skin of his back. His lips trail across my cheek and follow the path down my neck to my collarbone. He takes his time tasting and teasing me with his lips.

"Graham." I breathe his name. I don't know what I'm even asking, but it's the only word that I'm able to form on my lips as his kisses make me lose all train of thought.

"These fucking pajamas," he grits out before gripping my thighs and lifting me.

Instinctively my legs wrap around his waist, and my arms around his neck. I don't ask him where we're going. I don't care. All I care about is his lips on mine. The way his hard cock feels nestled between my thighs, and what happens next.

I don't have a plan, and to be honest, I don't think he does either. What I do know is that this feels right. His hands on me, his lips locked with mine. It feels oh so right.

He moves us to the couch, where I'm now straddling his lap. "No bra," he says huskily. He rakes his thumb over my hardened peak, causing goose bumps to break out across my skin. "So sensitive."

His touch, even through the thin fabric of my pajama top, is electric. Tilting my head back, I thrust my chest forward, giving him better access to me and allowing me to close my eyes and just feel. I don't know what this means or if I'll ever have the pleasure of this man's hands on me ever again, so I want to soak it all up. I want every caress, every kiss to be engrained in my memory. This is a moment I never want to forget.

He slides his hands under my thin cotton shirt, slowly making their way to my breasts. When he rolls a hard nipple between his thumb and index finger, I grind my center against his dick in retaliation.

"Fuck." His voice is gravelly and deep. "This needs to go." The next thing I know, my shirt is over my head and laying somewhere behind us on the floor. "Noah?" he asks.

"What?" I try to clear my mind to understand what he's asking me.

"Noah. Is he asleep?"

"Yes." I nod with my reply, still not sure why he's asking.

"Do we have to worry about him coming down here?"

"No. He'll call down the stairs first."

"You sure?"

"We can stop this—" I start, but he's already shaking his head and pressing a hard kiss to my mouth.

"We're not stopping. I just wanted to make sure the little man was all set. This isn't exactly a good position to find us in."

"I happen to think it's a very good position," I say, rocking my body against him once more. The move is meant to tease him, but it backfires when he slides his hand through the leg of my shorts and uses his thumb to gently trace my pussy through my panties.

"So wet for me, Addy," he says huskily.

"Oh, God," I moan. My body starts to tremble from his touch. I've never responded to a man like this. Never.

"What do you need, Addy?"

"I-I don't know."

"I can't give it to you unless you tell me. Do you want me to pet this pussy?" he asks, again sliding his thumb over my panties. "Do you want to ride my cock?" he asks. One strong hand grips my waist as he assists me with the rocking motion of my hips. "Tell me what you want."

"You."

"I'm right here."

"You know what I mean."

"Tell me."

"Just touch me. Kiss me. Just do... anything." I pant as his hand dances up and down my back.

"Where?"

"Everywhere. Anywhere. Just... don't stop touching me." I don't know how to ask him for what I want. Part of that is because I'm not sure how he feels about this. I don't know what this means for our friendship and my current living situation. I should be more concerned with both of those things, but I'm not. I've wanted this. I've wanted him for far too long to let those things stop me. Besides, we're both consenting adults. Whatever happens, we can deal with it like the mature, responsible humans that we are.

It's on the tip of my tongue to tell him that I'm his for the taking, but something stops me. Instead, I ask, "What do you want?"

"I want to watch you come."

I whimper, and my pussy throbs. "I want that too," I confess.

Pulling his hand from my shorts, he grips my hips. His blue eyes hold me captive as he begins to assist me with rocking back and forth on his cock. I brace my hands on his shoulders and block everything out but this very moment. This blip in time where I have his attention, and he has mine—this moment where he wants me, Addyson Sinclair.

"Give it to me, Addy. Let me watch you fall apart." His voice is deep and gruff and so damn sexy.

Closing my eyes, I tilt my head back and focus on the friction between my thighs with each glide of my body over his. His hands are still gripping my waist. His hold is firm, as if he's afraid I might suddenly decide this isn't what I want and run away.

"Addy, look at me." It's a demand, and I want to give it to him, but I'm afraid if I move out of this position, I'll lose the delicious tingle starting to form in my core. "Addyson." More commanding this time. My eyes pop open and lock with his.

Liquid blue pools of heat stare back at me. Just moments ago, I was afraid to open my eyes, and now I'm afraid to close them. My thighs quiver, and I dig my nails into the flesh of his shoulders. I'm close, so close, but I'm not ready. I don't want this to be over. I don't want to face what happens next. I just want to live in this moment.

"Your breathing is shallow," he rasps. "Your hands are shaking, even through your iron hold on me. Let go, baby. Just feel." His words are barely audible over the rapid beat of my heart, but my body heard him just fine. Without needing further prompting, my orgasm crashes through me like the waves of the ocean. It's unlike anything I've ever felt before.

When my body finally stills, I squeeze my eyes closed, prepared for him to tell me this was a mistake. However, that's not what happens at all. "Come here." His words are soft, but I hear them.

He somehow manages to move us so that we're both now lying face-to-face on the couch. His strong arms are wrapped around me, and his grip is firm as if he never wants to let me go.

"That was the sexiest fucking thing I've ever seen in my entire life."

"Stop." I bury my face in his neck, hiding my embarrassment.

"Addy?" He waits for me to lift my head from his neck and open my eyes. He cradles my cheek and leans in, pressing his lips to mine. This time his kisses are slow and tender, and tell me, without his words, he's in no hurry to end this.

I don't know how much time has passed. It could be minutes, could be hours, when he pulls away. "It's getting late. You have your first day tomorrow."

"Right." I move to sit up, and his grip tightens.

"What's that look?"

"What look?" I'm playing dumb, and we both know it.

"Your face fell."

"I just... wasn't ready for bed."

"Addy, you have to be up in a few hours to wrangle first graders. I'm guessing you need some sleep."

"But we need to take care of you." I reach for the waistband of his shorts, but he stops me.

"You already took care of me. You gave me what I wanted."

"This should be beneficial for both of us." I try again for his shorts, but again he stops me.

"I told you I wanted to see you come, and you gave me that."

"It's fine. I get it." This time I am able to tug out of his grip and stand. I search the floor for my top and hastily pull it over my head.

"Stop." His arms snake around my waist. "What's going on here? Why are you mad at me?"

"It's fine, Graham. I'm a big girl. I can take it. I don't need your pity orgasms."

"What the fuck are you talking about?"

Hot tears prick my eyes. "I'm talking about how you don't want me. Not like that. You let me use you because you're a nice guy, and now I'm being dismissed. I get it."

"Hold the fuck on." One arm is locked around me while the other hand tilts my chin up to look into his eyes. "Nothing that happened between us tonight had anything to do with pity." He drops his hand and takes hold of my wrist. "If you think for a single fucking second that I don't want you, let me prove it to you." He places my hand over his cock that's hard as stone. "Does this say I don't want you?"

"Then why? Why won't you let me?" I ask, stroking his cock through his shorts. The fear of rejection mixed with desire has my emotions in a whirlwind.

"Addy," he grits out. "Please stop." I halt my movements but don't remove my hand. "You're not just a quick fuck."

"What am I?" I ask softly. I need to hear him say it. His sweet words, I need to know what they mean. I need him to spell it out for me before my heart decides on its own. That's too dangerous.

He tucks my hair behind my ear. "You're Addyson. Sexy as fuck, a kick-ass mom, a loving sister and daughter, and the woman I can't stop thinking about."

"You think about me, but you don't want me?"

"I want you. I want to feel your pussy grip my cock more than anything, but it needs to be more than just some quick fuck in my basement. I want to take my time exploring you. I want to taste you and ravish you, and I'm going to need time for that. Time that we don't have tonight. It's late, and I don't want to worry about you being exhausted because I couldn't control my cock."

"Then let me control it." I smile at him, squeezing his cock through his shorts.

"Fuck," he hisses.

I watch as his eyes close, and he takes a few deep breaths. I continue to stroke him over his shorts, wishing I could feel the weight of his cock in my palm. "You know, it's a crying shame we both have to be up early." I smile at him.

"You can say that again," he mutters. "We really should get to bed."

"I'm afraid to."

"Talk to me," he says gently. "What could you possibly be afraid of?"

"I'm afraid to walk up those stairs and lose this. Whatever this is. I-I don't want to lose this feeling of being close to you. This feeling of being with you… like this."

"Tell me what you want."

I drop my hand from his cock and stand up tall, squaring my shoulders. I look him in the eye and pause, making sure I have his full attention. "I want you."

He swallows hard and nods. "Okay."

"What does that mean, Graham? Okay? Okay, you heard me? Okay, we're going to make a go of this? Okay, you'll fuck me? What does okay mean?"

"It means if you want me, you can have me. It means that if you want me to fuck you, then that's what I'll do, but I'm going to love you hard right after. It means that if you want to make a go of this, we can do that too. However, I'm going to need to talk to your brother."

"No. No. This is between us. This has nothing to do with Adam."

"He's my best friend, Addyson. He has been since we were kids.

You're his little sister. I can't do this. We can't do this until we talk to him."

"And what about tonight? Are you going to call him tomorrow and give my big brother a play-by-play?"

"Of course not."

"Can we just... not? Let's sleep on this. We can talk tomorrow night, and, Graham, I won't hold it against you if you decide to back away from this."

"I think taking some time to think is good. If we do this, there is no going back. I can't be inside of you one day and just be your friend the next. That's not how I'm wired."

"Is that what you told Brianne too?" It's wrong to bring her up, and I know it. However, I want his reaction. I want some kind of reassurance from him. If I know anything about Graham Morgan, it's that he's honest and doesn't play games.

"No. It wasn't like that with Brianne. We were just hanging out."

My gut twists at his words. "And is that what I'll be? Just hanging out with you?"

"No. If this happens, that makes you mine."

"Yours?"

"Mine." He bends his head and kisses me softly. "Come on. I'll tuck you in." He laces his fingers through mine. It's a small gesture yet an intimate one that sends my heart a flutter, and leads me to the stairs. Once we reach the top, he turns off the lights and softly closes the door. We don't speak as he guides me down the hall. He stops just outside Noah's room and gently pushes open the door. My traitorous heart skips a beat knowing that he thought to check on my son. Once we've both peeked in, he closes the door and continues down the hall to my room.

"I thought you said you were going to tuck me in?" I ask when he makes no move to step inside the room.

"I'm pretty strong-willed, Addy, but I can't go in there. I need to take care of this." He grips his cock. "And if I take one step into that room, it won't be my hand that's taking care of my issue. It will be your pussy. We don't have time for that." He bends and kisses me hard. "Get some sleep." He steps back until his back rests against the opposite wall of the hallway. My breathing is labored and I feel so damn needy for his touch. I crave it. I crave him.

I'm tempted to tease him, but I can tell from the set of his jaw that he's barely maintaining composure. So, instead, I blow him a kiss. "Goodnight, Graham." I'm glad that one of us is showing restraint, especially with Noah sleeping just down the hall. A lot has happened tonight, and I think we both need some time to sleep on this new development and determine where we go next.

"Night, Addy. Dream of me."

"I always do." I disappear into my room with a smile on my face. He has no idea that my confession was one that has been my reality for years. He has no idea I'm smiling because I know I'll see him again in my dreams.

Seven

Graham

I refill my coffee cup and check the clock once more.

It's almost time.

Reaching into the cabinet, I pull out two travel mugs, filling the first to the top since Adam prefers his coffee black, and filling the second three-quarters of the way to leave room for Addy's creamer. Just as I'm screwing Adam's lid on, I hear the thunder of running feet on the hardwood floor.

Why does that simple sound make me smile so damn much?

"Graham!"

I turn around as Noah barrels into the kitchen with an eager grin on his face and his dinosaur backpack positioned on his back. "Good morning, No. You ready for your first day?"

He nods emphatically, his eyes so wide with excitement, it's almost comical. "Mommy says the bus will be here soon!" he exclaims.

"About ten minutes," I confirm over the rim of my cup.

"Are you walking with me to the bus stop?"

Walking over to where he stands, I ruffle his hair and meet his questioning eyes. "Of course I am."

I'm rewarded with a huge smile. "Yay!"

A knock sounds at the door, followed quickly by a loud, "Hello?"

"Uncle Adam!" Noah bellows before turning and sprinting toward the front door.

I grab the full cup and follow in his wake, meeting the two of them at the entrance.

"And then Graham bought me a new backpack. *And* it had the lunch box too! It was the last one, Uncle Adam. The *last one*!"

My friend chuckles at his nephew's enthusiasm and kisses him on the forehead. "That's awesome, buddy."

"Please tell me there's coffee," Addyson says from behind me, hurrying down the hallway in our direction.

When I turn, I have to force myself not to react to her standing there. She's in black capris and a blue and white flowy top that subtly enhances her curves and makes her brown eyes pop. "On the counter. I'll grab it," I reply, moving back to the kitchen. I pour a little creamer in the cup, hoping it's the way she likes it, and make sure the lid is on tight.

Returning to where everyone waits, I catch the end of Noah's story. "And as soon as I finished my cereal, I put on my favorite dinosaur outfit that Mommy helped me lay out last night before Graham read me a story."

Adam flashes me a look. It's part surprise and bit happiness at his nephew's announcement. "What do you say we head down to the bus stop?" he asks.

Noah practically sprints out the door the moment it's open. "Wait, No. You have to hold your mom's hand as you walk," I instruct, falling into step behind him and Addy.

"How's it going?" Adam asks quietly, walking with me.

My mind flashes to the stolen moments I've shared with his sister, especially last night's incident in my gym. Of course, that's not exactly something I can tell my oldest friend. No one wants to hear those details when they're about your own flesh and blood, so I go with, "Good."

"Aren't you usually at work by now?"

"Yeah, but I didn't want to miss Noah's big morning. I texted my tech and told her I'd be a few minutes late," I confirm as we reach the corner where a few kids anxiously wait for the bus, their parents hanging back. With a sip of coffee, I add, "I'll head in as soon as the bus picks him up. He's talked about nothing else for two days."

Adam studies me for several seconds, his gaze intense, and I start to feel a little sweaty in the pits. Can you see moisture through my white dress button-down? Did he see the dirty thoughts parading through my brain like it's Thanksgiving Day?

I'm saved from being put under the microscope when Noah cheers, "It's coming!"

The group of kids and parents all turn in the direction of the big yellow school bus, the kids displaying a mix of emotions, but I focus on the two people beside me. Noah's eyes are dancing with anticipation, his little body practically vibrating and barely able to contain his excitement. Then there's Addy, who's watching her baby boy get ready to get on the school bus for his first day of kindergarten. Her brown eyes are shining with moisture, and I can tell she's fighting to keep them at bay.

I want to reach for her, to pull her into my arms and reassure her he's going to be fine, but I don't. Not with Adam standing on the other side of me.

As the bus approaches the stop, Noah turns to face his uncle. "Have a good first day, buddy," my friend says to his nephew, holding out his fist for a knuckle bump.

Noah grins at Adam. "I will," he says, tapping his much smaller knuckle against the big one.

When he turns to me, an unexpected lump forms in my throat. Not wanting to make a big deal out of this and risk upsetting him, I hold out my own fist and plaster a big smile on my face. "See you tonight, No."

He doesn't tap my fist, at least not right away. His eyebrows draw together in worry. "Will you read to me again when I go to bed?"

Instantly, I drop to my knees and ruffle his hair. "Of course I will. When I get home from work, I want to hear all about your first day, okay?"

Noah relaxes and nods. "'Kay."

Flashing him a quick smile, I say, "You better give your mom a quick hug before she explodes from excitement."

Noah's eyes widen. "She's going to explode?"

Addy's there, crouching down beside her son. "Not literally," she replies with a chuckle. "Graham just meant I'm super excited for you." She swallows hard again, meeting his gaze, just as the other kids start to climb on the bus. "When you get done with school, I'll be in my classroom just down the hall from your classroom."

He nods. "I know."

I watch as a single tear falls down Addy's cheek. "Okay. Have a good first day on the bus, and remember to listen to the bus driver."

"I will."

Addy kisses his forehead before standing up, and Noah walks over to the open door to climb on. When he gets there, he grabs the handle, his short body looking so small compared to the size of the door and steps, as he takes the first leap up. My heart hammers in my chest at how brave and eager he is, how's he's been anticipating this exact moment.

Just before he disappears, Noah turns our way, a big toothy grin on his face as he waves wildly. The sound coming from Addy is a combination of a sniffle and a laugh as she waves back.

Then, he's gone.

The door closes.

The bus slowly pulls away.

Addy bursts into tears without caring there are other parents nearby to witness her breakdown. Adam moves before I can, throwing his arm over her shoulder and drawing her into his chest. "That was brutal," she mutters into his shirt.

Adam sighs. "It was, but he's a great kid, Ads. He's going to be okay."

I want to add it's only a short drive, and she'll be at the school when the bus gets there, but I'm not sure how well that'd go over. The truth is I don't particularly know what she's feeling right now, but I do understand the magnitude of this moment. He's her baby, and he just took a giant leap forward in his childhood.

We walk back to my house, Adam trying to keep his sister's thoughts occupied with small talk. When we reach my driveway, he pulls her into his arms again and hugs her. "Tell my buddy to call me later so he can tell me all about his first day."

"I will," she mutters, looking a little forlorn and dejected.

"Later, man." Adam throws me a wave before heading to his truck to go to work.

"You okay?" I ask the moment he pulls out of my driveway.

She nods and gives me the faintest smile. "I am. This was just... hard. He's been my little boy since the moment he was born, and today, well, he was so brave to take this first big step. I cried the morning I took him to preschool, but this was so much worse. That was two and a half hours a couple mornings a week. This is... school."

I'm moving in her direction before I can even think better of it, and the moment she's in my arms, I feel like I can take a deep breath. "You're raising a great kid, Addy. He's brave because of you."

She gazes up at me, those brown eyes and full lips causing an inappropriate reaction in my pants. I wonder if she's going to go up on her toes and kiss me. I wouldn't even care we're outside and standing in my driveway. I'd fucking return that kiss, claiming her lips with my own as if it were a necessity to my very existence.

But she doesn't.

"We both need to get to work."

I nod, continuing to hold her against my chest a few seconds longer. "How about I bring dinner home tonight? We close at six, and I can grab pizza."

"You don't have to."

"I want to. We'll call it a treat for Noah's first day of school."

She gazes up at me. "You're too good to us."

I don't really know what to say, mostly because no one has ever accused me of being too good to them, especially a woman.

Addy backs out of my arms and walks to the driver's side of her Malibu. Before she slips inside, she pauses. "Graham? Don't forget the breadsticks. They're Noah's favorite." She flashes me a grateful smile, climbs into her car, and backs away, heading off to school with the spare key I gave her.

I'm left standing here, anxious for closing time to roll around so I can come home to Addy and Noah.

What does that mean?

"Graham Morgan."

I glance up from the pills I'm counting and smile. "Miss Millie, how are you this morning?"

"Just as wild and free as a fart in the wind," the old woman announces loudly, catching the attention from everyone in the building.

With a chuckle, I finish filling the bottle, add the label, and bag the prescription. Once the task is completed, I take the script to the counter, waving off Anne, the pharmacy tech. "Do you have your license handy?"

"Well, of course I do," she replies, digging into her massive handbag for her identification. "Just ignore the expiration date." Before I can comment, she bellows, "Oh! I ran into Brianne at my doctor's appointment earlier. She said you two broke up."

"We did," I confirm, taking the driver's license of a woman who probably has no business having one, and scan the barcode on the back.

"Because she's too uptight or because she's husband hunting and you're not ready for that?" the sweet old woman I've known since I was two asks.

I arch a single eyebrow in question.

"Too uptight, huh? Did you know she color-codes the patient charts and uses labels on everything? She even labels her pens, Graham. Her pens. I imagine she's probably that way in bed too."

I practically choke on the air I breathe. She gazes up at me expectantly. "Uhh, no comment?"

She waves her wrinkled hand my way. "Probably for the best. Anyway, I hear you've already moved on. What does Adam think about you dating his sister?"

That catches my attention. "I'm not dating Addyson," I insist, ignoring the nagging voice in my head arguing the fact I may not be dating her, but I'd like to. "Her apartment flooded and she's just staying with me while her place is getting fixed."

"Oh, yes, yes. I heard all about that when I was at Euchre Club at the church last night. Nancy Granger told Sierra Andrews that Bella and Jackson Horner were out for a walk with their new puppy and saw the fire trucks leave the station. They called his sister, who works at the grocery store next door, and she said Cooper Bing was working as the carryout. Anyway, he texted his girlfriend on that Chat Snappy app all the kids are using, and she said her neighbor's sister-in-law's boss lives right next door and lost all water pressure. That poor woman was in the middle of washing her towels when suddenly, bam! No water."

My head is spinning a little as I try to keep up.

"So...," I start, not really knowing what to say next.

"Anyway..."

I finish ringing up her prescription. "Do you have any questions?"

"About Addy?"

I blink once, twice. "No, about your prescription."

She waves her frail little hand. "Of course not. I've been taking this since Nixon was president."

"Well, all right then," I state, stapling her receipt to the bag and sliding it across the counter.

"Listen, if you're not dating that sweet young mother, I have the perfect man to set her up with. You remember George from the gas station? His grandson, Henry, came for a visit and just loved our little town. He's planning to relocate his law firm here next month. I thought I'd pass along Addy's phone number to him when he arrives."

The hairs on the back of my neck stand up. "What?"

"Oh, they'd make a lovely couple. He reminds me of David Hasselhoff from that TV show with the talking car. The ladies will swoon over him, just like a young Don Johnson," she informs me, nodding adamantly.

"Don Johnson?"

She leans in, as if about to share a big secret, and whispers, "*Miami Vice.*"

"Ahh."

"So, do you think it would be okay if I pass along her phone number? She's such a wonderful woman, and she needs to find someone to help take care of her and that sweet boy."

My eye twitches at the thought of "someone" stepping into that role, whether he looks like David Hasselhoff or not. I'll be damned if I'm going to sit back and watch some polished douche canoe slip into their lives.

Or into her bed.

Fuck that. If she's going to be in anyone's bed, it's going to be mine.

"You know, Millie, she's got a lot going on right now. I'm not so sure setting her up is the right thing to do," I state as casually as possible.

"No?"

"Well, she started school today, so she'll be pretty busy for a while." It's a lame excuse—I know it—and I just pray she doesn't call me on it.

Instead, she just grins. It's wide and friendly, but there's an underlying hint of mischief on that sweet ol' lady's face. "You're probably right, Graham. I'll just wait until things settle down for her before I pass along her number."

Relief settles in my chest as she takes her bag of medication and slips it into the large one on her arm. "All right, Miss Millie. You have a good afternoon."

"You too, young man. If you want me to pass your number along to Suzie at the church, you let me know. We've been telling her it was time to get back on the horse, you know?"

"Yeah, well, I'm good for now, but thanks." Suzie is in her mid-fifties and lost her husband to a heart attack three years ago. Not only is she a good twenty years older than I am, but I draw the line at dating my second-grade Sunday school teacher.

Hard pass.

I watch as she shuffles toward the front entrance, pausing to greet everyone she passes on her way out the door. Then, I shake my head, oddly frazzled by Millie's suggestions at setting Addy up on a date.

Over my dead body will that happen.

If anyone's going to date Addyson, it's going to be me.

As I return to the back counter and clean up the station to prep for the next prescription, my mind replays all those phenomenal kisses from last night. Vividly, I recall what it was like to watch her come, to hear those amazing noises slip from her lips as she rode me and rubbed herself against me.

I had to jerk off twice when I got back to my room.

Now, as I do everything I can to keep those same memories from completely taking over my brain, I think about what's going to happen when I go home. I'll pick up dinner from the pizzeria down the street and take it home to Noah and Addy. I'll get to hear him recount his entire day, from start to finish, while he eats, and then get to read him a story after his bath.

When he's fast asleep, I'll finally be able to talk to Addy. We both agreed to think hard about taking our friendship to the next level, to be sure we're both on the same page, and I've done that.

I want her.

I want them.

If I have it my way, Addyson Sinclair will be mine by the end of the night.

Eight

ddyson

"He's here!" Noah cheers from his spot next to the window. He's been sitting there for the last thirty minutes waiting for Graham to get home from work. He called to tell me he was on his way, and Noah has been bouncing with excitement ever since.

"Graham!" Noah rushes him as soon as the front door opens. "You're here."

"Hey, No. Let me set this down, and I want to hear all about your first day."

"Oh, it was so much fun—" he starts, but I interrupt him.

"Noah. Go wash your hands for dinner."

"Do I have to?" he whines.

"If you want some of this pizza and these delicious breadsticks, you do."

"Breadsticks! Yay!" He shoots off down the hall like a bolt of lightning.

Graham chuckles as he makes his way into the kitchen and sets the two boxes on the counter. I'm standing just close enough that he can snake an arm around my waist and pull me into his chest. "Missed you," he rasps as he touches his lips to mine. The feel of his lips against mine causes desire to pool between my thighs.

"Noah," I remind him.

"I know, but I couldn't help it." He releases me reluctantly.

"I missed you too." I smile up at him.

"I'm going to go get washed up." He kisses me one more time before he too disappears down the hall.

I can hear him talking to Noah. My hands touch my lips, and I smile. I've thought about him all day today. When I wasn't worried about how Noah was doing, I was thinking about Graham and last night.

"Ready," Noah says, sliding into the kitchen.

"All right, kiddo. Take a seat at the table. I'll make you a plate."

"Thanks, Mommy. Oh, can I have milk?" he asks.

"Milk sounds good to me," Graham says. He walks past Noah and ruffles his hair before going to the cabinet and pulling out a cup with a lid and straw that I use for Noah. He gets to work pouring him a glass of milk. "Addy?"

"Uh, just water for me. Milk and pizza are... just... no." I shake my head.

He laughs. "Have you tried it?"

"No. I'm not a big milk person unless—" I start, but he finishes my sentence for me.

"—unless it's chocolate." He smiles. "I know." He winks as he sets Noah's glass in front of him, a big glass for himself, and a bottle of water for me on the table.

"That for Noah?" he asks, pointing to the paper plate in my hand.

"Yeah."

"I'll take it. Make one for yourself." He takes the plate and sets it in front of Noah. "Eat up, my man."

I quickly make a plate for myself, as does Graham, and we sit at the table. "All right, No, let's hear it. Tell me all about your first day."

Noah grins. "It was—" he starts, but I hold my hand up to stop him.

"Chew your food first." I laugh. He nods and chews as fast as he can and makes a production of swallowing.

"It was so fun!" he says excitedly. For the next five minutes, he tells us all about his day. This is the second time I've heard it, but it's definitely with the same enthusiasm as the first round.

"I'm glad you had a good day, bud." Graham smiles softly at him.

"And now I get pizza, and you're still going to read me a story, right?" he asks Graham.

"You bet. You better finish up so we can get you in the tub," Graham tells him.

And me, I sit here watching the two of them together. We've been here for a few days, and Graham is already onto Noah's routine. It's nice to have someone around to help and just be here. I have my parents and my brother and sister-in-law, but something about this feels different. More intimate. As if this is what Noah's and my life could have been like had his father not been a spineless asshole. I shake out of those thoughts because that man is the last person I want to think about.

The rest of dinner is more talk about Noah's day. Graham asks him about lunch and any new friends he made, and my heart is so damn full it could burst.

"I want more, but my belly says it's full." Noah sits back in his chair and rubs his belly, making us laugh.

"Why don't you go grab some jammies, and I'll be there in a minute to start the bathwater?" I ask my son.

"Okay." He climbs out of the chair and shoots off down the hall. He only knows one speed these days.

"I've got this," Graham tells me. "Go take care of Noah."

"You bought dinner. The least I can do is clean up."

"It's a few paper plates and a pizza box. Go, I've got this." He stands, and before I know what's happening, he's pressing his lips to mine for the third time tonight. "I'll finish up and come up to read him a story."

All I can do is nod and do as he says. I find Noah in the bathroom. He's sitting on the rug butt naked, playing with one of his bath toys.

"Mommy, I didn't think you'd ever get here. I gots jammies." He points to the closed toilet lid and the dinosaur pajamas laying on top.

"I see that, and it's I *have* jammies." I smile at him before starting his bathwater. He plays with his toys and talks my head off about his first day, and I feel his excitement. I hate that my baby boy is growing up so fast, but I love how much he enjoyed his first day. I admit it's easier knowing that I'm in the same building as him.

By the time I get him out of the tub, his eyes are drooping, and I know he's ready for bed. It's a little earlier than normal, but today was a big day for him.

"Graham!" Noah calls as the man himself steps into the doorway. "Wow. That was fast!" Graham just chuckles, running his fingers through Noah's wet hair.

"Come on, kiddo, let's read that story." Graham offers Noah his hand, and he accepts it with ease. "Coming, Addy?" Graham asks.

"I'll be right there. I'm going to clean up."

Graham winks and leads my son out of the bathroom and down the hall to the room he's claiming as his during our time here. I clean up the toys and make sure we don't leave a mess behind before following the low deep timbre of Graham's voice. I stop just inside the door to see Noah already fast asleep.

"He's out, isn't he?" Graham whispers.

"Yeah. Today was a big day." I make my way into the room and to the opposite side of the bed. I pull the covers up over Noah and kiss his forehead.

Graham puts the book on the nightstand and waits for me at the foot of the bed. He offers me his hand, and I take it just as easy as my son did. It's easy to see that Noah is getting attached to Graham, and that scares me.

Graham surprises me when he leads us to his room instead of the living room. Once we're inside, he softly closes the door and pulls me into the best hug I've ever had. "I missed you," he whispers.

"I missed you too."

"Did you happen to think about us today?"

"Only all day."

"Me too," he confesses.

"Yeah? Come to any conclusions?"

"Did you?" he counters.

"Nope. That's not how this works. I asked you first."

"Yeah, Addy, I came to a conclusion. If I'm being honest, my mind was made up last night."

"Care to share with the class?" I ask, quirking a brow.

"Is it wrong that I just had a naughty teacher fantasy filter through my mind?" He leans in and kisses the corner of my mouth.

"Depends. Who's the teacher, and who's the student?"

"We'll take turns," he says, his eyes heated.

"Oh, it's you and me in this fantasy?" I tease.

"Woman. There is no one else." His voice is strong and no longer playful.

"What does that mean?" My heart is beating so hard I'm sure he can hear it.

"It means that you're mine."

"What if I don't want to be yours?" My tone is teasing. We both know I want to be his. There is no hiding or denying it.

"Then I guess I'll have to convince you." He pulls out of our hug but keeps his arm around my waist and guides me to the bed. He nods for me to lie down, and I do. He follows me. Lying on his side facing me, he raises his palm to rest against my cheek. "What do I have to do?"

"Noah is already so attached to you."

"He's a great kid."

"He is, but I don't want his heart to be broken when we leave and this ends."

He narrows his eyes at me. "Who says that this ends when you leave? Hell, who says you have to leave?"

"Graham." There is a flutter in my belly at his insinuation that we never leave, and that we keep this going between us. I want that more than I ever realized.

"Addyson."

"I don't know what this is. It's all happening so fast."

"This is me telling you that I'm all in. I want to talk to Adam, and I want the world to know that we're dating. This is me telling you that you and Noah can stay forever."

"That's... not what I expected you to say. Graham, you don't really do serious. Not living together serious." He's been adamant in the past about needing his space.

"Then that should tell you how I'm feeling right now. Like I never want to let you or Noah out of my sight. I want to be here when he comes home from school to hear about his day. I want to lie here in bed next to you when he's gone to bed and talk about ours." He leans in and kisses me softly. It's just a quick peck on the lips, but no less potent than if he was devouring me. "I want to kiss you anytime I want. This morning, I wanted to pull you into my arms at the bus stop so damn bad, but it was Adam who got that privilege. I want it to be mine."

"I can't just move in here with my son." The thought sends a thrill through me. I've wanted him for so long, but now that he's telling me everything I could ever want to hear from him, something is stopping me.

"Baby, you already have."

"It's temporary."

"Is it?"

"Do you hear yourself right now?" My head is spinning like a top. There have been so many changes in the past few days that I'm having trouble keeping up.

"Fine. When your apartment is ready, we reassess."

"Now, it's your turn. Tell me what you want." He pulls me closer. His warm hand slides under my shirt and rests on the small of my back.

"Did you know that I had a crush on you?" I ask softly.

"What? When?"

"Always. I can't remember a time when I didn't."

"Why did you never say anything?"

"Why would I? I was your best friend's little sister. You never once gave me any kind of look or sign that you would be interested in me. When I found out I was pregnant with Noah, I just sort of pushed it to the back of my mind. I had a baby to care for, and I already knew you were not one for commitments, and I now had a son to think about."

"I didn't know."

I nod. "That's why I told you. This is hitting a little different for me than it is for you. I've dreamed of you holding me and kissing me so many times that I can't even count them. And now, here you are with your arms wrapped around me, kissing me like I'm yours, telling me that you want me to be."

"Glad we're clear on that." He grins. It's playful, and not at all the grimace I was anticipating from him hearing about my crush on him growing up.

"What I'm saying is that if this had happened between us before I had Noah, I would jump all in. Headfirst. No questions asked. Now things are different. It's not just my heart that I have to think about. It's Noah's too, and he already loves you. Idolizes you."

"I would never hurt you or Noah. Never."

There is so much conviction in his voice that I know he's telling the truth. Besides, Graham isn't one to hide behind lies. He's always been honest about what he wants. "You always said you weren't ready to settle down. I'm not talking about a marriage proposal, but I have to think about Noah and the men that I bring into his life. Right now, you're Graham. His uncle's best friend and the guy who bailed us out of a jam. What happens when he grows even more attached, and you decide we're not what you want. I'm a package deal, Graham."

"You think I don't know that?" He almost sounds hurt. "Do you think I don't care about both of you? That little boy in there is a part of you, Addy. He's bright and funny and cute as hell. I know what it means to be with you. I know that Noah is a huge part of that, and I'm still here next to you, telling you that I want you to be mine. Both of you."

Tears well in my eyes, but I blink hard, trying to keep them at bay. "I want you too, but I have to protect his heart. He doesn't have his dad, and I just... I need to know that this is real, Graham."

He nods. His blue eyes never leave mine. "You have all the power here, Addy. You're a mom first, and I get that. I know it's a lot to ask, but if you could carve out a little of your time for me, that's all I'm asking."

His eyes tell me he's asking for more than that, and we both know it. However, he's willing to take this slow. That's what I'm hearing. "I don't want to tell Noah." He jerks his head back as if I've slapped him. "Not right away," I'm quick to add. "I just... I have to protect him, Graham." I lose my battle with my tears as one slides down my cheek.

"Hey." Graham wipes at my cheek with his thumb. "I'll follow your lead. No tears, baby. I can't take that." His lips press against my cheek. "I can get on board with not telling Noah. I can control myself when he's around, but I want to talk to Adam."

It's on the tip of my tongue to argue, but I don't. Adam is my brother, and his best friend. They have been best friends for a lifetime, and who am I to tell him how he wants to handle this. "What are you talking to him about exactly?" I ask.

"I'm going to tell him that we're dating. That I can't stop thinking about you. I'm going to tell him that I know that you and Noah are a package deal and that I want both of you."

"What if he's mad?"

He shrugs. "Then he's mad. Look, Addy, Adam and I have been friends our entire lives, but this isn't about him. It's about us. I know he's your brother, but you're a grown woman, a mother, not just his sister. You have the right to choose who you spend your time with. If you tell me that you're in this with me, then what Adam says isn't my concern. He can get on board, or he can watch from afar."

"You can't mean that."

"Miss Millie came into the pharmacy today. She heard you were staying with me. She asked if she could pass your number along to George's grandson, Henry. Just the mention of that had me getting defensive. That's never happened to me before. I've never been with someone who I would be upset about them leaving or finding someone else. Hell, Brianne and I dated for months, and I didn't even miss her when she ended things. And today, Addy, I missed you like fucking crazy. I missed you, and I missed Noah. That tells me all I need to know. This is different. This is more, and I couldn't give a fuck what Adam thinks as long as you're happy. You and Noah."

"Okay. You can talk to Adam. Actually, let me talk to him."

"I want it to be me. Man to man, I need him to know that this is real."

"This is all happening so fast. I think we need to ask ourselves if we're truly ready for this. For each other, and bringing Adam into the fold."

"We've known each other for years. I'm not a stranger you met off the street. This is me, and you, and Noah. This is the start of what will be."

"You're awfully confident."

"I've never been one to hide behind my feelings. I've just never had feelings this strong. I don't want to hide them or you, but for Noah, I can agree to that. However, it won't be forever. I'll prove to you that we're it. That you and I are the real deal."

"Graham?"

"Yeah?"

"Kiss me." He doesn't reply. He moves in and presses his lips to mine. He kisses me soft and slow for so long I lose track of time. Eventually, he pulls away and hugs me to his chest. "I should go to my room." I don't really want to, but I know it's what I need to do.

"Stay here. Just a little longer."

"Okay." I snuggle into his chest, and within no time, I feel myself dozing off. I keep thinking I need to get up and leave, but he's warm, and his arms wrapped tightly around me make me feel safe. I've never fallen asleep in a man's arms. I want my first to be with Graham.

Nine

Graham

As soon as I start to rouse from a deep sleep at first light, I draw her closer.

I know she's here, wrapped in my arms. I knew it last night when she fell asleep, and I didn't wake her. I knew when I started to drift off sometime well after her and still held her close. And I know it now, not just because I can smell her shampoo or feel her leg pressed against my erection. No, I know she's here because I feel content and comfortable in a way I've never felt before. It's terrifying, if I'm being honest, but so right at the same time.

Addy shifts in my arms, her petite hand sliding down to rest on my lower stomach. She's so close to my hard-on, it's difficult to think of anything but how dangerously near she is. My dick, of course, is incredibly ecstatic about her nearness. He's twitching and seeping with pre-come excitement, practically begging to be let out from his confines to play.

Her hand inches down, and I hold my breath, waiting. Slender fingers glide across my erection before palming my hard length. I hiss as a flood of pleasure sweeps through my entire body. She moves her hand again, slipping it beneath the waistband of my shorts. Warm, soft skin glides over me, and it's hard to think of anything but this euphoria. "Addy," I grit through my tight jaw.

"Yes?" she whispers just as her fingers wrap fully around me, giving a gentle squeeze.

Somehow, I'm able to get words past my Sahara-dry throat. "What are you doing?"

She doesn't respond right away, at least not with words. Addy continues to stroke my cock, drawing me closer to the edge of control with every move of her hand. She looks up, catching my heated gaze as she replies, "Something I've dreamed about doing since I was old enough to have dirty thoughts."

I groan, closing my eyes and letting the pleasure take over. I need to stop this, but I can't. I'm too far gone. The feel of her hand wrapped around me, stroking me off, is too much to take.

Addy moves, releasing my dick and kneeling beside me. She tugs on the waist of my shorts. I lift my hips and drop the moment they're down enough to free my cock. I'm about to ask her what she's doing when she looks up at me with lust-filled eyes, licks her lips, and lowers her head.

"Fuck," I moan the moment her warm tongue runs down my shaft.

My fingers slide into her hair, not to control her movement, but to ground myself and to keep from flying over the edge.

It works—for a second.

When she grips my shaft at the root and lowers her mouth around the entire length, taking me almost completely down her throat, my control snaps. My hips thrust up, the head of my cock slamming against the back of her throat. Addy gags but doesn't pull me out. Instead, she relaxes her throat even more and glides her tongue along the underside of my dick.

"Addy." Her name is a groan, a plea for mercy. I've been in her mouth for mere seconds, and I'm already about to blow, but there's no time to be embarrassed about my lack of stamina. She twists her hand slowly as she goes down on me again, sucking and licking at the same time. My balls are tight, the tingle at the base of my spine spreading up my back, and I know I won't be able to hold back. "Addy," I repeat, this time as a warning. "I'm going to—"

The words completely die on my tongue as she sucks my cock deep in her mouth like she majored in it in college. There's no stopping my orgasm racing through my body, taking over like a damn spiritual possession.

I come so hard, I have no control over anything. My hips thrust, desperate for more of the amazing warmth, wetness, and tightness of her mouth. My entire body spasms and shakes so violently, I briefly worry I've suffered some sort of permanent damage. And apparently, I holler loudly, because her hand comes up and covers my lips to muffle my cries.

When I'm finally able to draw oxygen into my burning lungs and crack open my eyes, I whisper a harsh "Fuck, Addy."

She sits up, smiling widely. She looks so fucking pleased, so damn sexy with hair slightly mussed and her nipples pressed firmly against her shirt. A fresh bolt of lust sweeps through my veins. Of course, there's no way I'm getting hard again right away. At least not without a few minutes to collect my thoughts.

Hell, I might need a nap.

But I refuse to give in to the euphoric exhaustion.

Instead, I dig deep for a burst of energy and flip our positions. Addy's sprawled out on my bed—an image I fucking love, by the way—and looking positively edible, like a Thanksgiving Day dessert buffet. My mouth waters.

"You're wearing entirely too much clothing," I inform her, helping to relieve her of her pants. The moment I slide them down her legs, exposing her panties, my cock twitches and I can tell it won't be long until I'm fully hard once more.

I toss her capris over my shoulder, my eyes zeroing in on her lilac panties. They're basic cotton and boy-cut with little positive sayings scrolled across them. My lips turn upward as I read the words beautiful, happiness, and joyful in different fonts and colors.

"What's that smile for?" she asks, noticing my attention to her panties.

"I was just thinking I have a few different words for these," I state, sliding my finger beneath the material above her thigh. When she raises her eyebrows in question, I go on. "How about edible," I suggest, bending down and running my nose over her covered clit. "Mouthwatering," I add, running my tongue over the wet material and getting a taste of her sweetness. "How about hard-on-inducing gorgeous?" I suggest, wrapping my mouth around her mound and sucking.

Addy whimpers softly. "That might be too long to print on panties."

I tsk, slipping my fingers beneath the waistband, anxious to remove them from her body. "You might be right, but that doesn't mean it's not true." Holding her gaze, I gently slide the material down her hips. What I find has my cock hard and ready to go once more. "When did you do this?" I ask, my throat dry.

"Yesterday morning when I showered."

My gaze never diverts from her shaved pussy as I finish taking off her underwear, casting them to the side. I drag my eyes away and somehow meet her gaze. With shaky fingers, I glide them over the wet, soft flesh. "Did you do this for me?"

She swallows hard before nodding. "Yes."

The groan that erupts from my throat sounds pained as urgency settles in. I *need* to taste her. Now.

I push her top up, exposing a matching lilac cotton bra. Without releasing the clasp, I carefully tug down the cups, freeing her gorgeous tits. I should take the time to remove the bra completely, but I'm already moving between her thighs and lowering my mouth to her sweet pussy.

The first swipe of my mouth over her clit has us both moaning in pleasure. Her wetness coats my tongue, surrounding me with her scent and fueling my desire to make her come. Like a man possessed, I go down on Addy, sucking her clit and sliding my index finger in and out at a steady pace.

I shift my shoulders, spreading her legs farther apart. She's glistening with moisture as I add a second finger, stretching her pussy wide. My mouth latches onto her clit once more, and she bites down on her bottom lip, a muffled whimper breaking through the silence.

My mouth still against her flesh, I flick my tongue across her swollen nub hard. "I want to feel you come, Addy. Come on my fingers. Flood my mouth with your release," I request before latching onto her clit once more and sucking on her sweet flesh.

She cries out, shoving her hand over her mouth to muffle the noises she's making. I curl my fingers upward, searching for that magical spot deep inside her that will send her soaring. I know the second I find it too. Her pussy clenches around my fingers and her body starts to shake.

"Come," I demand once more, watching as her release grabs hold and won't let go.

Addy's cries are stifled by her hand, her eyes tightly closed, as she comes with a vengeance. It's the most amazing thing to witness, feel, and taste. Her hips gyrate against my face, her internal muscles squeezing so tightly it almost hurts. All I can think about is what this moment will feel like when it's my cock buried inside her instead of my fingers.

I can't fucking wait for that moment.

When her orgasm starts to subside and her body relaxes, I gently release the pressure of my mouth around her clit and remove my fingers. I lap up every ounce of wetness she created, savoring the unique taste that's pure Addyson. Like a drug addict, I take everything I can get, not wanting this moment to end. And when it's finally done, I still want more.

Falling onto the bed beside her, I lick my lips, trying to recall the last time I enjoyed going down on a woman like that. I've always been a fan of the act, but I've never felt this bone-deep desire to draw every last drop of release from someone's body the way I did with Addy and wanting to do it over and over again.

She crawls onto my lap. My cock is hammer-hard, ready for her to shift just a bit and take me inside that tight, wet pussy. Unfortunately, I know our time together is almost over. The clock's reading is a blaring reminder that we both need to get moving for work, that her son will be waking soon for breakfast.

"Addy," I grind out through gritted teeth.

"Yes?" She rocks her hips and coats my cock with wetness. She rakes her nails across my chest, the bite causing my dick to jump with eagerness.

"We need to stop." I don't know where I draw that energy from, but somehow, I'm able to speak the words my body is trying to overpower.

"We have a few minutes," she whispers, leaning forward and pressing her tits against my chest. She nips at my jaw before soothing it with her tongue. Those magical hands of hers start to trek down my sides, and I know exactly where they're headed. My cock jumps with joy.

This woman is dangerous.

I stop her hands and roll us both over. It would be so easy to press inside her right now. Her legs wrap around my waist, opening herself up for me, but I refuse to move, refuse to push inside the way we both want. "When I slide between your thighs for the first time, it's not going to be a quickie before work, Addy. I'm going to savor and take my time, exploring your entire body with my hands and my tongue. I'm going to make you come so many times you lose count and forget your own name."

She shivers beneath me. "When?"

Now, now, now!

"Soon," I reply, exhaling deeply and running my nose down her neck. She smells familiar, like vanilla and sunshine, purely my Addy. I want to lie with her like this all day. I realize quickly I'd probably be able to and never tire of it.

See what I mean? My drug.

Another thought prickles the back of my mind. "I want to talk to Adam first."

She tenses beneath me. "Adam?"

"I want to tell him we're dating before I sink into you for the first time. I don't want anything hanging over us."

Addy exhales and curls her arms around my back, her fingers drawing lazy circles over my flesh. "I guess that makes sense."

Going up on my elbows, I meet those gorgeous brown eyes. "That's going to happen, Addyson. Believe me. I'm going to talk to him soon, and then we're going to figure out how to steal a night away, because if there's one thing I've learned in the last thirty minutes, it's that I'm going to need an entire night with you. Even then, it may not be enough."

I claim her mouth with my own, wishing we didn't have to stop but knowing we must. Our time is up.

"Graham?" she whispers the moment I release her lips.

"Yeah?"

"I can't wait for that night."

I suck in a greedy breath of air. "Me either, sweetness."

She sighs in resignation, my cue to roll off her and let her go. Addy sits on the edge of my bed and adjusts her bra, covering up those amazing tits once more. She reaches for her capris and slips them on, disregarding the panties I tossed somewhere on the floor.

When she's dressed, she turns her attention back to me. "Tosha and I have plans to take Noah to the jump park on Saturday afternoon. He's been begging to spend the night with her so he can play with her chocolate lab, Piper. If she agrees to take him, maybe we can... hang out."

I get up, ignoring the fact I'm naked from the waist down and hard as steel, and step directly in front of her. "If she agrees, we're not hanging out, Addy. I'm taking you on a proper date."

Her eyes brighten at the suggestion. "Yeah?"

"Hell yes," I reply, placing a kiss on the tip of her nose.

"And after?" she asks, desire swirling in the depths of her brown eyes.

"After I feed you, I'm going to bring you back here and explore every inch of your body. I'm going to taste, lick, and fuck you, Addy. All. Night. Long."

She smiles. "I like the sound of that," she whispers, sliding her hands up my chest. "What will we do until Saturday night?"

Wrapping my arms around her, I draw her close and breathe her in. "We'll steal a few moments whenever we can, because there's no way I'll be able to go until Saturday night without kissing you."

She goes up on her tiptoes and swipes my lips with her own. "I like kissing you too."

"I'm going to call Adam too and see if he'll meet me for a few beers Friday after work. The quicker I have that conversation, the quicker we're out in the open and can stop worrying about what he's going to say or think."

She nods and rests her cheek against my chest. I can't help but wonder if she's listening to the rapid thunder of my heart. It seems to do that whenever she's near. "Okay."

I hug her tightly, risking a quick glance at the clock and realizing we're running late to start our day. "Go shower. I'll run through mine and head down to start Noah's breakfast. Take your time and join us when you're ready."

"You don't have to do that," she insists, but I'm already shaking my head.

"I want to," I declare, kissing the tip of her nose one last time before releasing my hold on her. "Go. Now. Before I say fuck it all and drag you back to my bed."

Addy giggles the sweetest sound before lifting her chin and stating, "That doesn't sound so bad, actually."

I groan and close my eyes, picturing her coming on my tongue. "You're trouble. Go."

"All right, all right." As she reaches the door, she turns. "Thank you, Graham. For helping me with Noah."

"I'm honored to," I say, meaning every word.

With one final small smile, Addy slips from my bedroom, quietly shutting the door behind her. I'm left standing here, my cock hard and pissed off he's not getting any more attention, especially with the parade of memories filtering through my brain. Addyson Sinclair is a pleasant surprise I didn't see coming. Sure, she's every bit as strong and independent as I've always thought her to be, but now I can add sensual and sexy when she comes to the list.

So. Fucking. Sexy.

I glance down at my cock. "Sorry, buddy, but you're just going to have to deal with my hand for the next few days."

Saturday.

Saturday is when I'm officially making her mine, and I'm not just talking about in bed, though I plan to make her mine that way too. I'm referring to her—us. I want to share in the joys of her day and be a partner when it comes to caring for Noah. I want to make her laugh and carry the burden of what makes her sad. I want the relationship I've never even realized I wanted.

Me.

The king of casual dating. The one who never took a woman home to meet his parents or invited her to family dinners.

The thought of sharing those moments with Addy doesn't cause uncertainty and fear like it always did with other women. No, with Addy, I'm anxious and eager to do all of that and more. I want her by my side. More importantly, I want to be by *her* side.

I've also never pictured myself stepping into a parenting role before, yet here I am, ready to fill those particular shoes for Noah. I've never dated a single mother before, never really wanted to. Yet I'm anxious to get to know Noah more and spend as much time with him as possible.

It's a terrifying thought. I've never wanted this kind of relationship, this kind of intimacy. I'm sure I'm going to fuck up—probably a lot—when it comes to being this kind of boyfriend, but if anyone is patient and understanding while I figure it out, it's Addy.

I'm ready to prove to her she's more than just a casual fling.

She's my endgame, and she doesn't even know it.

Ten

ddyson

I've been a nervous wreck all day. Graham is having beers with Adam tonight. He says that he's going to tell him about us. That we're... dating. Adam is a pretty laid-back guy, but I have no idea how he's going to feel about this. It's had me on edge all day.

"Mommy!" Noah races into my classroom. "Look at my flower!" He thrusts a piece of construction paper at me.

"Wow." I take the paper from him. "This is so pretty," I praise.

"I'm good at kindagarden," he says, botching the word.

I chuckle. "You are very good at kindergarten," I say, pronouncing the word slowly.

Ignoring me completely, he groans dramatically. "I'm starving. What are we having for dinner?"

"Well, Aunt Joy is coming over to visit with us."

"Uncle Adam too?" he asks hopefully.

"Not tonight. Uncle Adam and Graham are going to dinner."

"What are they eating? I should eat with the boys." He puffs his chest out, and I have to bite down on my cheek to hold on to my laughter.

"They're going to a place kids are not allowed to go."

"That's a terrible place," he counters, and this time I do laugh.

"Probably," I say, agreeing with him. "What if we pick up Chinese on our way home?"

"Oh, can I have the roll thing? And rice with that red sauce and chicken?"

"Absolutely. I'm going to call Aunt Joy to see what she wants."

"Oh, can I do it?" He reaches for my phone. I tap Joy's contact and hit Video Call. Noah dances around my classroom as he waits for the call to connect. "Aunt Joy!" he cheers.

"Hey, Noah." Joy's sweet voice greets him.

"Look!" Noah rushes back to my desk, grabs the piece of construction paper, and holds it against the screen.

"It's too close, bud." Joy chuckles.

"Noah, let me talk to Joy," I tell him.

"Are you hungry?" he asks my sister-in-law.

"I am. Are you hungry?" she asks him.

"Starving," he says theatrically. "Mommy said you're coming to our house, but we're not there. We live with Graham now. Did you know that? He reads me stories, and he found me a new dinosaur backpack and lunch box!"

"Okay, buddy. Let me have the phone. Why don't you go pick a book to look at while I pack up my things and talk to Aunt Joy?"

"Okay. See you, Aunt Joy." He waves at the phone before practically tossing it toward me and rushing off toward the reading corner in my classroom.

"I wish I had just a little of his energy." Joy laughs.

"You and me both. We're going to pick up Chinese on the way home. Text me what you want."

"That sounds so good," she groans.

"I thought so too. I'm lucky that Noah eats pretty much anything these days."

"I hope that when Adam and I have kids, they're as good as Noah."

"He's not without his faults," I remind her.

"Oh, I know, but that's just human nature. He's a good kid, Addyson. You've done a great job with him."

"Thank you." I smile as I glance over at my son arranging the books on the bookshelf. He's used to helping me clean up my classroom. He just knows what to do.

"I need to go. I'm heading home soon. I'm going to stop by our place and change, and then I'll be over. Do you need me to bring anything?"

"Nope. Just you. I'll see you later."

Ending the call, I check on Noah and go back to my desk. I'd love to get through these parent emails before going home so I can leave my job here for the weekend. As soon as I'm back at my desk, I get a text alert.

Graham: I won't be home. I'm just leaving the pharmacy and meeting Adam at Hank's.

Me: Okay. Be safe. Good luck.

Graham: It's all going to be fine, Addy.

Me: You say that now. Maybe we should call this off.

Me: I'm just nervous. This is a big deal.

I hit Send before I can stop myself from speaking about what's been going on in my head. Instead of a text reply, my phone rings. I eye Noah, who is occupied with a book. "Hello," I answer softly.

"What's wrong? Where are you?"

"Nothing. I'm still at work. Noah is here with me."

"Got it. Good, you can just listen. Are you listening, Addy?"

"Yes."

"Your brother is my best friend. He has been for as far back as I can remember."

"I know."

"Listening, Addy," he reminds me. He doesn't expect a reply, so I don't give him one. "What we're building, it's… not something I ever expected. It's everything I never knew I wanted, or hell, even existed. If he doesn't like us together, he can get over it. I'm not giving you and Noah up."

My heart stutters in my chest when he talks about Noah. He's so good with him, but dating a single mom is a big deal. The thought of him walking out of not only my life but Noah's is terrifying. "Adam wouldn't do that. At least I don't think that he would. I don't know. This is such new territory. Now that the time has come to tell him my nerves are all over the place. And Noah, he's so attached to you already. He's never had a man live with us as if he were a father figure."

"I agreed to not tell Noah. I know that we need to protect him, but, baby, what you don't understand is that there is nothing to protect him from. This is new. We're new, but I've never in my entire life ever felt this way about anyone. That extends to Noah too. My house feels like a home with the two of you there. So, regardless of what Adam says or how he feels about us, we're not calling this off. I'm too far gone."

"It's been days," I remind him, still struggling to process the speed of us getting together and the declarations he's making.

"I've known you our entire lives. It's not like we're strangers. We already had a relationship, Addy. This is just taking it to the next level."

I have a choice to make. I can let my fears come between us, or I can stand behind him. I can stand behind this relationship. I don't ever want to choose my family over the person I'm dating, but Graham isn't just someone. He's everything.

"Call me after?"

"I will." His voice is softer. "Have Noah call me before bedtime."

"You don't—" I start, but he talks over me.

"I want to, Addyson."

"Okay. Be safe. I'll see you when you get home."

"Home," he whispers. "You and Noah, you're making my house a home."

If I wasn't certain that it wasn't possible, I'd think that my heart literally stopped beating for a few seconds. I clear my throat, calming myself. "Are you sure you don't mind if Joy comes over tonight?"

"Not at all. You don't have to ask, Addyson."

"I'll see you later," I say, as Noah's head jerks up.

"Who you talking to, Mommy?" he asks, racing toward me.

"Graham."

"Oh, I wanna talk." He wiggles around, holding his hand out for my phone.

Selfishly, I place the phone on speaker so I can hear their conversation. "Graham, Noah wants to say hi," I say.

"Hi, Graham!" Noah shouts.

"Shh, bud, you don't have to scream."

"Sorry," he says, offering me a toothy grin. "Graham, I drawed a flower."

"You did? That sounds fun. Do I get to see it?"

"Yes. We can hang it on the fridge."

"I'd like that, No."

"Why are you and Uncle Adam going to eat where kids can't eat? That's not a nice place, Graham."

Graham's deep chuckle fills the room. "How about the next time Uncle Adam and I bring you along? We'll be sure to go somewhere kids are allowed."

"Tonight?" Noah asks excitedly.

"Not tonight, bud. We'll talk to your mom and Uncle Adam and set up a day."

"Mom, can we call Uncle Adam now?" Noah asks.

"Not right now." What I don't say is that Adam and Graham might not be on speaking terms in a few hours. I hate to disappoint my son, but I can't very well tell him yes or no in this situation.

"Please?" he begs.

"Noah, you need to listen to your mom," Graham tells him.

"Ah, man," Noah whines.

"You be good for your mom. Call me before you go to bed, so I can say goodnight."

"What? You won't be home to tell me a story?" he asks.

"I... Yeah, little man, I'll be there," Graham commits.

"Graham, you don't have to do that."

"I don't do anything I don't want to do, Addyson. I'll be there to tuck Noah in."

"He can stay up a little later since it's the weekend." Noah cheers at my confession. The idea is exciting to him, but he's had a long day and will be passed out at bedtime, if not before.

"I'll be there, Addyson." There is a note of conviction in his voice. It's sexy and thrilling, and it brings a wave of contentment over me.

I've been doing this single-mom gig since the day I found out I was pregnant. To have someone other than my parents or my brother to help carry that load, it's different and makes me want things for Noah and me that I'm not sure we will ever have.

"Okay."

"Okay. Noah?"

"Yeah?"

"You're the man of the house while I'm gone. You got to watch out for your mom and Aunt Joy, all right?"

"I can do it." Noah stands a little taller.

"I know you can, bud. I'll see you later."

"Bye!" Noah shouts.

I take the phone off speaker. "I'll see you soon," I say softly.

"Yeah, you will." With that, he ends the call.

Somehow, I manage to work through the rest of my parent emails while Noah draws on the whiteboard. Forty-five minutes later, we're packing up and heading home.

"Can I go play in my room?" Noah asks after dinner.

"Sure, bud." I manage to ruffle my fingers through his hair before he jets off up to the room he's been staying in.

"Spill it," Joy says as soon as Noah is out of earshot.

"What?"

"Come on, Addyson. You've been distracted all night."

"Fine." I look over my shoulder to make sure Noah's not standing anywhere close. "Graham and I are... dating."

"It was only a matter of time."

"What? What do you mean it was only a matter of time? This is new. So new."

"Maybe the part where the two of you make it official is new, but the fact that this was inevitable was not."

"What are you talking about?"

"See, my dear sister..." She grins. "I'm an outsider looking in. I see the way you've always looked at him and him you. He's always been protective of you. Why do you think he showed up with Adam the day you called about your apartment? He could have gone home, but he didn't. He needed to check on you." She smiles smugly.

"No. You're crazy. Okay, not completely crazy. I've crushed on him since I was little, but this is altogether different."

"It's not."

"It is."

"Joy!"

"Addyson!" she mocks me. "I'm just calling it like I see it. Now, I need the details."

"I don't know. It just sort of happened."

"You're blushing."

I cover my face with my hands and groan. "He makes me feel like a damn teenager. I'm a mom. I don't have time for crushes."

"Hold up. Just because you're a mother doesn't mean you're not entitled to happiness."

"That's not what I meant. I know that. I need to think about Noah first, though. I can't just jump in with both feet and let whatever happens happen. The last time I did that, I ended up alone and pregnant."

"Maybe," she muses. "However, from where I'm sitting, that turned out pretty damn good for you too. That little boy is a light."

"He's my entire world. That's why I have to think about him first. I can't let him get too attached to Graham, and then when this ends, whatever this is, he's going to be destroyed."

"He will be, but, Addyson, you can't protect him from life."

"He's already missing a dad, and he loves Graham so much. He would be devastated."

"And what about you?"

"What about me?"

"If this ends between the two of you, you're going to be devastated too."

"Yes," I admit. "But I can handle it. I just don't want to do that to Noah."

"Kids are resilient. I think you should do what feels right. Maybe give it a little more time before telling Noah, but don't keep him in the dark. That little boy of yours is smart as hell. He's going to figure it out."

"I really like him, and our chemistry... it's unlike anything I've ever felt before. Explosive even."

"Oh." She grins. "Tell me more."

"Stop." I laugh. "I'm serious. I've never responded to a man just being near, the way I do with Graham."

"Can I let you in on a little secret?"

"Always."

"That's how it was with Adam and me. It's still that way for us. That kind of connection isn't something that you just walk away from."

"I can't tell you how many times growing up I thought about being his. How many times I've thought about kissing him, and let me just confess that my imagination did not do the man justice."

"Let it happen, Addyson. Let the cards fall where they may. Noah will be fine, because he has you... and me and Adam and your parents. My gut tells me that you're both going to have Graham as well."

"I love my son. He is my greatest gift in this world, and I can't imagine my life without him. However, the last time I just let go and let whatever happens to happen, I ended up a single mom. Again, I love my son with every ounce of my soul, but I never thought I'd be doing this on my own, you know?"

"I can understand that, but sometimes the risk is worth the reward."

"Was that in your fortune cookie?" I ask with a laugh, before blurting, "He's telling Adam tonight."

Joy waves her hand in the air. "Nothing to worry about."

"How do you figure? They've been best friends since they were knee-high to a grasshopper. Isn't dating your best friend's little sister against the bro code?"

"Probably." She shrugs. "But Adam isn't blind, Addyson. He's seen the same things that I've seen. He even said there was something more when the three of you took Noah to the bus stop. He was surprised that Graham was going too, but then again, he wasn't."

"You really think he's going to be okay with it?" I ask her. Even as I ask the question, I know it won't matter. What I feel for Graham, what we're building is too strong. I hate that it could come between them, but I know for me, and for Graham if Adam balks at the idea of us together, it won't matter.

"If he isn't, then that's on him. I love my husband, but he has no say so in who you or Graham date. He needs to learn to suck it up and move on."

"You make it all sound too easy, and how could Adam have a suspicion and not mention it?"

"I can't answer that. All I know is that he's made comments before that he'll be surprised if the two of you don't end up together one day." She gives me a knowing smirk, and my heart soars. She's telling me without telling me that this is going to be okay.

I glance down at my watch. "I guess we're going to find out soon. Graham promised Noah he'd be here to tuck him in."

"Aw, see." She points her index finger at me. "He wouldn't do that if he wasn't in this. Graham knows what's at stake. He knows how your lives are intertwined, and he understands that Noah is a part of you. Don't overthink it."

"I wasn't overthinking it this morning," I mutter under my breath, but my sister-in-law has supersonic hearing and catches me.

"That." She wiggles in her seat, getting more comfortable. "Tell me about that."

"No. No way. You've heard enough about me. Tell me, what's going on with you?"

"I want a baby," she blurts. Her eyes widen at her confession.

"Have you told him?"

"No. We talked about kids, and we both want them, but we never really set a timeline. But I want to start sooner rather than later."

"You should tell him."

"I've been trying to work up the courage."

"He's going to be a great dad. He was great with Noah, and you're going to be the best mom."

"I want our kids to grow up together, and Noah is already five."

"He can be the protective big cousin."

"Who knows, maybe he can be a big brother sometime soon."

"I'd love to have more kids. I love being a mom. I just want to make sure I do it right the next time. I want a man to be there to stand beside me through it all."

"I think you've found him, Addyson."

I nod but don't reply. In my heart, I think I've found him too. My mind, however, isn't exactly on board just yet. I know that Joy is right. I need to stop stressing and just let it happen. When I'm with Graham, in his arms, there is no stress and no worry. He has this way of making me feel as though it's all going to work out. We'll see how the next few weeks go. If we're still both into this, we can tell Noah.

Eleven

Graham

I pull open the heavy wooden door to Hank's, the sound of classic Alabama and the scent of stale beer hitting me in the face as soon as I cross the threshold. The place is pretty busy, but considering it's Friday night, I really shouldn't be surprised.

I spot my friend sitting at the bar and head in his direction. Of course, Mr. Heckleman and Mr. Jordan stop me first, asking how my dad is doing and if I think the rumor of a big chain pharmacy coming to town will come to fruition.

"I hope not. You get a lot better, more personal service from a family-owned business," I reply diplomatically, slowly keeping my feet moving.

"That's right!" Mr. Heckleman agrees, holding up his draft beer in salute.

The moment I reach the stool beside my friend, I sigh in relief.

"Long day?" he asks before taking a drink from his beer bottle.

"The longest," I mumble, sliding onto the stool.

The moment Hank sets a cold drink in front of me, Adam asks, "Have you heard the rumors?"

Again, I sigh and lean back in my seat. "We heard them. Dad and Mom stopped by to work on payroll when Norma Heller came in and said the city got an inquiry for a development. The request didn't give too many details on the business but did mention a national chain pharmacy."

All afternoon, I kept thinking about what Norma told my parents, which I guess, actually helped keep me from overanalyzing the conversation I was going to have with Adam. Unfortunately, it was just trading one stress for another.

"What did your pops say about it?"

I take another pull of my beer. "He said we're not going to worry about it. The best thing to do is focus on what we do day in and day out, but I caught the look he shared with my mom. Honestly, he's not worried about them. He's nearing retirement age and is looking forward to slowing down more so than he already has. What he's worried about is me." I meet my friend's gaze. "He's afraid the business my family built won't be around long enough for me to enjoy the fruits of their labor."

Adam nods. "I get it. They worked hard to build the business and reputation, which is why I think if some big chain comes to town, you guys will be okay. Everyone knows the Morgan name, and no way are they gonna trade in excellent customer service and friendly service for a CVS."

I hope he's right, but I'm just not sure. At the end of the day, they'll go where they can save a few bucks.

"Anyway, how was your day?" I ask, eager to change the subject.

"Water main break over on Highland. We've got a boil order for that corner of town," Adam replies.

"You boys ordering?" Hank asks, approaching the bar with two fresh beers.

"Definitely. Joy's over at Graham's with my sister, so I'm on my own," he states.

I glance down at my watch while Adam orders, noting the time. I know it's a Friday night and Noah can stay up a little later, but I don't want to be gone too long. We've fallen into a solid routine these last few days, where I get to read him a story at bedtime, and I don't want to miss it.

"And you?"

I glance up, finding Hank waiting for me to place my order. "Oh, sorry. Just a burger and fries."

"You sure? We got meatloaf, corn, and mashed potatoes tonight for the special," he informs me.

"I'll take that then."

Hank nods before disappearing to put in our orders with the cook.

We make small talk for the next ten minutes, all while I try to figure out how to lead in to the conversation we need to have. It's not every day I tell my best friend I'm going to date his sister, whether he likes it or not. Do you step into the discussion slowly and with finesse, or is this one of those instances you just rip off the Band-Aid and blurt it out?

"Gonna take Joy to a UK football game next month. Wanna go?"

I glance over at my friend and snort. "And be your third wheel? Hell no."

Adam just grins. "You wouldn't be the third wheel. I was gonna see if Addyson and Noah wanted to go."

That grabs my attention and perks me up a little. "I'm in."

His eyes don't give anything away, nor does he say anything about my quick response. "Noah's been wanting to go, and since T-ball is done now, I figured they'd be able to get away for the day."

The door is cracked open.

"About Noah and Addy," I start, just as Hank appears, delivering two steaming plates of Donna's homemade meatloaf, mashed potatoes, and blanched corn from the farmer's market.

Adam grabs his silverware and dives in, and even though I'm hungry too, I'm too anxious for this conversation to just jump into my food with Adam's gusto.

"Shit, this is delicious. Joy's been trying new recipes at home."

"Yeah? How's that going?" I ask, taking a smaller bite of my mashed potatoes and gravy-covered meatloaf.

He glances over and pins me with a look. "Well, she's trying. And I've gotten really good at positive reinforcement."

I snort a laugh, wondering what it would be like to be in Adam's situation. Newly married with a wife who's learning to take care of a house and husband. From what I've heard, Joy didn't know much about cooking, and many of their early pre-wedding meals were boxed kits or takeout. But Adam isn't the type of guy to remark about her lack of cooking skills. Instead, he'd encourage her to keep going and eats whatever she puts on the table at the end of the day, helping out and cooking meals for her on the nights she works.

"I cook as much as I can too, so we've been learning together. We tried this chicken and potato dish she found online and ended up ordering pizza when the chicken turned hard and chewy and the potatoes chalky and bland," he adds, a huge smile on his face.

He'd do anything for his wife.

I glance at my watch, again noting the time, and set my fork down. Most of my food is untouched, but I feel as if I'm going to burst if I don't get this out soon. "Listen, I wanted to talk to you. About Addy."

That catches his attention as he turns his shoulder my way. "Everything all right? I hope you don't mind Joy went over there tonight for dinner."

He barely has his statement out of his mouth and I'm holding up my hand. "Of course I don't care she's there. Not only are you guys welcome there anytime, but it's also Addy's place too, and she can have any guest she wants."

"Okay," Adam replies, seeming a little relieved. "Then what's up?"

Taking a deep breath, I square my shoulders and meet my friend's gaze. "I'm taking your sister out tomorrow night."

His face doesn't give anything away as he stares back at me. "Out?"

"On a date."

Adam breaks eye contact by reaching for his beer and taking a drink. When he sets it down, he asks, "How long have you been dating her?" He doesn't seem mad, just curious.

Food completely forgotten, I turn on my stool and give him my complete attention. "I haven't been. Tomorrow will be our first date." I leave out the fact she's fallen asleep in my bed more nights than not. I don't want to push it.

He slowly nods. "What about Noah?"

My smile is quick and easy. "He's so fucking cool. I love spending time with him."

He returns my grin. "He is."

"We're keeping him out of it for now."

"So, you're just going to sneak around?" The look on his face shows his disapproval.

"No. I want the world to know we're dating, but when it comes to Noah, she's very protective. Not that I blame her. She's worried about him getting more attached than he already is." I check my watch once more, making sure I have time to get home before bedtime.

"What's that?"

When I look up, his eyes are narrowed on my watch. "What?"

"You keep checking your watch."

"Oh. Well, I promised Noah after school I'd be home in time to read him a bedtime story."

My friend's lips spread into a wide grin. "He's a pretty cool kid. Gets it from his uncle."

I roll my eyes dramatically. "Keep telling yourself that, but that kid is all his mother."

Adam concedes with a nod. "Listen," he starts, taking a deep breath. "If you want to date my sister, I'm not gonna stand in your way or get all weird about it. She's an adult, and I trust you. But as Addy's older brother, I have to ask, are you sure you're ready for the kind of relationship she deserves?"

The hairs on the back of my neck stand up.

As if sensing my immediate response to his question, he continues, "I don't mean that in a bad way, man, but you've never wanted a serious relationship. I suppose, if that's the type of relationship she's looking for, one that's just casual—and we promise to never *ever* discuss that—then so be it. But I think I know my sister pretty well, and she's not a casual fling kind of girl."

"She's not," I confirm. "It wouldn't be casual."

Adam's eyebrows draw together in question. "You'll be in a relationship? A week after ending whatever it was you had with Brianne?"

I totally get where he's coming from with his questions, really I do. I don't exactly have the best track record when it comes to women, mostly because I've never wanted anything serious. But with Addy, I can't imagine us together in any other way. I don't want a fling with her. I want dates and holding hands. Cuddles on the couch. Long talks on the swing in my backyard on a warm summer's night. Slow kisses goodnight.

"I can already tell this is different than what Brianne and I had. I never wanted more with her and made my position on the subject very clear from the start. Now, with Addy, I see something I never thought I'd want. A future."

He seems to consider my words. "You know, I told Joy on Wednesday when we met for lunch that I suspected something was up with you two. I couldn't exactly put my finger on it, but I saw the way you looked at her. It was… different. Much different than when we'd hang with Brianne or the ones who came before her. Just the mention of her name and you had this glint in your eye."

I nod, understanding exactly what he means. "I really like her. After just spending five minutes with her in my home, it was like I saw a whole new Addy. She wasn't just your little sister anymore. She's, well, she's genuine and real and a fucking knockout. She takes my breath away." And does things to my dick just by thinking about her, but I leave that part out too. I shake my head, as if trying to find the right words. "Everything about her is beautiful, inside and out."

Adam stares back at me for several long seconds before reaching out his hand. "Good, and maybe a little gross on the details," he says the moment I place mine in his. "I worry about her. She's the toughest, strongest woman I know, but even Ads needs help every now and again. No, not help. She needs a partner. If you were just looking to, you know, do things we won't *ever* talk about in this particular situation, I'd tell you to stay away, but you're probably the best man I've ever met, so if you want to date my sister, maybe even give her the life she and my nephew deserve, I'm all for it."

My shoulders relax for the first time since I left work and headed in this direction. "Thanks, man. Means a lot to me."

He nods and smiles solemnly. "Just know if you fuck with my baby sister, best friend or not, I'll kick your ass."

I bark out a laugh. "Deal, man. But just so you know, I don't ever plan to hurt her."

Adam shrugs and picks back up his fork. "No one ever plans to hurt the person they're with, but it happens sometimes. The key is to unfuck the fuck-up you made."

His comment makes me snort. "Poetic."

Adam shrugs and finishes off his meatloaf in one huge bite. "That's me. Mr. Poetic," he mumbles with his mouth full.

"How about you? Everything good at home?"

As soon as he swallows, he glances over with a shyness to his features I've never seen before. "Yeah, good. Real good, actually. I've been thinking a lot lately."

"About?" I encourage when he doesn't continue.

"About having kids. We talked about it before we got married, and we both want them. Every night when I go home to her, I picture Joy pregnant with my baby or with a baby in her arms."

I can't help but smile over at my best friend. "You'll make a kick-ass dad."

His grin is a little sheepish. "She'll make the best mom."

"Then why are we still here?" I ask, pulling my wallet out of my pressed trousers and tossing too many bills on the counter beside my uneaten food. "Let's head to my house so you can get your wife and take her home."

Now, he's smiling ear to ear. "Sounds good to me." He pulls out his wallet and does the same before adding, "Besides, you have a bedtime story to read."

My chest tightens with a foreign emotion. "I do."

I'm practically giddy the entire drive back to my house, despite the fact my best friend is behind me. I get to see Addy and Noah in just a few minutes, which has my foot pressing down on the accelerator a little harder than normal. Even the somewhat shitty day I had doesn't seem to matter. I'm excited to go home, to see them both in my space, waiting for me.

I pull into the driveway and park my truck in the garage beside her car. Earlier in the week, I jockeyed around a few things so she could park in the first bay, so they are closer to the entrance. Addy argued, of course, not wanting to take the spot I've been using since I bought this house, but I refused to listen. I could walk an extra few feet from the far side of the garage to the side door if it meant Addy and Noah were closer.

I leave the garage door up so Adam can follow, and the moment I open the interior door, I'm surrounded by laughter. By *Addy's* laughter.

As soon as I cross the threshold, my best friend practically barrels past me, knocking me into the door with a thud. "Dick," I mutter over his laughter.

"Where's my wife?" he says loudly as he leaves me standing in the mudroom to close the garage door.

"Uncle Adam!" Noah hollers, the sound of little running feet bringing another big grin to my lips.

I walk into the kitchen and find a smiling Joy sitting at the island and Addy leaning against the counter on the opposite side, both watching Noah launch himself at his uncle and giving him a huge hug. I move toward the woman who monopolizes my thoughts—both waking and sleeping—and step in beside her. I want to take her in my arms, but not with an audience. Instead, I subtly inhale her sweet vanilla scent, wishing I could run my nose down her slender neck.

Addy looks over her shoulder, her eyes filled with happiness. "Hi."

"Hey," I reply quietly, reaching over and giving her hip a gentle squeeze.

"Graham!" Noah declares, grabbing my attention. I turn and brace myself just as the boy rounds the island and throws himself at me. I easily catch him and stand, returning the big hug I'm greeted with. "I've already had my bath," he informs me, his brown eyes so eager. "And I already picked a book to read at bedtime. I brungded it home from school."

"Brought it home from school," Addy gently corrects, patting her son on the back.

"I can't wait," I tell him, preparing to set him down. But he doesn't seem to be in a hurry to go anywhere. Instead, he wraps his legs around my waist and gets comfy on my hip.

"You about ready, wife?" Adam asks Joy, kissing her lips before she can answer.

I steal a glance over at Addy, who's trying to hide her smile behind her hand. "I bet I know what they're going to do when they get home," she mumbles just loud enough for me to hear.

"What? What are they gonna do? Play Connect Four? I love Connect Four!" Noah proclaims, making everyone laugh.

Joy blushes ten shades of pink, while Adam just gives a cocky smile. "I love me some Connect Four too, buddy."

"Uncle Adam? Next time you and Graham go to dinner, I get to go too. Graham said so. You have to pick a place for kids."

Adam grins at his nephew. "Deal, little man. Next time the girls want to hang out, we'll do a dudes' night."

"With me?" he asks.

"With you too."

"Yes!" Noah exclaims, throwing his hands up in victory.

A few minutes later, we walk Joy and Adam to the door and wave as they drive away. The moment they're out of sight, Noah tugs on my arm. "It's time!"

I laugh at his excitement. "Why don't you run to the room and get the book ready. I'll be there in just a minute."

Once his feet hit the floor, he takes off like a bullet. When he's no longer within sight or earshot, I reach for Addy and pull her into my arms. "I've been dying to kiss you all day," I whisper, turning us so she's out of sight in case her son returns.

"Yeah? Prove it," she whispers, her sweet voice all breathy.

"My pleasure," I reply, one hand wrapping around her hip, while the other slides up her neck and tangles in her hair. I pull her body flush against mine and press my lips to hers.

At first, the kiss is gentle and soft, but it only takes one swipe of my tongue against hers to turn ravenous and urgent. My cock is raring to go, aching to strip away the clothing barriers between us. Unfortunately, I know this isn't the time or place to take this further. The last thing I want is Noah to walk out and see my hands all over his mother because I can't control myself.

"Are we set for tomorrow night?" I ask, trying to catch my breath and not think about the way her body feels against mine.

"Yes. Tosha and I are meeting at the jump park at two, and then she's taking him home with her for the night. I already told Noah, and he's super excited. Did everything go okay with Adam?"

My palm caresses over the swell of her ass because I have no control. "Everything went as expected. And what about you? Are you excited?"

Her eyes sparkle as she nods and bites down on her bottom lip. "Very."

I groan, wishing I was the one doing the biting. "Good," I reply, punctuating my comment with a chaste kiss on her lips.

"Graham, you coming?" Noah hollers, drawing out the last word in a singsong voice.

Addy and I both chuckle. Reluctantly, I release my hold on her and take a step back, knowing I have mere moments to get myself under control. Specifically, my cock. "Be right there," I call over my shoulder.

"You better get going. He picked a baseball book, and he's anxious to hear it."

"Then I best not keep my buddy waiting."

With another kiss on the tip of her nose, I turn and head toward the guest room where Noah is staying, wishing I weren't leaving her behind.

But I also know this is an opportunity for just me and Noah. Last night was the first night I read to him without Addy nearby, and I'm anxious to do it again. It makes me feel useful, giving her a little time to herself. Plus, I get one-on-one time with Noah.

It's a win-win.

Tonight, I'll spend a little extra time with Noah, because tomorrow, his mother is all mine.

I can't fucking wait.

Twelve

Addyson

"So, where is he taking you?" Tosha asks me.

My gaze is on Noah as he jumps to his little heart's content. "I don't know. To be honest, I didn't even ask."

"Definitely something with easy access." I don't have to look at her to know that she's smiling.

"I'm living in his house, and you're going to have Noah all night. I'm pretty much a sure thing," I counter.

"That's a big move. A date is one thing, but sleeping together, that's completely different."

"I know." This time I turn to look at her. "I know it changes things, and I know it's a risk to my heart because this is Graham, and I've always wanted him. I know all the risks involved to my heart, but I also know that if our night leads to that, and let's be honest, I hope it does, I won't be saying no."

"I'm not trying to deter you. Not at all. Besides, you told me about all your conversations, and he talked to Adam. That's a big damn deal. As your bestie, I just want to make sure this is what you want, and you know the risks."

"I know. I just don't care." It's true. I've played this over and over in my mind a thousand times. I can deal with the heartbreak. "It's Noah I'm worried about. He's already so attached to him."

"He's a great kid, and kids are resilient. If it doesn't work out, he'll heal just like his momma."

"We're not going to tell him. At least not right away. We want a few dates and to just see how this goes before we tell him."

"He's a smart cookie, that boy of yours. He's going to figure it out. I mean, he might not realize that Mommy and Graham are playing hide the salami, but he's going to know something is going on."

"Really, Tosh?" I laugh.

"I'm just saying." She grins, taking a sip of her soda. My phone rings, and when I pull it out of my pocket, I see Graham's name. "Can you keep an eye on Noah?" I ask my best friend.

"You know I will."

"Hi," I answer.

"Hey, babe. How's it going?"

"Good. Noah is jumping his little heart out."

"I had to run to Mom and Dad's, and I'm not far from there. Can I stop by?"

"Do you want to?"

"Yeah. I know little man is going to be all kinds of excited, and I kinda want to see it, and him. He's going home with Tosha, so I won't get to see him until tomorrow." My heart melts at his words.

"He'd love that."

"I'm in the parking lot." I can hear the grin in his voice. "I'll be there in a few."

"Okay." I end the call and place my phone next to me on the bench.

"One phone call and the man's got you all swoony." Tosha waves a hand toward me.

"Trust me. It's with good reason."

"Details, woman."

"He's here. He said he was driving by and wanted to stop and see what this place was all about because he knows that Noah will be excited about it."

"That caused this?" She points to me. "You're holding your heart like it aches."

"He said that he won't get to see Noah until tomorrow since he's going home with you, and he wanted to see him."

"Oh. Damn. He's good." She nods.

"Yeah," I agree as strong hands grip my shoulders.

Graham bends down and places a kiss on my cheek. His body hides the act from Noah, who isn't paying us a bit of attention as he bounces away. "Hey, babe."

I tilt my head back to look at him. "Hi."

"Graham, good to see you," Tosha greets with a knowing smile.

"Hey, Tosh," he replies. "Where is he?" he asks, scanning the room.

"There." I point to where Noah is jumping around and doing flips with a few other kids who appear to be his age.

"I'm going over." He kisses the top of my head and stalks off toward my son.

"Damn," Tosha mutters. "That's hot."

I don't need her to explain it because I know exactly what she means. A man like Graham, or hell, any man for that matter, who wants to give his time and affection to a kid that's not his own... ovary explosion.

"No wonder you're jumping in with both feet."

"See what I mean, though?" I nod to where Noah's face lights up, and he launches himself at Graham. Graham, of course, catches him with ease and settles him on his hip. Noah has his full attention as he tells him all about his day so far. "Noah is already so attached to him."

"Okay, so I need to retrace my steps here. Forget everything I said about being careful and the risk. There is no risk."

"What?" I peel my gaze away from Graham and Noah to look at my best friend. "What are you talking about?"

"Addyson, my dear friend, you did not see how that man looked at you. His eyes got all soft and shit. And that—" She points to where Graham and Noah are. My eyes find them once more. Graham has his head tilted back, laughing, and Noah is shaking with his laughter still in Graham's arms. "—that is some heavy real. He's in this."

"You can't know that."

"I've known Graham as long as you have. We've been friends for a lifetime, and I'm telling you. He's smitten with both of you."

"I know he is, but if he changes his mind... Graham isn't one to make long-term commitments. You can't deny that."

"Sure, that's how it's been up until now, but he's different with you. It's the first time I've seen you two together since all of this, and the way he looks at you, damn girl, if I had a man look at me that way, I'd be climbing him like a tree."

"Mommy!" Noah comes rushing toward me. "Look." He turns to point at Graham, who is smiling from ear to ear. "Graham's here. He come to see me."

"*Came* to see you," I correct him.

"That's what I said. Can we get ice cream? Graham said I had to ask you first."

"Sure." I reach for my purse, but Graham's deep rumble stops me.

"I've got it, Addy. You ladies want anything?" he asks.

"No, thanks," Tosha replies.

"I'm good too. Be good for Graham." I point at Noah.

"Mommmm." He drags out my name. "I'm a big boy now. I'm five." He holds up five fingers before slipping that hand into Graham's.

Graham winks at me and then gives Noah all his attention once more as they make their way to the concession area to grab some ice cream.

"You're in trouble, my friend," Tosha quips.

"Why's that?"

"There is no way you are resisting that." She motions to where Noah and Graham are standing.

"I don't want to," I admit. "I just don't want Noah to get hurt."

"It's too late for that, Addyson. He's already attached. Just roll with it and see where it goes."

I know she's right. Just seeing the two of them together and the way Noah's eyes light up, tells me she's right. However, it's not just Noah. Graham made a point to come to see him knowing it would be tomorrow before he got to. That means something. Maybe Tosha is right. Maybe keeping this from Noah is extra stress we don't really need.

I'm in my room and giving myself a final once-over when I hear the doorbell. I wait to listen for Graham, but the house is quiet. I hear the doorbell again, so I venture out to the living room. "Graham?" I call out. No reply, but the doorbell rings again. Making my way to the door, I pull it open, and my mouth falls open.

Graham is standing on the other side with a bouquet of wildflowers. He's wearing a pair of jeans that look as though they were made for him and a solid black T-shirt that does nothing to hide what's going on underneath.

"You're beautiful," he tells me. He leans in and gives me a peck on the lips. "These are for you," he says, handing me the bouquet of flowers.

"I—They're beautiful. Thank you." I bring the flowers to my nose, and the heavenly scent wraps around me.

"They're your favorite, right?"

"They are. How did you know?"

He shrugs. "I've been paying attention."

"I don't recall any time in recent memory saying that I loved wildflowers."

"I've been paying attention for a while. I just didn't understand why or that the information would one day come in handy." He gives me a boyish grin, and it makes my heart soar.

"Thank you. I'm just going to put these in water."

He follows me into the house, closing the door behind him. "I heard you calling out for me." He grins.

"I definitely wasn't expecting to find you standing at your own door."

"I wanted to pick you up. Surprise you with flowers."

"And when you bring me home tonight?"

"I'm definitely staying over." He winks.

"We could just stay in. Order something for delivery, and just... stay in."

"Tempting, but I'm taking my girl out on a date. What kind of boyfriend would I be otherwise?"

"That's a pretty serious title."

"It's one that I take seriously." He moves to stand behind me where I'm posted at the sink, arranging the flowers in a pitcher since I couldn't find a vase. He wraps his arms around my waist and trails kisses down my neck. "There is nothing I want more than to stay home with you so we can just... stay in," he admits. "But I need to show you that this is more to me. That you are different than any woman before you. I need to take you out on a date and spend some time with you before we come back here and I have my wicked way with you."

Placing the flowers on the counter, I manage to turn to face him. "You think I'm a sure thing, huh?" I tease, wrapping my arms around his neck.

"I know that I am. When it comes to you and to Noah, the two of you get all that I am."

"Graham," I whisper his name.

His lips find mine in a kiss that literally weakens my knees. When he finally tears his mouth from mine, he pulls me into his chest for one of the best, if not *the* best, hugs I've ever received. "I'm all in, Addyson. Me, you, and Noah."

It takes me a minute to get my emotions under control before I can speak. "You make it impossible for me not to fall for you."

"I'll catch you. My arms are wide open. I'll catch you both."

This time words escape me completely, so I just hug him as hard as I can, willing my tears to stay away.

"Come on. We've got a date to get to." I feel his lips press to the top of my head before he steps back. I miss his heat instantly.

"I just need to grab my phone and my purse."

"I'll be right here."

I scurry off to my room to find my phone and slide it into my purse. I take one last look in the mirror. I chose a jean skirt that hits a couple of inches above my knees. I'm in a flowing tank top that's royal blue and wearing wedge sandals. My makeup is very minimal, and my hair is pulled up in a twist of curls. I was worried it was too simple, but the way Graham devoured me with his eyes, I'm guessing he approves. Shutting off the light, I make my way to him, ready to get this date started.

"This is so good," I moan as I pop another homemade pita chip covered in spinach and artichoke dip into my mouth. Graham sits across from me, smiling, as he reaches for another chip as well.

"Any word on your apartment?" he asks.

"Nothing. I called my landlord yesterday on my lunch break. Apparently, he's still waiting to hear back from the insurance adjuster."

He nods. "I hope it takes them a while." He winks, running a chip through the dip. "I like having you and Noah close."

Butterflies swarm my belly. "Thank you for taking us in. I appreciate it more than you know."

"When I offered my place, I didn't anticipate we would be here. But being that close to you, you were impossible to resist."

"Do you think it's a close proximity thing? The feelings you're having?"

"No. That's not it at all. That might be what forced my hand and initiated this between us, but that's not what this relationship is about."

I nod and avoid his gaze by taking a drink of my sweet tea.

"Addy, look at me."

Taking a deep breath, I glance up and find him staring at me with a serious expression on his face. "You and Noah staying with me is not the reason we're sitting here right now. It's because I can't even think about you without my cock twitching in my jeans. It's the way you look at me with those big brown eyes, and how your scent of vanilla seems to follow me everywhere I go. It's the way we laugh and the mother that you are to Noah. You're an incredible woman, and I'm honored to call you mine."

I take a minute to let his words sink in. "I've wanted you for so long," I reply softly. "Over the years, there were so many times I would lie awake at night and picture what it would be like being with you like this. It was a crush, and I knew it, and I was convinced that it was all it would ever be." I pause, taking a drink to collect my thoughts. "When I got pregnant with Noah, my life changed. I didn't have the liberty to crush on anyone. I was going to be a single mom, and my baby boy needed all my time and attention. I let you go, or at least I thought I did. Suddenly, all those old feelings are front and center, and I don't know what to do with them."

He reaches across the table and places his hand over mine. "You give them to me, baby. Every single one of them. The happy, the sad, the fear, the pain, I want it all, Addyson. Every single fucking part of you, I want it. Not just you, but Noah. I know that he's the most important person in your life. I know that he comes first, and I'm okay with that. I know that any future children we might have will be loved just as fiercely, and that hits me here." He taps his chest with his other hand, right over his heart.

I sputter and cough. He removes his hand and slides my drink my way. I take a hefty sip and swallow before meeting his eyes. "Future children?"

"I can see it. You growing round with our baby. Noah would be the best big brother." He smiles, but it looks pained.

"What's wrong?"

"Nothing." He takes a big gulp of his own tea.

"Graham. Tell me."

"We shouldn't be having this conversation here."

My eyes dart around. We're at a little Italian restaurant in Harris, and it's slow tonight. We're sitting in the back corner, and the tables around us are empty. "I think you're safe. No one heard you." I try not to be offended that he wants those things with me but wants no one else to know about them.

"I couldn't give a fuck less who hears me, Addy."

"Then why?"

"Why? Because my cock is hard as stone beneath this table. The thought of making love to you bare, making a baby with you, is hot as fuck, and my cock is ready to play."

"Oh." My mouth drops open in shock.

"Yeah, oh." He shakes his head. "Can we table this for home?"

"Here you go." Our waiter delivers our meals. "Can I get you anything else?" he asks.

"No, thank you," Graham and I say at the same time. Our waiter nods and scurries away.

"Eat," Graham says gruffly.

"What are we doing after this?" I ask, picking up my fork and taking a bite of my chicken alfredo.

"Going home."

"Date night is over?" I ask with a grin.

"Not over, just changing directions."

"And what direction is that?" I ask coyly. I can see it written all over him. If he could only feel the wetness between my thighs, he'd be demanding we package up our meals to go.

"My bedroom. Now hush and eat so I can think about things that are not remotely sexy to take care of this problem."

"I can help with that," I offer.

"Addy," he growls, and I laugh. "Minx." He smiles.

"I'll be good."

"Just until we get into the car, babe. I just need to make it out of here without anyone seeing my cock throbbing for you, and we're good."

"I... never mind. Let's eat."

He shakes his head and digs into his own meal. We eat in comfortable silence while I let him calm himself down. I guess women have it easy. We can hide our need from those around us.

Thirteen

Graham

Is it possible to have some sort of permanent damage from an erection? Like, so hard and painful for extended periods of time it'll never subside no matter how many times you beat off? Can you imagine going to the doctor for an everlasting hard-on? I always made fun of those commercials on TV, the ones talking about seeking medical assistance for erections lasting longer than four hours.

Now, I'm contemplating my options.

Tonight has been perfection, even if I was in pain most of the meal, but can you blame me? Addy is wearing a simple jean skirt—making her legs look fan-fucking-tastic—and a blue top. Both beg to be slowly removed from her body, and, boy, do I have plans for that when we get home. I've gone over it so many times in my head since she opened the door, I could have amnesia and still give a play-by-play.

"Thank you," she says softly as I take her hand and lead her from the restaurant.

"You're very welcome," I reply, pushing through the exit and escorting her to my truck. When I open the passenger door, I don't want to release her. I love the way her hand feels nestled inside mine.

Addy stares up at me, her eyes shining with an eagerness I've come to love and appreciate. She's a genuinely happy, optimistic person, and when those sexy brown eyes are locked on mine, I can't help but feel a little excited to be under their spell, secretly praying a little bit of her sunshine seeps from her body into mine. I can see exactly why she's in the profession she's in.

"Hey, you." Addy faces me and slides her hands up my chest.

I wonder if she can feel the thundering of my heart beneath her palms.

Before I can say a word, Addy goes up on tiptoes and presses her mouth against mine. I forget about everything, including the fact we're standing in the middle of a parking lot, and just feel. Her lips are soft and taste faintly like tea, the strawberry cheesecake we shared for dessert, and something uniquely Addyson.

I want more.

My fingers curl, digging into the hair at the base of her neck, as my tongue delves deep. I wonder if I'll ever tire of this. Of kissing her, feeling her skin beneath my fingers. Of craving a person, and not just for her body.

It still freaks me out how drastically I saw a change. One minute, she's Addyson, my best friend's sister. The next, she's Addy, the woman I can't stop thinking about throughout the day and the one I picture when I beat off in the shower.

Daily.

"Get a room!" someone hollers from across the lot.

Ripping my lips from hers takes Herculean strength, but I manage. Her eyes are glazed over, and when they finally focus on mine, a blush creeps up her neck and stains her cheeks. "Umm…"

I clear my throat, grab her around the waist, and lift, gently setting her in the passenger seat. Addy squeals, grasping my shoulders as she moves. "Buckle up, Addy," I instruct, placing a chaste kiss on her lips before stepping back and shutting the door.

I take my time walking to the driver's side, subtly adjusting my cock to conceal my hard-on. By the time I climb inside the cab, Addy's buckled in and grinning. As I start the engine, she asks, "So? What now?"

"Well, we can do anything you'd like. I don't have a definite plan set. We can run over to the theater and see what's playing or we can take a ride out to the trails and watch the sunset."

She reaches for my hand and laces her fingers with mine. "Or we could go back to your place and continue that kiss." There's no denying the fire dancing in her eyes, nor the way the same heat spreads through my veins.

"Or we can do that," I confirm.

She smiles, so I throw my truck in reverse and prepare to make the drive back to Cedar Hills.

"So, how was your first few days of school?" I ask to make idle conversation. Mostly, I do it in hopes of keeping my eyes on the road instead of on her.

"It was good," she responds, grazing my hand with her soft fingers. "I have a great group of kids this year."

My throat goes dry. Does she realize she's doing that? Stroking my skin and basically driving me wild. "Good," I mutter, my tongue sticking to the roof of my mouth.

Just as we hit the edge of town and the road opens up a little, she moves our joined hands, bringing them to her mouth. Her warm breath tickles my skin moments before I feel her lips dance across my flesh.

"How about you? How was work yesterday?" she asks.

My brain short-circuits though, and it takes me a few seconds to recall what she asked. "Busy," I mumble, shifting in my seat to alleviate the discomfort in my pants.

"Busy is always good," she replies.

That's when I feel her tongue. Her warm, wet tongue glides across my knuckles in a way I never would have thought I'd find sexy until this exact moment. Until *her* mouth. Risking a glance in her direction, I'm hypnotized as her eyes lock on mine and she sucks my index finger into her mouth.

"Fuck," I bite out harshly as I jerk the wheel. Addy giggles as I rip my eyes away from hers and straighten out the truck. "Jesus, Addy, don't do that. I'm trying to drive."

"So it would be a bad idea to do this?" she asks right before she sucks two of my fingers deep into her mouth, her tongue swirling around them like she were licking a popsicle.

"No. Yes." I exhale deeply, trying to keep my composure.

"Well, which one is it?" she asks, her question laced with humor.

"Yes, it would be a bad idea, because I'm having a hard time concentrating on the road."

"Oh," she replies, releasing my hand. Immediately, I wish I could take the words back, tell her I was just kidding, but I don't get the chance. Instead of begging her to hold my hand, she says, "So it would probably be a bad idea for me to do this then, huh?"

I glance over and watch as she shimmies her panties from beneath her denim skirt. She slides them down her legs until she's holding them up. The satiny blue material hangs from her fingertips, and the scent of her arousal fills the cab.

"Jesus," I groan, stealing a quick glance at the road before returning my eyes to those fucking blue panties. "Yes, that's probably a bad idea too."

"Huh. I should probably just put these back on then," she teases, holding them up so I can see just how skimpy that scrap of material is. A thong. She was wearing a fucking thong beneath that skirt, and I'm suddenly so hard, I can't think straight.

I swallow and stare at the road in front of me, even though I'm dying to steal another peek at those damn panties. "Yes, I think you should."

Does she put them back on? Hell no, she doesn't. My little vixen sets them on my lap. She reaches over and places her wet thong that smells like her sweet pussy on my dick, the very one that's trying to Hulk from my jeans at this exact moment to try to get close to her. "Maybe in a few minutes," she replies, clearly ignoring my suggestion.

When her fingers tap across my cock, I jump in my seat, gritting my teeth. "You're not playing fair, sweet Addy."

She palms my aching cock and whispers, "No, probably not, but I figured it serves you right."

Risking a quick glance her way, I ask, "What?"

"That I tease you the way you've been teasing me."

I practically swallow my tongue. "How have I been teasing you?"

Addy leans over but isn't able to get as close as either of us would like, thanks to the seat belt. "Well, let's see. The other night, you kept touching my arm when I was making dinner. You knew how you were affecting me, Graham. I caught you staring at my nipples, which were so hard and achy from you touching me. Then this morning, you walked around the house practically naked after your workout."

"I was wearing shorts," I argue lamely. I could see exactly how my shirtless state affected her.

"With no shirt. Plus, you were all sweaty, and that reminded me of sex."

I can't help but grin as I glance her way. "My sweat reminds you of sex?"

"Your sweat reminds me of how hot it got that morning you went down on me in your bed."

A groan flies from my mouth as that particular image comes back in Technicolor.

"Did you know you walking around shirtless and sweaty was like an aphrodisiac, Graham? Did you know you made me so wet, I had to go take a shower with my purple vibrator while Noah was playing to relieve the ache?"

My eyes are wide as I look her way. She leans back in her seat, taking her hand with her as she goes.

"Show me."

"Show you?" she parrots, the corner of her mouth turning upward as a wicked glint fills her brown eyes.

"Show me. Now." I'm playing with fire. I'm driving down the highway, ten minutes from home, but I can't seem to stop myself. Desire is leading the charge, fueling my words and my actions. My eyes bounce from the road, which thankfully is basically empty at this point, and the woman sitting beside me.

Addy shimmies in her seat, lifting her skirt up her thighs. I can't see her pussy, but I don't need to. The sound she makes when her fingers touch herself paints a beautiful fucking portrait.

"Are you wet, Addy?" I ask in a voice that doesn't sound like mine.

"So, so wet."

"Let me see," I demand, keeping my focus straight ahead.

Her fingers appear in front of my face, all glistening wet and smelling like heaven. Before I can say another word, she swipes those two digits across my lips, coating me in her wetness. My mouth opens and my lips latch on to her fingers as I suck. Her taste hits my tongue like fireworks on the Fourth of July. Explosive. Dramatic. So fucking intoxicating, I need more.

I lick and suck them clean, only to have them removed from my mouth once more. Addy returns her fingers between her thighs and groans. "Don't make yourself come."

"Please," she whimpers, her hand moving a little faster now.

"No. That release is mine," I growl, eternally fucking grateful when I see the city limits sign. We're less than three minutes from home, but I have a feeling these three minutes will be the longest of my life.

"What are you going to do when we get to your house, Graham?" she asks breathlessly.

Carefully slowing my truck to the speed limit, I turn off the main road and start weaving my way through the side streets. "I'm going to eat your pussy like a starved man. Then, when you've come at least once on my tongue, I'm going to fuck you. Probably hard the first time, because I'm not sure I have the ability to do slow and sweet yet."

A soft whimper fills my truck cab. "I don't want slow and sweet, Graham."

I look over for only a fraction of a second, but it's enough to see her fingers buried in her pussy. I bite my tongue and press down a little harder on the accelerator, just praying I can get us home in one piece.

Finally, I turn the corner and see my house. I almost sigh in relief. The moment I pull into my driveway, I press the button to lift the garage door, driving my truck inside the second it clears the moving door. Then I lower the door just as quickly, finally surrounding us in solitude.

Addy moves first, ripping off her seat belt as I turn off the engine. She climbs across the seat, straddling my lap and slamming her lips down on mine. I grip her bare ass, the denim skirt she wore now pushed up and over her hips. She rocks, grinding down on my cock. The friction is glorious and frustrating at the same time.

Her hands drop to where she sits, deft fingers frantically pulling at my fly and tugging at the button. "Addy," I mumble against her eager mouth. "We can't do it in my truck."

She leans back a bit, her breathing labored and her eyes wide. "Why not?"

A small smile graces my lips. "The first time I'm inside you shouldn't be in a truck, sweetness."

A mischievous grin crosses her swollen lips. "I beg to differ. I think the first time should most definitely be in a truck." To prove her point, she palms my cock again and swipes her fingers through her folds. Only then does she bring that finger to my mouth and slide it between my lips.

Automatically, I suck her finger hard. "I see your point."

"Good," she replies, diving back down for my zipper and button and practically ripping them open.

I lift my hips and shimmy my pants down past my knees, which is a pretty big feat, considering she's straddling my waist. My cock is finally free, moisture seeping from the head in anticipation.

Then, something hits me. "Addy, grab my wallet."

She digs for the back pocket of my pants, which is a little tricky, but she hits pay dirt. As if knowing exactly why I asked, she opens it up and finds the single condom I put in there earlier today. I don't know why I did. My plan was never to take her roughly in my truck, but damn, am I glad I did.

Addy rips the foil package open and meets my gaze. "May I?"

I can't seem to find words, so I nod eagerly. She positions the rubber at the head of my cock and slowly starts to slide it into place. Having her hands on me this way is heaven and hell, all wrapped into one. Heaven because there's no better feeling, and hell because it only makes me want more.

When I'm sheathed, I shift our position so she's poised over me, her back pressed against the steering wheel. "This is going to be hard and fast, Addy, but I promise to take my time with you on the second round."

"Yes. Yes. Hard and fast," she pants, moments before slamming down on my cock, taking me all the way inside her sweet pussy in one stroke.

We both groan. And feel.

So. Much. Pleasure.

I almost don't want her to move.

Almost.

Unfortunately, my body's natural need to move takes over, and before I know it, I'm lifting her up and thrusting back inside. Addy rocks her hips and moans, her internal muscles squeezing. "Fuck, Addy."

"I'm so close, Graham," she whispers, gyrating on my cock like it's her job.

"I can feel you, sweetness. Ride my cock," I practically demand, thrusting up over and over again.

She cries out and her pussy squeezes. Hard. I feel my balls draw up; the tingling starts at the base of my spine. I'm teetering on the edge of release, praying I can hold off just a few more precious seconds so she comes too.

Reaching between us, I press my thumb against her clit as I thrust up. The result is another cry from her mouth and her pussy clamping down on me. Addy whimpers as I roll my hips and fill her completely once more. Like a beautiful bomb, she detonates, flying over the edge. I can feel her wetness coat my cock as she comes. Her mouth falls open and her body spasms spectacularly, triggering my own release.

"Addy," I grunt moments before I finally let go, following her over the edge of pure bliss.

I've had sex plenty of times before, but nothing compares to this.

To her.

When my body finally stops jolting, I struggle to catch my breath, mostly because this feels different. This wasn't just sex. This wasn't just a release. This was something greater, something magnificent.

Like the setting sun meeting the horizon, it takes your breath away.

"My God," I mumble, leaning my head forward against her chest. She's panting, her arms lazily wrapping around my neck as she holds me close.

"Mmmm."

We sit here, both trying to get ourselves under control. My fingers dance across the globes of her ass, causing her to shimmy against me and making me smile. "That was... wow."

"Mmhmm," she whispers, turning her head and placing her lips against my neck. She kisses me softly before shifting and snuggling against my shoulder. "The windows are all steamy."

I snort a laugh. "I'm not surprised. That was pretty fucking hot."

Addy sighs and I feel her internal muscles relax a bit around my cock, reminding me I'm still very much buried inside her. Usually, this is the point I'd move. I'd head to the bathroom and clean up, but with Addy, I want to stay right here and hold her. I want to eventually move to my bedroom, lay her down, and continue my exploration of her body, from head to toe.

And when I'm done? I want to do it all over again, just in case I missed something.

. Shifting her in my arms, I take her lips with mine. The kiss is soft, tender even, as my tongue slides against hers. My fingers slide into her hair as her chest presses firmly against mine, and just as quickly as it had before, the flames of lust ignite one more time.

Just by holding her in my arms.

My cock twitches and starts to grow.

She must feel it because she gasps and wiggles against me. Just like that, I'm fully hard and itching for more.

With one last lingering kiss, I squeeze her ass, rocking her against me, grinding her clit against my pelvis. "Let's get you inside, beautiful. I have big plans for round two."

Fourteen

ddyson

My legs quiver as I climb out of the truck. I step back and wait for Graham to join me. He's holding his pants up, and I watch as he discards the condom, dropping it into the trash can in the garage.

"Keep staring at me like that, sweetness, and we won't make it to the bed." His voice is gruff, and I feel it between my thighs.

I want *him* between my thighs.

"You still feel me, don't you?" he asks.

I ignore him. He knows I can; there is no point in agreeing. Instead, I say, "You promised me round two."

He lets his jeans fall to the floor of the garage. "I did." He grips his cock, and strokes it. His arm flexes as his large hands mimic what my pussy just did for him. "Addy?" I force myself to look from his cock to his eyes. "Inside. Now."

"I don't know. I was enjoying the show," I tease. I may be trying to wind him up a little, but I really was enjoying the show.

I watch as he bends over and unties his boots before pulling them off. He kicks his jeans and his boxer briefs to the side, and they land somewhere beneath his truck. Next, he reaches behind him, in that sexy way that men do, and grips the back neck of his T-shirt, and pulls it over his head. I don't know where it lands because I'm too busy taking him in. He's chiseled to perfection. His body is a work of art that I could stare at for hours.

His hair is a little longer on top, and his five o'clock shadow covers his strong angular jaw, and he's every woman's fantasy come true. He's definitely mine, and he was just inside me.

My eyes trail from his washboard abs to his hard cock. His hands are on his hips as he lets me look my fill. His cock twitches, and my mouth waters. That's never happened to me before. I've never craved to taste a man.

Not until Graham.

"Addy, baby. Inside." His voice almost sounds pained as he instructs me where he wants me, but I'm not ready for that yet. He wants round two, and so do I, but I'll be good with an appetizer before the main course.

"What if I don't want to go inside?" I ask coyly.

"Tell me what you want, Addyson. Whatever it is, I'll make it happen."

I wonder what he would say if I told him all I wanted was him. I want him to be mine forever. Instead, I continue with this seduction, something that's way out of character for me, but I've never been with a man like Graham.

Taking a step toward him, I place my hands on his chest and give him a small push backward. His back lands on the door of his truck. I take my time letting my palms wander over his torso, letting my fingers trace the planes and valleys of his abs. When I reach his cock, I fist him just like he did earlier and lazily pump my hand.

"You do that, and I won't last," he grits.

"Noah's not home," I remind him. "We have all night." I move to my knees and swallow hard as I come eye to eye with his cock. He's bigger than anyone I've ever been with. Blow jobs have never really been my thing. They were more take it or leave it. But with Graham, I want to give this to him. Hell, I want to give this to me. I want to feel the velvety smooth skin of his shaft sliding across my tongue.

I want to taste him.

"I want to come with your pussy wrapped around my cock."

I nod. "Round two."

"If you put me in your mouth, that won't happen."

"Graham, we just had sex in your truck, and you were ready to go in minutes. I'm not worried." With that, I place a kiss on the head of his cock. He hisses out a breath, and a thrill races through me. I take him into my mouth, letting my tongue tease him. Pulling back and going in for more, I take him deeper each time.

"Fuck," he pants, and his hands hit the side of his truck. I peer up at him under my lashes, and his eyes soften. "You're beautiful. I want to always remember you like this. With my cock in your mouth, riding me in my truck. Sitting across from me tonight. You're everything I've ever wanted." He brushes my hair out of my eyes.

I let him pop free from my mouth, and before I can go back for more, he's sliding his hands under my arms and lifting me to my feet. "I don't have any condoms out here, and when I come, it's going to be inside you."

"Yes, please," I reply, making him laugh.

"Wrap your legs around me, beautiful." He grips my ass and lifts me.

I do as I'm told and wrap my legs around his waist and hold on tight while he carries us into the house. He doesn't stop until we're pushing through his bedroom door. He still doesn't put me down. Instead, he carries me to the bedside table and commands, "Get a condom." I lean over in his arms and manage to pull the drawer open and grab a condom.

"Put it on me."

"How am I going to do that?"

"I've got you. I won't let you fall."

"Just set me down."

"No. No, I'm not setting you on your feet so that wicked mouth of yours can suck me off. I'm going to bury my cock in your pussy."

"I'm still dressed."

"This skirt is my new favorite."

Fire shoots to my core at his demanding tone and at the thought that he wants me so bad he refuses to set me down. He walks to the wall and presses my back against it. I manage to reach between us and sheath his cock. No sooner than my hands land on his chest, he aligns himself at my entrance and pushes inside. We both moan at the connection.

"So fucking tight," he hisses. "Your pussy was made for me." He bends his head and trails kisses down the column of my neck.

"Graham."

"What, baby?"

"I need more."

"Oh, now she wants to play." He chuckles. "What was that in the garage?" he asks.

"I wanted to taste you."

"Jesus," he pants. "This is how this is going to go. I wanted to make love to you, and we will, but the truck, and the garage, and... I have to fuck you."

I wiggle my hips, and I'm shocked when he smacks my ass. My skirt is all the way around my waist, giving him nothing but bare skin, and he's taking full advantage.

"I'm going to take you hard and fast."

"Promise?" I taunt him, and he grins.

"You know I'd never make a promise I can't keep. Not to you and not to Noah." With that, he pulls out and pushes back in. He pounds into me over and over and over again. He steps away from the wall, and I wrap my arms tighter around his neck. With his feet planted on the floor, he lifts me off his cock, before slamming me back down. I cry out in pleasure.

"There. Right... there," I pant.

"You there, baby? I need you to get there."

"Don't stop," I plead.

"Touch yourself."

I don't listen. Instead, I hold on, letting my nails dig into his back. A slow burn starts in my pussy, and I can feel it. I'm so close. "C-Close," I tell him, my eyes rolling back in my head.

"Give." Thrust. "It." Thrust. "To." Thrust. "Me." Thrust.

Before the final word is out of his mouth, I'm falling over the edge of orgasmic bliss that can only be achieved by Graham Morgan.

He's ruined me for all other men.

He calls out my name as he stills and releases inside me. We're both breathing heavily, and there is a delicious ache between my thighs that I know I'll be feeling for days to come.

"You okay?" he asks, his voice like gravel.

"I'm perfect."

"You are." He kisses me softly. "How about a bath?"

"Only if you take one with me."

"We're taking advantage of being kid-free, remember?" He smiles. Slowly, he lifts me off him and sets me on my feet. I wobble, and he keeps hold of me until I find my balance. "I'm going to take care of this." He points to his latex-wrapped cock. "And start the bathwater. Come in when you're ready."

With a kiss on my temple, which is a complete contrast to the man who just fucked me within an inch of my life, he disappears into the bathroom. On shaking legs, I walk to the dresser to take in my appearance. My hair is a mess, my makeup is smeared, and my clothes are askew, but there is a smile on my face.

A dopey love-sick smile.

Needing to be near him, I quickly strip out of my clothes and then realize I don't have my phone. I grab one of his T-shirts, rush to the garage, and grab my purse. I have to get down on my hands and knees to grab his discarded clothes.

"That's something I don't see every day," he says from behind me.

I stand with his jeans in my hands. "Got 'em." I grin.

"I would have gotten them."

"I know, but I came to get my phone to check on Noah."

His eyes soften. "How's our boy?"

My heart squeezes at his question. Digging in my purse, I pull out my phone and see a message from Tosha.

Tosha: He's such a ham.

. . .

It's followed by a picture of Noah with two cheese puffs hanging out of his mouth like fangs.

Me: Why is he still up?

Tosha: Because he's with Aunt Tosha.

She hits me with an eye-rolling emoji, and I can't help but laugh.

Tosha: He wants to say goodnight.

"Call her," Graham says from behind me.
"I can't believe he's still up. It's almost eleven."
Graham shrugs. "He's with Aunt Tosha."
"I'm sure she gave him anything he wanted and had to wait for his sugar high to crash."
"Maybe, but it's the weekend."
I hit Tosha's number for FaceTime. It's not until Noah picks up and asks where Graham's shirt is that I realize I didn't think about what we both looked like.
"I'm getting ready to go to bed, but your mom said she was going to call and tell you goodnight, and no way was I missing that," Graham replies.
"Next time, you and Mom should come with me. It's so much fun at Aunt Tosha's," Noah boasts.
"We'll see, bud." Graham laughs. "Have you been good?"
My chest does that tightening thing again. The way he cares about my son makes him even hotter, and I never thought that was possible.
"So much fun. But I miss my story. Aunt Tosha doesn't do the voices right," he tells us.
"Tell you what. Tomorrow night, we'll read two stories."

"You promise?" Noah asks.

"Yeah, I promise. Be good for Aunt Tosha."

"I will. Love you, G. Love you, Mommy." He waves at the screen, and I have to fight back against my tears.

I swallow hard. "Night, Noah. I love you."

"Love you, No," Graham tells him, and with one more wave, the call ends. "That's the first time he's ever told me that he loves me."

"I tell him so often he doesn't realize."

"Don't. Don't you dare take this moment away from me."

"I'm sorry. That wasn't my intention. I guess I don't know how you feel about it, and didn't want to put any pressure on you."

"It hits me here." He places his hand over his heart.

"Yeah." I know exactly what he means. The love of my son does that to me too, and to see him openly love Graham, and for Graham to return that love, it warms my soul. Dropping my phone to the bench my arm is barely down when I get a text message.

Tosha: I need details.

Me: Night, Tosh.

Tosha: Night.

Graham wraps his arms around me from behind, and that's when I realize he's still naked as the day he was born. "Graham!" I scold. "What if Noah saw you? Or Tosha?"

"I knew you had to hold the phone up for both of us to be on the screen with my height. We were fine."

"What am I going to do with you?"

"I can think of a few things, but right now, we're going to take a bath before the water gets cold." Before I can stop him, he's lifting me bridal style and carries me into the house. I have his clothes, my purse, and phone clutched to my chest, laughing the entire way.

Once we're in his room, he takes me to the bed, and I toss everything before he carries me into the bathroom. He places me on my feet and peels his T-shirt over my head. Without words, he steps into the tub and gets comfortable before holding his hand out for me. I settle between his legs, my back to his chest, and he wraps me in his arms. The water is warm and feels incredible.

"This is nice," I say after a few minutes of silence.

"I agree." His lips press to the side of my head.

"You're good with him. With Noah."

"He's a good kid."

"You told him that you loved him."

"He's an easy kid to love."

I want to tell him that I love him too. This dynamic between us is new, and he's already told me that he's all in. There is no point in scaring him away by dropping that three word confession. Even if I feel the words, I feel the love that I have for him deep in my soul.

"It's weird, but I miss him. I've loved our night together. I wouldn't change that, but I miss him," Graham confesses.

"Yeah," I agree. "It's quiet when he's not around."

"Have you heard anything about your apartment?" he asks.

"No. The last I heard, it was going to be weeks."

"Why don't you tell them you want out of your lease?"

"I've thought about it, but looking for a new place doesn't sound like a good time." *And I'm not ready to leave you.* I keep that confession to myself.

"You don't need to find a place. Your place is here with me. Yours and Noah's."

I turn to look at him over my shoulder. "What?"

"This house, it's a home with the two of you living here. We're doing this, you and me. We might as well go all in."

"We're not telling Noah. I mean, not yet."

"Yeah, about that. I think that we should tell him."

"What?" Am I hearing him right? I turn around and straddle his lap. I need to see him for this conversation.

He wraps his arms around me, locking his hands at the small of my back. "I think we should tell him. He's a smart kid, Addy. He's going to know something's going on with us. I don't think I can hide. In fact, I know that I can't hide it. You and Noah, you both mean too much to me."

Holy shit. Is this really happening? On the one hand, I want that more than anything. I want to stay here with him and see where it takes us, but on the other hand, I have my son to think about. If Graham changes his mind, Noah will be crushed. *I'll* be crushed.

"It's really soon."

"I know."

"That's a big step."

"I know."

"I have to think about more than just what I want."

"Addy, I know. You don't have to give me an answer tonight. I just need you to know that's what I want. I want you, I want Noah, and I want you both here."

"Can we just... see how it goes?" That's my mind talking while my heart is screaming for me to agree and call my landlord to start the process of getting out of my lease. I've acted on words before. I've let myself believe the words of a man who betrayed me, and even though Graham is good to me, and he's good to Noah, I still need some time. I promised myself when I found out I was pregnant that I would always put my son and his needs first.

This is me doing that.

"We can," he says, kissing me softly.

"Are you mad?"

"Am I mad that you're an incredible mother who thinks about her son? No, Addy, I'm not mad. Besides, I know what I want. I also know I'll wear you down." He winks.

"You think so?" I ask, the mood growing lighter.

"Yep."

"How do you plan to do that?"

"I'm going to woo you."

"Woo me?" I laugh.

"Yep. I'm going to make you fall in love with me."

"My heart has a lot of cracks."

"That's fine by me. I plan to fill each and every one of them." My heart squeezes in my chest at his words. He kisses me, holding my face in his hands, and making me lose all train of thought.

I kiss him back, letting my tongue slide against his. That's the only way I can prevent myself from telling him that I'm already falling in love with him.

Fifteen

Graham

Something wakes me up, and unfortunately, it's not the beautiful woman tucked against my body.

I glance over, taking in her beautiful sleeping form. The way her lips are slightly parted, her dark eyelashes delicately resting against the soft skin beneath her eyes, and her hair fanned out, are a stark contrast to her sandy-blonde hair against my navy-blue sheet.

My cock notices other things. The warmth of her naked skin pressed against mine, the weight of her full breast laying on my chest, and the heat of her pussy close to my erection, yet not nearly close enough.

Just as I'm about to roll her over and wake her with an epic good-morning orgasm, I hear the noise once more.

I know what it is, and I'm not happy about it.

I consider ignoring it, really I do, but if I know the asshole in my kitchen, I know he won't leave until he's damn good and ready, which probably won't be for a long time out of spite. Cockblocking asshole.

With a deep sigh, I gingerly extract myself from my bed, my cock protesting with each move I make, and grab a pair of shorts. I slip into my bathroom and relieve myself, grateful my erection is slowly subsiding. After washing my hands and brushing my teeth, I slip out of my bathroom and head in the direction of my kitchen to confront my intruder, leaving behind a sleeping Addy.

"I should call the police and report a break-in," I mumble the moment I cross the threshold for the kitchen.

Adam grins widely, looking all bright-eyed and chipper for—I glance at my watch—nine in the morning. Shit, I thought it was earlier than that, but I suppose staying up half the night, balls deep in the incredible woman I left in my bed, does something to your internal clock.

"You can't call the police when you give me a key, asshole," Adam replies, smiling at me over his mug. "I made you coffee."

Ignoring him, I move to the cabinet and pull out a cup, filling it to the top. Only when I've had my first sip do I turn and face my best friend. "What are you doing here?"

He tries to look innocent, but I know better. We've been friends far too long for me to fall for that shit. "What? Can't a guy stop in and have coffee with his best friend?"

Taking another sip, I lean against the counter and just stare. "Sure, but you knew damn well last night was my date with Addyson. You're here cockblocking."

He pulls a face.

Serves him right.

"Let's not say cock and my sister's name so close together."

I shrug. "You're the one showing up at my house at nine in the morning, knowing full well what you may interrupt."

Again, the look on his face is priceless. "I didn't think this through."

"Clearly not," I quip, feeling a little vindicated as I sip my coffee.

"Anyway, without going into any gory details, I take it last night went okay? The *date*, I'm referring to, not anything else disgusting that may have transpired afterward." Adam shudders.

"Yes, Mom. The date went well. I had a great time, and I hope to see her again soon." Glancing at my watch again, I add, "Probably within the next thirty minutes or so."

"Probably less. Joy has been itching for details since before the sun came up," my friend confirms. "I'm guessing she was already texting Ads the moment I left."

"Speaking of, why are you here anyway? Aren't you wanting to baby-make with your wife? Shouldn't you be, you know, making a baby, and not here, bothering me?"

"Wrong time of the month," Adam confirms with a sad little nod.

"Ahh. I take it you had the conversation?"

He grins. "Friday night. Actually, I didn't have a chance to bring it up. Joy did."

"That's awesome, man. Hopefully, you're successful right away."

"Me too." Adam jumps into a short tale of some employee trouble he's having, telling me all about the young twentysomething guy, who has now been caught napping in his truck on two occasions, while he's supposed to be mowing city-owned property. Usually, over coffee, I'd share insight in past experiences I've had at the pharmacy, where employees are concerned, but all I want to do now is push my best friend out the door so I can get back to his sister.

Who's in *my bed*.

I start to drink my coffee a little faster, my brain exiting the conversation and jumping into plans on exactly what I want to do to Addy when I return to my room. My tongue tingles at the prospect of running along her smooth, soft skin, discovering every nook and cranny of her delectable body, listening to every coo that slips from her mouth.

I look up, ready to throw my best, oldest friend in the world out the damn door, when I catch movement. Naked. Movement. Addy walks around the corner and stops. Realization sets in. Her eyes widen and her mouth drops open. Fortunately, her brother's back is to her, since he's facing me.

My own eyes must widen a fraction before I rip my gaze away from the naked beauty standing behind my best friend. Her brother. Adam narrows his eyes at me and starts to turn around, as if knowing something is happening behind him. As if realizing what's happening, Addy bolts back around the corner, nearly being caught by the one man she'd probably rather die than have see her standing there naked as the day she was born.

Adam, realizing no one is there, slowly turns back to face me. I try to school my expression, but he must be able to read my thoughts, because his dark eyes narrow on me. He lifts his cup and chugs the contents, and all I can do is hope he's not scorching his throat.

The moment he walks over and sets his cup in the sink, he says, "Well, clearly I've overstayed my welcome."

I wish I could argue with him, but I can't. I love visiting with my friend, but he definitely needs to go.

Without saying another word, Adam heads toward the front door. Before he pulls it open, he hollers over his shoulder, "Bye, Ads. Call Joy later." With that, my friend throws me a wave and leaves the same way he entered, ensuring the door is locked as he goes.

With a chuckle, I make my way to my bedroom, praying Addy hasn't freaked out enough to put her clothes back on. That would be a real shame. When I step inside my room, I find a large lump sitting in the middle of the bed, covered by a blanket.

Without moving, she mumbles, "Please tell me he did not see my ass when he turned around."

"Your ass was safely hidden from your brother's eyes."

She pulls the blanket off her head and lets it fall. Much to my delight, she's still naked. "Thank God. I never would have heard the end of it."

"Actually, I think he probably never would have brought it up. You know, considering it was his sister's bare ass," I tease, shucking my shorts and making my way toward her.

Her eyes darken as they zero in on my hardening cock. "You may be right."

"I'm always right," I insist, climbing onto the bed and reaching for Addy. "But let's not get into that right now."

She moves at the same time, straddling my legs the moment I sit. "What do you think we should *get into* then?" she asks coyly.

I can't stop the grin that spreads across my lips. "You. I'm definitely going to get into you."

"I'll clean this up," Addy insists, grabbing the empty pan from my hands.

"You cooked. You don't clean up," I argue, reaching for the dirty dish. "In fact, Noah and I will tackle these dishes together."

"I can help?" Noah asks from his place at the table.

"Of course. When a woman cooks us a delicious meal, it's our responsibility to share the workload and clean up," I inform him, taking the pan one last time from Addy. "Why don't you go relax."

"Relax? What's that?" she jokes, but the way she awkwardly chuckles lets me know she's a little serious too. I can't imagine a single mom gets a lot of free time to relax and unwind.

"Go grab your book. You can take it out to the swing unless you're afraid of mosquitoes carrying you away." I don't move until she slowly retreats, heading to her room to grab whatever she needs to relax.

"What can I do?" Noah asks, drawing my attention away from where his mother just stood and back to him.

"You're going to help me load the dishwasher. Let's take these dirty plates and silverware to the sink."

Noah immediately takes his dirty plate and fork and carries them to the sink. He slides them onto the counter beside the pan, while I return to grab my dirty stuff, as well as Addy's.

"Now, this is very important to make sure we're filling the dishwasher properly. This way, we can get as many dirty dishes in it without wasting space." I rinse off the first plate and hand it to him.

He nods, carefully placing the plate into the rack. "Like this?"

"Perfect, No."

We work together to fill the dishwasher, as well as filling the sink to handwash the pan the Italian chicken was baked in. "Why do you have to do that? Can't it go in there?" he asks, pointing to the open dishwasher.

"Well, I always handwash my pans, especially if they have baked gunk on them. Since this one has a lot, it may need to soak in the sink for a while."

"Like with me and the bathtub?"

Smiling, I reach over and ruffle his hair. "Exactly. Sometimes, when you're extra dirty, you have to wash a little harder to get that dirt off."

He nods insistently. "One time, Uncle Adam and I have really muddy at the river and Mommy gave him a mad look. I had to take a shower to get it all off my skin. I don't like showers because I can't play with my boats. Do you have boats when you take a bath?"

"No, no boats or baths for me. I like showers," I tell him, filling the pan with hot soapy water. When he doesn't say anything, I look his way. His mouth is hanging open in shock. "What?"

"You don't like boats?"

I drop to my knees and meet his eye. "Of course I like boats, but I just don't play with them anymore in the tub."

He seems to consider my words before he asks, "Because you're a man?"

I fight the grin. "Well, because I grew up, yes. I played with boats and cups in the tub when I was a little guy like you."

His head turns slightly to the side, his wheels spinning. "Graham, can I ask you a question?"

"Of course, little buddy. You can ask me anything."

He takes a deep breath and asks, "Can you teach me to be a man like you? I don't have a daddy, and Gavin says his daddy is the man of the house. I have to be the man."

My heart is trying to pound out of my chest. Literally. It's beating so hard, I'm a little concerned about having a heart attack. But as I take in Noah's innocence, his genuine goodness and wholesomeness, all I want to do is wrap my arms around him and be the man he so desperately deserves. Not the man he needs. His mother is doing a phenomenal job filling both roles. The man he deserves.

The one they both deserve.

"Of course I'll help you, but can I tell you a little secret?"

He nods insistently.

"You're already an incredible boy, and I have no doubt when you get older, you're going to be the best man I know. Do you know why?"

He shakes his head.

"Because you have the best mom. And the best grandpa. And the best uncle. They've all been perfect examples to you and provided you with guidance to becoming a great man someday."

"And you?" he asks, his voice cracking a little.

I feel it at this moment. I feel myself falling hopelessly in love with this little boy. How could I not? He's simply amazing, with those trusting big brown eyes and unruly sandy-blond hair. "And me," I confirm. "I'll always be here if you need me."

Noah throws his arms around my shoulders and hugs me tightly. "Okay."

When he pulls back, I give him a smile, but I can still see a look on his face. "What?"

"One more thing, Graham."

"Shoot, buddy."

"Can you teach me to use those weights downstairs?"

With a little chuckle, I reach out and ruffle his hair. "Since your mom is relaxing, how about we go downstairs and work out together?"

"Really? Now?" he asks, his eyes dancing with delight.

"Yep. Though, we'll have to take it a little easy, since we just ate."

He nods in understanding. "Okay."

"Tell you what, why don't you run to your room and change into tennis shoes. You never wear flip-flops at the gym."

Again, he nods, hanging on my every word. "What about my clothes?" he asks, looking down at his jean shorts and dinosaur tee.

"Those are fine," I confirm.

"Are you wearing those clothes?" he asks, indicating my khaki shorts and Margaritaville T-shirt.

"No, I'll change into gym shorts and a tank top."

The moment the words are out of my mouth, he spins around and heads out of the room. "Then I'm gonna change too!"

I follow the eager five-year-old, only to stop in my tracks when I find him in the living room. Addy is there, curled up on the couch with a thin throw I'd never use in the middle of August. Her book is sitting on her lap, but she's not reading it. Instead, her eyes are closed.

Noah carefully walks over to where she sleeps and gently takes her book, setting it on the coffee table. Then he grips the blanket and pulls it over her arms to cover her.

My throat is so thick with emotion, I can't even draw air into my lungs. He turns and finds me standing behind him. He gives me a sheepish grin before heading to his bedroom to change his clothes.

I follow and before he can enter his bedroom, I say, "Hey, No?" When he turns around, I say, "Do you know how I know you're going to be a great man someday?"

Noah hesitantly shakes his head, his eyes riveted on me. "How?"

My lips curl. "Because of that right there. What you just did in the living room. You took care of your mom without being told to do it, because you worried she might get chilled while taking a nap, and that's how I know you're going to be a great man someday."

His entire face breaks out in a huge grin.

"Change your clothes and meet me at the basement door, but don't go down, okay?" I don't want him to get on a machine and hurt himself.

"'Kay!" he declares, disappearing into his room and making me chuckle at his eagerness.

I throw on a pair of athletic shorts, a sleeveless tee, and my tennis shoes quickly, because something tells me Noah is already waiting for me. My assumption is confirmed when I step out of my room and find him waiting at the closed basement door. First thing I notice is the fact he changed his clothes into a pair of athletic shorts and a tank top.

I can't help but smile.

"Ready?" I whisper, careful not to wake Addy.

Together, we walk down the stairs into my home gym. "The rule for working out is you can't come down here without supervision. Understand, Noah?"

"What does that mean?"

"You can't come down these stairs without me or your mom," I state, before adding, "Or your uncle Adam." My friend comes over every now and again and uses my gym too. "Deal?"

"Deal."

"Perfect. Now, let's start with a couple of stretches. We never work out without stretching."

"We have to stretch in PE too."

"Yep. Stretches are just as important as the actual workout. You do them before and after."

"After too?"

"Yes, sir. Always after too. It's part of the cooldown process."

We go through a series of stretches, Noah mimicking and hanging on my every move. Only then do we move to a piece of equipment. It's hard to pick what to use, considering he's small and will likely not be able to lift any of the weights I have, but I refuse to let that stop us.

"I'll go first and show you how to do it," I state, placing a twenty-pound weight on each end of the bar. It's considerably less than what I normally bench, but it'll work for tonight. "Okay, you stand back so I don't accidentally hit you with the bar. It weighs eighty-five pounds total, so it can definitely hurt you if you get too close."

He nods and steps back.

I bench press a set of ten before replacing the bar on the stand. "Ready?"

He doesn't look convinced. "With all that weight?"

Sitting up, I reach out and take his hand. "Well, by yourself, no, but with me helping, I bet you can do it. Want to try?"

He nods again.

I jump up and wave at the bench. His body looks so small on the bench, which makes me smile. His little arms reach up. "Okay, I'm going to stand at your head and bring the bar down to you. You grab it and wait until I tell you to bring it down."

"Kay!"

I lift the bar and place it in his little hands, making sure I have the entire weight of the bar. "All right, slowly bring it down to your chest and then push it back up." He does exactly as instructed. "One. Do it again." He does. "Two."

By the time we get to ten, he's panting a little.

"Wait until I put the bar back in the holder before you sit up."

He does exactly as coached and is all smiles the moment he's allowed to sit up. I hold up my hand for a high-five, which he promptly gives me with gusto. "I did it!"

"You sure did, No."

"I can't wait to tell Mommy! She'll be so proud of me."

"She will," I confirm, and when I see movement out of the corner of my eye, I realize we're not alone.

Addy is sitting on the stairs, watching, just like she was earlier in the week when I worked out. There are tears in her eyes as she smiles at me, mouthing a "Thank you" from across the room.

I nod before taking a knee and ruffling his hair. "Ready to try some dumbbells?"

Noah practically jumps up and down with excitement. "Yep!"

"Let's do it."

Sixteen

Addyson

I've been lying awake for over an hour. I was too amped up to sleep. Today is Graham's birthday, and I have all kinds of surprises for him. That starts with making him breakfast before he leaves for work. He works every other Saturday at his family's pharmacy and refused to take it off because it is his birthday. It's just another day, he said.

It's not just another day. It's the day that this amazing man was brought into the world, and we most definitely will be celebrating.

Noah and I have been staying here for over a month, and celebrating his birthday is just another way for me to thank him for all that he's done for us.

When my alarm turns over to six thirty, it's time to get up. The pharmacy opens at eight, so Graham will be leaving for work in an hour. That's plenty of time for me to make him a birthday breakfast. I didn't tell Noah because I was afraid he would spill the surprise, but I'm about to. I know he'll want to help, hence the menu.

Carefully, I slip out of my room and into Noah's. Graham's bedroom door is closed, but I still need to be quiet. Sitting on the side of Noah's bed, I run my fingers through his hair. "Wake up, buddy." He grumbles as his eyes flutter open. "Guess what?" I whisper excitedly.

"What?" he asks in his sleep-laced voice.

"Today is Graham's birthday."

His eyes light up. "It is?"

"Yep. And guess what else?"

"What?" He sits up in bed. I've got his attention.

"We're going to make him breakfast before he goes to work."

"We are?" His eyes widen, and he wiggles where he sits.

"Yes. Go potty and brush your teeth. We need to get busy so he can eat before he goes to work."

Noah gasps. "He has to work on his birfday?"

I chuckle. "Sometimes adults have to do things like work on special days."

"He needs lots of food then." He moves to climb out of bed and rushes out the door to the bathroom. I just hope that Graham is already in the shower and didn't hear him.

I wait in the hallway for Noah and take his hand, leading him to the kitchen. I lift him to the island and get to work gathering everything that we need.

"What are we making, Mommy?" he asks.

"Pancakes."

"Oh! I'm good at stirring," he tells me.

"I know you are. Let's get to work."

Fifteen minutes later, the counter is a mess. Noah has batter on his nose, but we have a big plate of pancakes and a fresh pot of coffee ready when Graham walks into the kitchen.

"Happy birfday pancakes!" Noah cheers.

Graham's smile lights up the room. Who am I kidding? That smile lights me up inside too. "Did you do all of this?" he asks Noah.

"Me and Mommy." Noah nods proudly.

"Thank you, No." He leans in and hugs him before swiping at the batter on his nose and wiping his hands on a dish towel.

"Mommy needs a hug too, G. She helped me. I'm only five," Noah reminds him.

"Right. Mommy needs a hug too." Graham slides his arm around my waist and buries his face in my neck. "Morning, beautiful," he whispers huskily.

He pulls back, and Noah smiles. "Now we eat. I'm so hungry," he says dramatically.

"Well, we can't have that." Graham lifts him from the island. "Grab a seat, bud. I'll make you a plate."

"We have to eat it all gone to get big and strong. Right, G?" he asks. I smile at Noah shortening Graham's name like Graham does for him. They really are two peas in a pod.

"That's right, No." He smiles at my son, and I was wrong. This is the smile that lights me up inside. It does more than that. It sets me on fire.

I work on cleaning up our mess while they begin to eat. "Addy, come sit," Graham tells me. Grabbing my plate, I sit next to Noah, with Graham on the other side.

"We did good, Mommy. Right, G?" Noah asks.

"Best birthday breakfast I've ever had," Graham tells him. Noah beams with pride and takes another huge bite of his pancakes.

"I hate to eat and run, but I need to get to work."

"Boo," Noah calls out. "Working on your birfday isn't a fun day."

"I don't mind it. I enjoy my job," Graham tells him. "Are you all done?" he asks.

"My belly is done," Noah replies, making us both laugh.

"Go wash up so I can have a non-sticky hug before I leave for work."

"Okay!" Noah climbs out of his chair and rushes down the hall.

Graham stands and walks to where I'm sitting. His palm rests against my cheek as he bends down and presses his lips to mine. "Thank you for this."

"You're welcome," I say as he kisses me one more time. The pitter-patter of Noah's feet coming down the hallway has him standing to his full height and walking to the sink. He rinses his plate and places it in the dishwasher.

"I'm ready," Noah says, sliding into the kitchen on his sock-covered feet.

Graham bends and opens his arms. Noah doesn't hesitate to walk into his embrace. "Love you, Graham. Have a good birfday at work."

"Love you too, No. Thank you for breakfast."

"Welcome," he chirps. "Mommy, can I watch cartoons?"

"Sure, bud. You need me to help you?" My heart is bursting at the seams seeing the two of them together.

"No. Graham teached me."

"Graham taught you," I correct him. "I'm going to clean up the kitchen and shower. Then we're going grocery shopping."

"Okay, Mommy." He runs off to the living room.

"Thank you for this. Having you and Noah here already made this the best birthday. This was just icing on the cake." He smiles.

He has no idea what I have in store for him. "Have a good day, dear." I smile sweetly.

"When we put Noah to bed tonight, you're mine."

"Oh, is the birthday boy making demands?"

"I miss you, Addy."

"I'm right here."

"I want you closer."

My heart sings from his words. "Have a good day."

"Thanks, baby." He kisses me one more time before grabbing his travel mug I had ready for him and exiting through the mudroom to the garage.

"Mommy, why did you clean so much?" Noah asks from his booster seat in the back seat of my car.

"Well, I just wanted to do something nice for Graham since it's his birthday. He's letting us stay with him, and I thought cleaning would be the nice thing to do." I almost slipped and told him about the rest of the day's plans. However, we just left the grocery store, and we're on our way to pick up Chinese and take it to Graham for lunch. I don't need him spoiling the surprise. I've managed to keep it from Graham and Noah this long. A few more hours won't hurt.

"We're stopping again?" Noah asks.

"We are. We're going to go in and pick up the food I ordered for Graham and take him lunch."

"Can we eat with him?"

"He only gets a short amount of time to eat, and we need to get home and get these groceries unpacked."

"I got muscles," he says.

Glancing in the rearview mirror, I watch as he flexes. "I see that."

"Graham and me, we work out," he tells me.

"So strong," I praise him, and he bobs his head in agreement. "Come on. Let's run in and grab our order, and we can head home."

"What are we eating?" he asks as I offer him my hand to climb out of the back seat.

"I ordered us some Chinese too."

"That sweet chicken stuff?"

"You know it."

"Yay!" He pumps his fist in the air.

Our order is ready when we get there, so it only takes a few minutes to grab it, get Noah back in the car, and head toward the pharmacy.

"Can I carry it?" Noah asks.

"Sure. Just be careful," I tell him, handing him the small bag that contains Graham's lunch.

As soon as we enter the pharmacy, Noah goes straight to the register. "Where is Graham?" he asks the young girl.

She smiles down at him. "He's back in the pharmacy." She points to the back wall. Noah grabs my hand and pulls me toward the back of the building. When we're halfway there, he spots Graham talking to a customer.

"Graham! We brunged you birfday lunch," he calls out.

Everyone in the store, I'm sure, heard him. The older lady that Graham is checking out smiles, wishes him a happy birthday, and steps away from the counter. I make sure there are no other waiting customers before telling Noah he can go to the counter.

"What did you bring me?" Graham asks him.

"Sweet chicken. It's yummy. Right, Mommy?" He turns to look over his shoulder at me.

"It's very yummy," I agree.

"It's been slammed all day. I wasn't going to have time to run out, and I forgot to pack something. I was so full from my delicious breakfast this morning," he tells Noah.

"It was Mommy's plan, but I carried the bag," he confesses.

A line starts to form, so I place my hand on Noah's shoulders, and we step back. The clerk steps to the next window and motions that she can help the customer. "We'll let you get back to work," I tell him.

"Meet me at the door." He points to a side door, and I nod. By the time we get there, he's pulling the door open and bending down to wrap Noah in a hug. "Thank you for lunch, No."

"Mommy too," Noah reminds him.

"I would never forget your mom," he tells him. Releasing my son, Graham stands to his full height and slides his arm around my waist. "Thank you, Addy," he says huskily. He squeezes my hip before releasing me.

"Tonight, Mom said we can have cake!" Noah says loudly.

"She did?" Graham, who still has his arm around me, gives me a side-eye. "You two have done enough for me today. It's been the best birthday ever."

"We're really good." Noah nods. Not one bit of modesty for this five-year-old.

"We'll see you at home later?" I ask.

"Yeah. I should be there a little after six or so."

"Great." I lean in to kiss him but pull back. It's easy to forget that we're not the only two people in the room when he's this close to me. His eyes darken, and he mouths, "Later" to me. With a fist bump for Noah, we're back in the car and on our way home.

"Do you need any help?" Joy asks.

"No. I don't know." I laugh. "I think we're all set." I glance around the kitchen at the many slow cookers and side dishes I've prepared and others have brought for tonight's party. "We have plenty of drinks, the cake is set up, and yeah, I think we're good," I say again with a laugh.

"This was really nice of you," she tells me.

"He's done so much for Noah and me, letting us stay here. It's the least I can do."

"How are things between the two of you?" she asks.

I exhale a heavy breath. "He's... everything."

"Have you told Noah?"

"No. But it's getting harder to hide it from him."

"Oh, Addyson, this is lovely. He's going to be so surprised," Tammy, Graham's mom, says, pulling me into a hug. "You and I both know that if I were to do something like this, he'd be grumpy."

"He has no clue," his dad, Alan, chimes in. "I stopped by the pharmacy earlier and tried to get him to let us take him to dinner. He thanked me for the offer, agreed to have dinner with us tomorrow, but said tonight he was coming home to the two of you." His blue eyes sparkle, reminding me so much of Graham. He has a lot of his father's features.

"Noah was excited about cake," I tell him.

"Oh, sweetheart, it's more than that. You and Noah are his family too."

Her words hit me in my feels. I want nothing more than to be Graham's family. Not because he's my brother's best friend, but because I've fallen hopelessly in love with him. Not just some teenage crush that's carried over. I've given him every piece of my heart.

"He's here!" Adam calls out.

The room is a flurry of activity as everyone halts their conversations and crowds into the kitchen. I had everyone park next door and those who could carpool. So he hopefully still has no idea until he walks into the house.

As soon as the mudroom door opens, Noah wiggles to be set free from where he's standing in front of me. I keep my grip on his shoulder until Graham steps into view. Then all bets are off. Everyone yells, "Surprise," and Noah launches himself at Graham. Luckily, Graham was ready and caught him easily, setting him on his hip.

"What's all this?" he asks Noah, nodding to his guests but still giving my son his attention.

"It's your birfday party."

"Did you do all of this?" he asks Noah.

"Mommy did, but I helped."

"Well, thank you." Graham hugs him tight before placing him back on his feet. Graham scans the room until his gaze lands on me. With a steady stride, he comes to stand before me. "You've been busy today," he says with a smile pulling at his lips.

"Meh." I shrug like it was nothing.

He surprises me when he bends his head, and his lips press against my forehead. "Thank you, baby." He whispers low enough that only I can hear him. But that doesn't matter because I'm sure everyone, all his friends and family, my brother, my parents, and my son, can hear the thunderous beat of my heart.

He turns to his mom, who has tears in her eyes, and hugs and kisses her on the cheek. He moves to his dad and works his way around the room.

"Damn," Tosha mutters.

"Yeah," I agree. She chuckles, and together we start getting the cold food items out of the refrigerator and guiding people to come and make a plate. I make one for Noah, but he barely touches it. He's too excited about all the people that are here giving him attention. He's a ham for sure, living it up.

The night goes smoothly, and no matter how many times I seek out Graham, he turns to find me looking at him. It's as if he can feel me. It's crazy to my own ears, but I don't know how else to explain it.

We had barely finished eating when Noah convinced Graham that it was time for cake. He does manage to eat the entirely too large piece as well as his big scoop of ice cream. I'll be lucky if he ever falls asleep tonight.

It's been a great night with lots of laughs, and so many showed up. Adam helped me reach out to some of their buddies. Mom and Dad, Adam and Joy, Tosha, and Graham's parents. They all contributed to the food and came by early to help decorate. Well, Adam mostly occupied Noah, but that counts for something.

I haven't had a spare minute to spend with him other than when he first walked in, but I know he's having a good time. The smile on his face and the laughter coming from the corner of the room tells me so. Most of his friends are gone, leaving our parents, Tosha, Adam, and Joy. It's well past Noah's bedtime, so I need to start that process.

"Noah," I call out. He's sitting on the floor playing with his trucks while Adam, our dad, Graham, and his dad carry on whatever conversation they're having. Mom and Tammy are in the kitchen cleaning up, and Tosha is in there with them. I walk over to sit on the arm of the couch, the same side where Graham is sitting. He reaches out and slides his arm around my waist.

I freeze because our fathers and Noah are sitting with us, but at the same time, I'm starved for his affection. It's hard to be here with him and not sneak kisses or subtle touches. He squeezes my hip and pulls his arm away.

"Noah. It's time for bed."

"No," he says loudly and goes back to playing with his truck.

I stand and reach for his hand, but he smacks mine away. "Noah," I scold.

"No. I don't want to go to bed."

"Noah." Graham stands and holds out his hand. "Bud, it's time for bed."

"I don't want to," Noah whines. He's exhausted and doesn't want to miss the action, so he's fighting it.

"Your mom says it's time for bed. Come on. I'll read you a story."

"No, Graham, it's your birthday party. Noah, come with me." I'm shocked when he crawls toward Graham and locks his little arms around his legs. "I want Graham."

Graham bends down and lifts him into his arms. He talks softly, but the room has fallen quiet, so we can all hear what he says. "No, you can't talk to your mom like that. You have to listen when she tells you it's time for bed."

"I want you to tell me a story."

Graham hugs him a little tighter at his confession. His eyes fall, and you can just see it written all over his face. He loves my son. Noah wants him over me, it's as if my son reached into his chest and wrapped his little fist around Graham's heart, and we're all here to bear witness.

His eyes find mine, and they're pleading. With one look, I know what he's asking. He wants to put Noah to bed. He wants to read him a story. My heart lurches in my chest. Noah is so attached to him.

He's not the only one.

I've fallen in love with him too.

I nod, letting him know that it's okay. He can take him to bed.

"All right, bud. Give Mom a kiss goodnight." Graham leans in, and Noah gives me a one-armed hug and a kiss.

"Night, Mommy. Love you," he says, his eyes already drooping.

"You all right with this?" Graham finally voices his concern.

"I'm good," I assure him. I watch them until they disappear down the hall and look back at three sets of eyes watching me intently. I can see it on all three of their faces. They know. They know there is something going on with us. Something more. Of course, Adam knows, but our dads, they don't. Scratch that. They didn't, but they do now.

Reaching into my pocket, I search for my phone as something to occupy me because I'm not ready to face our fathers. "I lost my phone," I mumble and go in search of it. I find it on the small table by the front door. I was taking pictures of Graham with a few of the guests as they were leaving. Picking it up, I see I missed a call from my landlord and that he left a message. Typing in my passcode, I bring my phone to my ear.

"Addyson, this is Mr. Garcia. Sorry to call so late. I wanted to let you know that the drywallers started today, and we are on track for you to be back in your apartment in two weeks. Three at the most. Give me a call, and we can discuss further."

Two weeks. Maybe three. That's all the time I have left. Noah is going to be crushed when we leave. Suddenly, I'm wondering if moving in with Graham temporarily was a good choice. It's not just Noah who is going to miss him. I'm going to miss him too. The happy lull of the evening comes to a grinding halt.

I don't know where we go from here.

Seventeen

Graham

Finally.

Finally, everyone is gone. Yes, I was incredibly shocked and humbled to find my house full of family and friends to help me celebrate my thirty-fifth birthday, but now I just want them all to leave so I can take Addy to bed.

To show her how much I appreciate what she did.

No one has ever done anything like this for me. Sure, my parents always take me to dinner, but a few years ago, it was convenient for Adam and me to meet at Hank's for a birthday drink. But then he started dating Joy, eventually marrying her, and his attention shifted from nights out with the guys to nights in with the woman he loves. I never understood it. Never wanted it for myself.

I do now.

After making sure the house is locked up and the lights are off, I head down the hall in search of the woman responsible for tonight. I find Noah's door closed, no sound coming from his room. Doesn't surprise me. Even though he fought sleep, which I firmly believe is why he got mouthy with his mom, he barely made it through the second page of the book he chose for me to read.

The next door is for Addy's room, which I find wide open, the room dark. I still peek inside, checking the small bathroom for her presence. That door is also open, lights off, so I head to the one place I pray she's at.

My room.

After spinning on my heels, I slowly open my closed door and step inside. The room is dark, but there's just enough light, thanks to a few battery candles sitting on the nightstands. But my attention isn't on those. No, my eyes are riveted to the beauty lying in the middle of my bed, wearing what can only be described as the world's sexiest scrap of lingerie.

"I would ask if it's my birthday to receive a gift like this, but..."

Addy smiles. "I don't know about a gift, but when I saw it online, I thought you might like it."

I start to unbutton my shirt, slowly stalking toward her. "Thought? No, no, sweet Addyson. I fucking love it, and I've only seen the front." When I reach the bed, I strip off my button-down, quickly followed by my undershirt. She watches me intently, her eyes laser-focused on my hands as I remove everything from the waist up before sliding my belt from my pants and dropping it onto the floor. I release the button on my trousers and slowly slide down the zipper, the sound of the teeth releasing echoes through the quiet room. "Do you know what I'd really like?"

"What?" she asks, not moving her gaze from where my pants remain open.

Reaching for her hand, I smile when she shimmies to where I stand, places her hand in mine, and allows me to help her stand. Only then do I take her place on the bed and slip my hands behind my head. "I'd really like to see the back of that outfit."

Addy seems a little reluctant, and perhaps a bit embarrassed, but my brave woman steels her spine, places her hands on her hips, and slowly starts to turn. The front is a lace body suit in a deep purple color, and it dips very low between her full tits. Two thin straps wrap around her shoulder, disappearing from view until she's fully turned around. She's a fucking wet dream.

And the back? The back is every bit as amazing as the front. The straps drop incredibly low, crossing in the middle of her back until they meet lace again at that sexy divot at her lower back. And her ass? On full fucking display. The lace tapers into a tiny little strip and disappears between the globes of her ass.

I groan. I try to say words, but they won't come. Instead, I make a noise. It's both of appreciation and one of pain, because right now, my cock is so damn hard, I could pound concrete.

She peeks over her shoulder, a coy smile on her plump lips. "I take it you like?"

"I fucking love." Suddenly, I'm moving. "Come here."

Addy meets me at the edge of the bed and is in my arms seconds later. My mouth claims hers, hard and insistent, my tongue pushing between her lips and tangling with a fury. My hands wrap around her hips before slowly sliding across the soft lace material until they meet the bare skin of her ass.

The moment I squeeze, she presses her body against mine, her frantic hands sweeping up my neck and diving into my hair.

"Jesus, I don't want to take this off, but I really want to take this off," I mumble against her lips, slipping my finger beneath the thong.

Addy chuckles, raking her nails against my scalp. "Wanna know a secret?" she asks, her voice all breathy and laced with desire.

"Tell me."

She nips at my bottom lip as she whispers, "This whole piece is stretchy."

I pull back and meet her lust-filled gaze. "Stretchy?"

Leaning forward, she runs her tongue up the side of my neck, making me shiver. "Stretchy."

As if needing confirmation, I tug on the little scrap of material between her ass cheeks and grin when it easily pulls from her body, as if made from some sort of elastic.

"It's the only way to get this get-up on, Graham."

"That means we don't have to take it off." It's not a question, but a statement.

Slowly, she shakes her head.

"Fuck, yes." My mouth slams down onto hers as I spin us around so her back is to the bed. My finger slides lower until it sweeps across her wet, swollen pussy. Addy shifts her feet, widening her stance to give me better access. Two fingers instantly push inside, her internal muscles clenching around me.

I carefully pull them out before thrusting them up once more. She cries out, her body starting to shake against mine, as I do it over and over again. Her body shakes harder, and even though my balls ache for release, I'm going to take my time with her. I'm going to savor this gift she's giving me.

Curling my fingers, I can tell the moment she's about to come. Her legs quiver and her pussy squeezes. She leans forward and rests her head against my chest, riding my fingers. "Take what you need, sweetness. I want to feel it."

And she does. Spectacularly, her release explodes like fireworks, her muscles tightening like a vise around me. I only wish it were my cock.

But it will be.

Soon.

When her orgasm starts to ebb, I kiss her a bit slower. My tongue strokes and tangles with hers, drawing out the pleasure and subtly reigniting those flames I saw dancing in her eyes.

Her fingers skip down my chest before slipping into the open fly of my trousers. Deft fingers wrap around my cock with enough pressure to make my eyes cross. "Now you?" she asks, trailing her mouth across my chin and down my neck.

"Not a chance, Addy."

She pulls back and meets my gaze, worry written in bold imprint across her gorgeous, flushed face.

"My birthday, right?"

She nods and confirms, "Yes."

"Then, I want to eat my dessert."

Realization sets in, and she chuckles as I guide her onto my bed. "I would have thought you'd want to *receive* your gift."

"Oh, this most definitely will be me receiving my gift. Now, get in the middle of the bed and grab the headboard." I reach over and toss the pillows out of the way and watch her every move as she gets into position at the head of the bed. "Perfect."

Then, I make my move. I slide on my back between her kneeling thighs, her pussy hovering just over my face. My mouth waters. My tongue tingles in anticipation. She's soaked, her first release coating her inner thighs and the purple lingerie stretched across her mound.

"Don't let go of the headboard, Addy," I command before swiping my tongue across the wet lace.

She jolts at first contact and rocks her hips, grinding herself against my mouth. I reach between her legs and move the lingerie to the side, exposing my dessert, and like a man starved, I eat.

I lick.

I suck.

I fuck her with my tongue until she's gyrating her hips, her body completely taking over in a race for release. Her thighs tighten around my head, but I don't care. It doesn't stop my tongue's assault on her clit.

"Too much," she mutters between gasps, squeezing her legs again to try to stop me.

It doesn't work.

"Never enough," I state before plunging my tongue into her pussy.

Addy cries out, her body convulsing, her internal muscles gripping my tongue, and spilling her sweet taste all over my mouth and face. Before the tremors of her release subside, she falls forward, her body boneless and spent.

If only I was finished with her...

I help move her, but she basically falls onto the bed, and I can't stop the smile that spreads across my lips. She's without a doubt, the most unbelievably sexy, intoxicating woman I've never had the privilege of sharing a bed with, but the kicker is I want her to stay.

Forever.

The last month has done nothing to diminish that, nor do I see the next one doing it either. Or the one after that.

"You okay?" I ask, standing up and sliding my pants and boxers down my legs and kicking them off to the side.

"You killed me," she mumbles, her face pressed into the blanket. When I chuckle, she turns her head, eyes focusing on my cock.

With one slow stroke from root to tip, I ask, "You tired, Addy?"

Her eyes remain locked on their target as she replies, "I'm starting to perk up a little."

"Just a little?"

She makes a noise but doesn't speak.

"You know," I start, taking a step toward the bed, "I have a vivid picture in my head of you in my bed."

"Yeah? What am I doing in your bed?" she asks, her cheeks flushing a gorgeous shade of pink.

"Well, coincidentally, you're wearing this sexy, purple, lacy lingerie," I state, climbing onto the bed and kneeling beside her.

Addy gasps with mock shock. "That is a coincidence."

"But in my fantasy, you're not lying on the bed."

"I'm not?"

"No. In my fantasy, you're on all fours in the middle of my bed. Your back is arched and you're looking back at me over your shoulder. I grip your hips as I slide my cock inside your pussy over and over again, until you're panting for more and begging to come."

She moves, spinning around and positioning herself on all fours. My cock twitches with excitement. "Like this?"

"Yep," I reply, my eyes glued to her entire body, my throat dry, and my heart trying to pound right out of my chest. "Just like that."

I move my position behind her, wanting to savor the way she looks right now, yet needing to be inside her more than I need my next breath. My hands have a slight tremble as I run them over her ass to grip her hips. My cock is ready, seeping moisture from the tip and about to explode.

Reaching over, I rip open the drawer of my nightstand and pull out a strip of condoms. With trembling fingers, I sheath myself in protection while still moving toward the goal, which is getting inside her body.

I slide the head of my cock along her ass, sliding lower until I'm at her entrance. "You know, one of these days, I'm going to claim you... here." I press my thumb against her ass. She gasps and presses back against my touch. "But not tonight, Sweet Addy. Tonight, this pussy is mine."

No, it's mine forever.

With that, I make sure the material of her lingerie is pulled to the side and thrust until I'm balls deep in pure euphoric heaven.

I set a punishing pace, driving in hard and fast. The tingle starts at the base of my spine almost immediately, but I refuse to let go yet. Not until she's had three, which might take a little extra coaxing.

Addy moves to her elbows, her delectable ass staring up at me in the perfect position. It's the stuff dreams are made of, as she rocks back to meet me. "Touch yourself, baby. I want to feel you squeeze my cock."

She rolls her hips, taking me even deeper. "I'm not sure I can."

"You can, Addy. Touch yourself."

She reaches between her legs, and I know the moment her fingers are working her clit. Her pussy convulses and tightens, making my eyes cross.

"That's it, sweetness. Are you close?"

Addy gasps, pressing back hard. "Yes. So close."

"Ride my cock, baby. Ride me and make yourself come."

She rocks her hips once more and cries out, her internal muscles choking my cock. It's pure heaven. I let myself go, my body completely taking over as it drives for release. When it hits, it's the force of a Mack truck, powerful and with enough of a punch, it's hard to draw air into my lungs.

"Addyson," I groan, going completely still as the first wave of pleasure courses through my veins. Suddenly, my hips move on their own, drawing out my orgasm, savoring the sensations of her pussy squeezing my cock.

We fall together in a heap of boneless limbs, panting and sweaty, but in the best way possible. After a few minutes of slowing our heart rates and catching our breath, I say, "I do think I like that outfit, Addy. You wear that, and every day will be my birthday."

She chuckles and snuggles into my embrace. "I'm not sure it survived the actual celebration," she replies, her voice laced with exhaustion.

I glance down as I slide from the warmth of her body, noticing the crotch area is extremely stretched. For some reason, a satisfied smile spreads across my lips. "Tell you what, we'll buy more. Many more actually. I think you should wear one every night."

The sweetest laugh falls from her lips, making me want to kiss them. "I'm not sure that's in my budget, but I could definitely see about getting another one."

"Deal," I whisper, leaning over and kissing her shoulder. "I'm going to run to the bathroom and take care of the condom. Be right back."

When I return a few minutes later with a warm washcloth, Addy's passed out in my bed, softly snoring. I can't help but grin as I slip back into bed, carefully extracting the blanket from beneath us and cleaning up the remnants of her release. I toss the washcloth through the open bathroom door and pull her against my body. Everything in me begs to lie here, to just hold her and memorize the way she feels, sleeping in my arms, but my eyes and brain won't cooperate.

Before I'm ready, sleep grabs hold and pulls me under.

I enter my house, only to find it quiet, which is completely unusual since Addy and Noah moved in. Setting my keys on the entryway table, I smile when I see a picture of me and my parents from the surprise party that Addyson threw for me. It's hard to believe that was almost two weeks ago. Time with them flies by, and all I want to do is slow it down.

As I walk down the hallway, I hear crying, instantly recognizing it as Noah. "But, Mommy," he whines and sniffles, "I want Graham to come."

The mention of my name makes me pause outside the open door. "I know you do, buddy, but he has to work. He has a commitment, and that's his first priority."

The hairs on the back of my neck stand up as realization sets in. I'm the reason Noah is upset. Or at least I'm part of it.

"But I drewded that picture for him. He *has* to see it at the art fair, Mommy," he says before crying once more.

"Come here, Noah," she replies. I want to peek inside the room, but

I'm not ready to let my presence be known yet. I hear the bed squeak, which tells me Noah probably climbed onto his mom's lap on the bed. "You'll be able to show Graham your drawing as soon as you get home."

The little boy doesn't reply, just cries harder, and I can't take it anymore. I step inside his bedroom, my heart breaking as I see him wrapped around his mom's abdomen, crying into her shoulder. "What's all this about?" I ask, startling them both.

Noah whips around, his tear-streaked face full of happiness the moment he sees me. "Graham!"

Addy gives me a sad grin over her son's head. I'm already reaching for him before she can say a word. As soon as he's in my arms and I hug him tight, I take a seat on the bed beside Addy and position him so I can see his face. "What's wrong, No? Tell me."

He sniffles and uses the back of his hand to wipe his nose, but that doesn't matter right now. Getting to the bottom of his despair is the only thing on my mind. "My art fair is tomorrow," he whispers, casting his eyes downward.

"Okay," I encourage, lifting his chin to meet his eyes. "That's good, right?"

Noah nods and sniffles. "I wanted to show you my drawing, but Mommy says you have to work."

I glance quickly over at Addy in confusion. "What time is the fair?"

"Four to six," she states softly.

Realization hits me. "Ahh. It'll be over before I get off work." The pharmacy closes at six. Even if we're able to close down right at the top of the hour, I don't always get out of there until six fifteen or later.

Hearing Noah cry, his little hands gripping my shirt, breaks me. I'm willing to do anything—no promise too great—to take those tears away. I know life is full of moments where you don't get your way, when disappointment isn't avoided—but this will not be one of those times. Not for Noah.

"I'll be there."

His little face jerks up, his eyes wide with a mix of eagerness and hesitancy. "You will?"

"Yes," I confirm, using my thumb to wipe the tears from his cheek.

"I'll ask my dad to come work for me for the last part of the day, so I won't miss your art fair."

"Graham," Addy starts, but I cut her off.

"I want to be there," I tell her, meaning every word.

"Yay! I can show you my drawing! I made it for you," Noah proclaims, throwing his arms around my neck and hugging me tight.

"I can't wait, No," I say, returning the gesture. When he pulls back, I meet his gaze and say, "I wouldn't miss it for the world."

And I wouldn't. Nothing could keep me away from that art fair.

From him.

From his mom.

I'm in love with both of them.

And as terrifying as that is, I won't fight it. I can't. I'm too far gone. I see a future with them both.

My future.

Eighteen

ddyson

"Morning, beautiful." Graham places his hands on my hips and presses a kiss on my cheek.

"Morning." I look over my shoulder at him and give him a soft smile. I try not to show him that my mom guilt is strong.

Last night when Noah cried for Graham, my heart cracked wide open. All this time, we've been focused on hiding our relationship from Noah. While I wasn't looking, my son handed Graham his tiny heart on a platter. He loves him. I know he does, but it's deeper than just love. They've bonded, and it's a special bond that has my heart full.

However, my head and my heart are conflicted. I know how easy Graham is to love. He showers us with his affection and his attention. But how do I know it's not because of our circumstances? How do I know that once Noah and I move out that he's going to feel the same way about us?

I wanted to protect my son, but I failed. If Graham changes his mind, if he realizes he doesn't want a woman who has a kid, we're both going to be broken. I never wanted this to touch Noah. I was naive enough to think I could prevent it.

I was wrong.

"Babe, are you—?" Graham starts, but the pitter-patter of little feet racing down the hall has him stepping away.

"Graham! You're still coming, right? To my art fair?" There is so much excitement in his voice he's practically vibrating with it.

"Of course I am. I called my dad last night, and he's going to come in and cover me so I can be there when it starts."

"The whole time?" Noah's voice is filled with awe.

"You know it, No. Are you ready for school?"

"Yep. I brushded my teeth and everything."

Pushing down my worry, I turn to smile at them. "Well, we need to get going. We don't want to be late. Go grab your backpack."

Noah comes over to Graham and wraps his arms around his legs. "I'll see you at my art fair. You promised." He looks up at Graham with so much trust.

Graham kneels before him and hugs him tight. "I promise, buddy. I'll be there at four." He looks up at me. "Can we maybe take our little artist out for pizza afterward?" he suggests.

Our little artist.

I don't know if he means it as it sounds. I don't know if it's just a figure of speech, but my heart heard him, and it's yearning for it to be true. For this to be not only our present but our future.

"What do you think, Noah? Pizza for dinner?" I ask my son.

"Yes!" He pumps his fist in the air and takes off like a bolt of lightning to get his backpack.

"So, this thing starts at four, right?" Graham asks.

"Yes, four to six, but, Graham, you don't—" I start, but he leans in and presses a chaste kiss to my lips.

"I want, Addy. I want to be there. I'll text you when I get to the school."

"Okay."

"I'll see you later, baby." Another quick kiss before he grabs his travel mug and walks out the door.

It's just after three when Noah comes racing into my classroom. "Is it time?" he asks, bouncing on the balls of his feet.

"Almost. I brought you a snack since we're not going home."

"I'm starving," he says dramatically, making me laugh.

"Well, then you better get over here." I pull a peanut butter and jelly sandwich that I've cut in half and a bag of apple slices out of my lunch bag. I get busy getting his snack ready before I settle back in to enter some grades.

Noah chatters about his day, making mine with his excitement for school and tonight's art fair. When my phone beeps with a message, I glance over to see Graham's name on the screen.

Graham: I'm here.

Me: We're in my classroom.

Graham: On my way.

Me: K.

"Noah, time to clean up the books. Graham's here, and it's almost time for the art fair to start."

"Yes!" He jumps to his feet and does a little dance in celebration. I don't know if I've ever seen him this excited about anything.

"Is that what you're teaching young minds these days?" Graham says from the doorway of my classroom. "I don't remember dance parties in elementary school."

"Graham!"

He has just enough time to brace himself before Noah crashes into him. "Hey, No." He chuckles. "Are you ready for the art fair?"

"You came."

"Of course I did. I promised you I would, and I don't break my promises." His eyes find mine, and there's something in his eyes, something I can't name, but it's gone before I get a chance to look further.

"So, how does this work?" Graham asks.

"Well, we have the gym set up. There are stations for each grade. Kindergarten through fourth."

"You don't have to work it?" he asks.

"Not this time. We all take turns for these kinds of events."

"Gotcha, well, shall we?" Graham offers Noah his hand, and he starts to offer me the other before dropping it to his side. His jaw tics, and if I hadn't been watching him so closely, I would have missed it.

Together the three of us make our way to the gym. It's still quiet, but it won't take long for families to come filing in to look at the art of their students. My parents are out of town traveling, and Adam and Joy are both working late. If Graham were not here with us, it would be just Noah and me. Something I'm used to after the last five years.

Until Graham.

We make our way through each section. The kindergarten exhibit is on the opposite side of the gym. We browse the other displays but don't stop. Noah is bursting with excitement to get us to his picture. He's still holding onto Graham's hand and trying his best to move us along faster, but Graham keeps a casual pace.

Each grade level had a theme this year. My first graders' theme was food, and my students loved drawing their favorites. "This is my students," I tell Graham and Noah.

"Mommy, can we come back?" Noah asks.

"Oh, I guess," I tease him.

He turns back and continues to pull Graham by the hand to the kindergarten exhibit. "There!" Noah points to the table on the right and starts pulling us that way. "Paxton!" he calls out to one of his friends.

Paxton turns, and so does his family or the adults that are with him. One of which is Brianne. Graham's ex's mouth drops open when she sees Graham holding Noah's hand. Her eyes flash to me, and her brows furrow. She can't understand why Graham is here with us.

"Graham," Brianne greets him.

"Brianne. Good to see you."

"You were the last person I expected to see here." She gives a nervous laugh.

"I couldn't miss my man Noah's art debut," he says, making Noah smile.

"Is that your dad?" Paxton asks.

"Paxton," a woman who looks like Brianne scolds.

"No. That's my Graham." Noah shrugs.

Brianne sputters a cough.

"Noah, why don't you show me your picture while Graham talks to his friend?" I suggest.

"Graham too," Noah insists.

"You bet, No." He smiles at my son. "It was good to see you," he tells Brianne and dismisses her, giving Noah his full attention. "Lead the way," he tells Noah.

Noah does just that. Grabbing his hand again and pulling us to the side of the table with his picture. Once we stop, Graham rests his hand on the small of my back. The heat of his palm, even through the thin fabric of my shirt, sears my skin.

"There." Noah points.

I scan the picture, and tears form in my eyes. The kindergarten's class theme was family. I should have put two and two together, as excited as he was for Graham to see his drawing. I'm staring at a family. A man, a woman, and a little boy, if my eyes are not deceiving me.

"See. It's our family. It's Graham, and Mommy and me." Noah looks up at us, his smile wider than I've ever seen it.

"N-Noah." Graham clears his throat. "It's a masterpiece," he tells him. There is no mistaking the emotion in his voice.

"Thanks." Noah beams. "Do you like it, Mommy?" Noah asks.

I have to swallow past the lump in my throat. "It's beautiful," I tell him. My heart is cracking wide open for my sweet boy. He loves Graham so very much, and I know Graham cares for him too. However, it's easy to get attached when you're living in such close quarters. I was a fool to think that this wouldn't touch Noah.

"Graham, can I talk to you?" Brianne asks.

"Come on, Noah. Let's go walk around for a bit."

"G, are you coming?" Noah holds his hand out for Graham.

Graham doesn't hesitate to take Noah's offered hand. "It was good to see you, Brianne, but there is nothing left for us to talk about." Her mouth falls open in shock, but he ignores her. "Where are we going next?" Graham asks Noah.

"Mommy's class." He starts leading the way, and I melt into a puddle when Graham places his hand back on the small of my back. He leans in and quickly presses a kiss to my temple. I hear Brianne gasp behind us, but I'm on the brink of my own breakdown, so I don't look back.

When Noah stops at the art displays, he moves to get a closer look, but we hang back. "Addy?" Graham asks.

I turn to look at him. There are worry lines creasing his forehead. "You, and me, and Noah. That's what matters." His voice is soft and almost pleading.

I nod because I can't form words. The worry lines don't fade, and neither does the churning in my gut. The unknown lies between us. The heaviness of the picture that Noah drew anchors that feeling even more so.

Somehow, we manage to get through the remainder of the exhibits without any further incidents and without Noah's smile slipping. "I need to run to my classroom to grab our things."

"Lead the way," Graham says, bending down and scooping Noah into his arms, making them both laugh. "You did good, No."

"You really liked it?"

"I did. You, my good sir, are an ar-teest," Graham pitches his voice.

"Can we hang it on the fridge?" Noah asks.

"Um, yeah, I'd be upset if you didn't. I think that's just what the kitchen needs."

"Me too," Noah agrees, bobbing his head.

Making it to my classroom, I quickly gather our things, and we head outside. Graham makes sure we're all set before we agree to meet at the pizza place. Noah chatters about the art fair and the fact that Graham loved his picture. I send up a silent prayer that my boy's heart doesn't get broken, that my heart doesn't get broken.

We're both in too deep.

"This is my favorite," Noah says, taking a huge bite out of his breadstick.

"Wipe your mouth." I hand him a napkin and smile. My phone vibrates, and I pick it up to see my landlord, Mr. Garcia, calling. "It's my landlord," I tell Graham. I place the phone to my ear. "Hi, Mr. Garcia."

"Hello, Addyson. I just wanted to let you know that your apartment is ready, and you are all set to move in."

"Really?" I ask, my voice cracking. I'm excited to go home but worried about Noah and me. What does this mean for our relationship with Graham? I know he asked us to stay, but I need to go home. I need to see how this plays out with us not living with him. I need to make sure this relationship isn't just due to convenience of our circumstances. I've been duped before, and I refuse to repeat that same mistake, even if it did give me Noah.

"I know it's been a long road. There were issues with insurance and contractors."

"When? When can we come back?" I ask, my eyes finding Graham's across the table. He sets his jaw, and I have to look away.

"Whenever. Tonight, if you want. You're working with your renter's insurance for items lost, correct?" he asks.

"Yes, we've actually settled. So, I'll have to replace a few things. Thank you for calling, Mr. Garcia." I end the call, placing my phone back on the table.

"Your apartment is ready?"

"It is." I nod and turn to look at Noah. "Hey, buddy. Guess what? We get to move back home."

"No!" Noah shouts, dropping his half-eaten breadstick to his plate, and crossing his arms over his chest. "I don't want to move."

"Noah, Graham was nice enough to let us into his home while ours was being repaired. Our place is fixed from the water."

"I don't want to go," he says, tears welling in his eyes.

"Noah, sweetie, we have to move home."

"No. We're a family. We live with Graham." Noah looks at Graham. "Right? We're family. You, me, and mommy. We live with you." There is desperation and so much heartbreak in Noah's tone of voice.

"No." Graham's voice cracks.

"Tell her," Noah demands. "We live with you. We're a family like my picture."

The waitress stops and drops off our check. "Would you like a box or refills to go?" she asks.

"We're good, thanks," I tell her. The last thing I'm worried about is a few extra slices of pepperoni and cheese.

"I'm going to pay this." Graham slips out of his side of the booth.

"Let me—" I start, and he pins me with a look that has me closing my mouth. "We're going to head out to the car."

"I'll be right there," Graham replies, and stalks toward the register to pay.

"Come on, Noah." I slide out of the booth, and with his hand in mine, I lead him outside. He gets into his booster seat without complaint, but he's mad. He's hurt and angry, and I know he doesn't understand, and that's on me. I didn't think this through.

I roll down my window when Graham steps up next to my car. "I'll see you two at ho—my place," he quickly corrects himself, his eyes flashing to Noah.

"We'll see you there," I promise.

The drive to his place is short and quiet. Noah stares out the window, ignoring me. I miss his constant chatter, and I hate that he's hurting, and it's all because of me.

"Time for a bath," I tell Noah once we are in the house.

"No. I don't want to take a bath."

"Noah." Graham's voice is firm yet kind. "Listen to your mom. It's time for a bath."

"Will you read me a story?" Noah asks him.

"Always, No. Go with your mom. I'll be in to read to you."

"Noah, go grab some jammies. I'll be right there," I tell him. He doesn't respond, but he does turn on his heel and move slowly down the hall.

"Addy?" Graham rasps.

"He'll be okay," I assure him. It's something I keep telling myself over and over since last night.

"I want you here. Both of you," he says.

"Can we talk about this later?" I ask him.

"Sure." He pulls me into his arms and hugs me close. "I'll be in to read to him."

"You don't have to," I start, but he stops me.

"I want to, Addy. What's it going to take for you to understand that? It's not a hardship to read Noah a bedtime story. In fact, it's a privilege, one that I don't take lightly."

"Graham." My voice cracks.

I feel his lips press to the top of my head. "Go take care of our boy. I'll be right there." He releases me, and a shuddering breath leaves my lungs. My legs tremble as I walk away from him. Why does life have to be so hard? I thought Noah's dad turning his back on us was the hardest thing I'd ever have to go through. I was wrong. Watching my son's heart break is so much worse. Knowing that I'm the root cause of that slices me to my core.

"Ready?" I ask Noah, plastering a smile on my face.

He doesn't reply, but he does begin to strip out of his clothes while I get his water ready. I nod, letting him know it's ready to get in. "I'm sorry, Noah. I know you like living here, but this isn't our home. Don't you want to go back to your old room and your toys?" I ask him.

"I have toys and a room here."

"Buddy, we were only staying here until our apartment was ready to move back to."

"But you're the mom. You can let us stay, right? Moms get to choose, so you should choose this house."

"It's not that easy, Noah."

He ignores me for the rest of his bath. All through me washing his hair, draining the water, drying off, and getting dressed. He doesn't say a word. What kind of mother does that make me that my five-year-old is giving me the silent treatment because I broke his heart? I only hope that the adjustment period will be fast and my smiling happy little boy will return to me quickly.

"You ready for your story?" Graham asks from the doorway of the bathroom.

Noah nods and walks across the hall to his room. "Let me talk to him," Graham says.

"I'll try anything," I tell him.

He leans in and kisses the corner of my mouth. "I'll get him to sleep, and then we can talk."

I nod and go back to cleaning up the bathroom. When I'm done, I stand in the hallway listening to Graham's deep voice as he reads Noah's favorite dinosaur book.

"The end," Graham says softly.

"G?"

"Yeah?"

"Can I ask you something?"

"You can ask me anything."

"Well, I was wondering?" Noah starts and stalls.

"No, you can ask me anything, buddy. Even when you and your mom move home, you can call me anytime. Just because you're not living here doesn't mean we're still not best buds."

My heart swells for this man. I know he wants us to stay here. He's told me so, but he's supporting my choices with Noah. I know he's going to challenge me later. He thinks he wants us to stay. But us leaving is what we need to do. I just need... reassurance that he really wants us, not just because we are convenient. I know he's never done or said anything to make me believe we were a convenience to him, but my past with Noah's dad has me being guarded. I just need a little time.

"I was wondering," Noah's soft voice brings me back to the present.

"What were you wondering?" Graham asks him.

"Well, I thought maybe that if you said yes, we could stay."

"What am I saying yes to, No?" Graham chuckles.

The room is silent for several heartbeats. "G, will you be my daddy?"

"Noah." Graham's voice is choked.

I have to cover my mouth to keep my sobs from breaking free. My heart is cracked wide open, laying here bleeding on the hallway carpet. My sweet, sweet boy.

What have I done?

Nineteen

Graham

How I keep it together is beyond me.

I remember crying a total of three times in my life. When I broke my arm on the playground in fourth grade, even though I kept those tears at bay until my mom picked me up from school. Then, when my mom's dad passed away. I was thirteen, and while I wasn't as close to him as I am my dad's dad, I felt a pain so deep, it consumed me. The third time? When I got my letter stating I passed my North American Pharmacist Licensure Examination, the final step I took to become a third-generation pharmacist. It was a mixture of relief and pride after eight long years of schooling.

And now?

The tears threaten to fall, but I somehow blink them back.

Noah looks up at me with so much hope and fear, I want to wrap my arms around him and declare yes. Yes! I will be your dad. It would be the greatest honor of my life, but I have to think about Addy. She's doing everything she can to protect her son, and I do know that includes protecting him from me. Even though I'm the last person on this earth who'd ever hurt or disappoint him, I do understand why she's keeping me at arm's length where he's concerned.

"Listen, No," I start, moving him so he's sitting on my lap instead of beside me. "This is a hard conversation to have with you, because you're still little."

"But I'm trying to be a man."

I instantly smile. "You are, and you're doing a great job. So let's have this conversation man-to-man. While I understand your request, I'm sorry to say, it's not that simple, but do you know what *is* simple? Me being your friend. I will always be available to you, whether you live at the apartment or across town or in Timbuktu."

Noah wrinkles his little nose. "Where's Tim-buck-too?"

"Far, far away. My point is, I will always be in your corner, Noah. You and your mom. If you need me, you call."

"Really?"

"Of course," I insist, holding him a little closer than before. Just the thought of him going back home makes it hard to breathe. No, not his home. His home is here.

With me.

But I don't say that. I don't want to make this separation harder on either one of us.

"G?"

"Yeah, buddy?"

"I don't have a phone."

I can't help but chuckle as I draw him close and hug him to my chest. "That's okay. You can use your mom's."

Noah sighs. "I guess that's all right. She lets me call Uncle Adam."

"Well, as long as your mom gives you permission, you can call me anytime you want."

He snuggles against my chest, and I can't help but wonder if he can hear my heart pounding in his ear. I feel like it's trying to drum out of my chest with nervousness and anxiety. About the conversation I know is coming with Addy. About them returning to their own place. About being left alone when all I want is to be surrounded by the two people who have come to mean more to me than I ever thought could.

We sit together in silence, Noah cuddled against my chest. After several minutes, his body becomes heavy, his arms falling as his breath evens out in sleep. Still, I don't move. Not yet. If this is the last night I get to have this, I want to hold on as long as possible.

Just when my arm starts to go numb from his weight, movement catches my attention in the doorway. I glance up and find Addy standing there, and even though there's a soft smile on her full lips, I can see the weight of the world swirling within those brown eyes.

"He's asleep," I state lamely.

She nods, her arms crossing over her chest as she leans against the doorjamb. "You're amazing with him, Graham," she whispers, her eyes bright with unshed tears.

I glance down, taking in his sleeping form. "He's easy to love."

Gingerly, I roll Noah to the side and onto the bed. He instantly snuggles the pillow and curls up with the blanket, sighing as he drifts back off to sleep. When he's settled, I climb off the bed and make my way to where Addy stands. I step in behind her, pulling her back to my front and hold her tight. Together, we stand here and watch her son sleep.

Finally, I say, "Come on, Addy. Let's talk." I flip off the overhead lights and pull the door closed, leaving it cracked open a few inches in case he needs us. Then I take her hand and slowly lead her to my bedroom. Not hers, mine. I need her in my bed tonight.

Once we're inside, I close and lock the door before turning my attention on her. She's still wearing what I'd consider her teacher clothes, so without a word, I carefully strip them from her body. When she's down to just a pair of blue cotton panties, I go to my dresser and pull a well-worn T-shirt out of the drawer. Neither of us say a word as I slip the shirt over her head and hold it out while she slides her arms in the holes.

Stepping back, I take in the absolute beauty before me, standing in the middle of my bedroom, wearing my shirt.

Just as it should be.

With our eyes locked, I quickly remove my tie, button-down, and trousers, until I'm left in nothing but boxers. Even though I'd much rather climb into bed commando, I know our conversation requires pants, so I grab a pair of athletic shorts and slip those on. Finally, I take her hand and guide her to my bed.

I climb on first, sitting with my back against the headboard, and help maneuver her between my legs. My arms wrap around her waist and just hold her close, breathing in the familiar scent of her clean shampoo.

"You have to go, Addy. I know. I want you here, both of you, but I do understand. You have to go," I repeat, as if trying to convince myself.

She sighs, covering my arms with hers, as if holding onto me while I hold her. "I do."

"When?" My voice is surprisingly strong as I ask this question, despite the fact my heart is on the verge of breaking in half.

"Saturday."

My throat is dry, my tongue heavy as she confirms what I've suspected. They're moving in just two short days.

"I texted my boss earlier and am taking tomorrow off. I need to finalize the delivery of the furniture we had to replace, and I'll have to go to the store. Joy is going to help me go through the rest of the boxes of stuff they took from our apartment. All of the kitchen stuff is fine but needs washing."

"I can take tomorrow off," I offer, hoping my dad is available.

She's already shaking her head in disagreement. "I can't ask you to do that. You already had your dad cover for you tonight."

I sigh, knowing she's right. Yes, I know my dad would gladly work for me if I told him why, but I also know Addyson, maybe even better than I know myself anymore. She needs to do this for herself, and most likely, by herself. Having Joy help is one thing. She's a girlfriend, as well as her sister-in-law, and I think right now, she needs that alone time with her. I get it. I don't like it, but I do understand. "How about I bring dinner? It's my weekend off, so I'll help Saturday." The thought of helping her move her belongings out of my house is enough to make me die a little inside.

"Okay. Adam is lined up too."

I nod, even though she can't see it. "I'm not going to ask you to stay,

Addy. I want to, with everything inside of me, I want to beg you just to stay. This is where you belong. You and Noah. This is where I want you to be. I also know it's fast and that scares you. But do you know what? It doesn't scare me. Not the way I expected it to. I'm not afraid of a relationship with you. I'm not afraid of dating and living together and raising Noah by your side. I've already told you spending time with him is an honor. But I *am* terrified of this ending, because I know in my heart you're my future. I see it so vividly.

"So if you need to move back home until you're ready to be on the same page, if we need to keep our romantic relationship away from Noah for a little while longer, that's okay. We can date. No, we *will* date, and I don't mean to sound like a bossy asshole, but I'm not ready to let this end, because I know when you're finally ready to be on the same page as me, that's it. *You're* it, Addy."

I hear her sniffle, her fingers gripping my arms as she holds on a little tighter. "Thank you."

Kissing the top of her head, I whisper, "I will never rush or push you, babe. Never. We can take this at your pace. I'll follow your lead."

I'm on the verge of telling her everything else in my heart, but I know it's not the right time. She needs to think, and the last thing I want is her to feel like I'm telling her I love her just to get her to stay.

The next thing I know, she's moving, spinning around, and straddling my lap. Her mouth is on mine with the same urgency I feel running through my veins. As if this may be the last time we're here together, even though in my heart, I know it won't be. That doesn't stop the fear, the anguish from grabbing hold and squeezing.

I turn us both, laying her down on my bed. My hands frame her face as I lower my body to hers, pressing her into the mattress. I memorize every piece of the way she looks right now in this moment, because I know I'll need those recollections to keep me company at night.

I brush my lips over hers, trailing them across her cheek, noticing they meet wetness spilling from her eyes. I kiss away her sadness before sliding my lips down the slender column of her neck. My tongue dances across her flesh, savoring the taste of my Addy.

I'll never get enough of her.

Ever.

My hands slide beneath the shirt covering her body, reveling in the softness of her skin. I want to explore every inch of her with my mouth, but the urgency to be inside her is too great. When I claim her with a kiss once more, she shifts beneath me as I slide her panties down her legs, followed quickly by my own shorts and boxers. We barely break the connection of our lips, as if it's what keeps us tethered together.

Reaching blindly for my nightstand drawer, she grabs my face with her hands and meets my gaze. "No. I want to feel you. All of you."

My heart hammers with the force of a thousand drums as I try to swallow over the lump in my throat. "You sure?"

She nods, hitching both ankles over my ass and drawing my body down to hers. "Very sure."

My cock meets wetness, and a tsunami of emotion swells in my chest. I want to move fast, yet slow down as to draw out this moment. One I'll remember for the rest of my life. "I'm not going to fuck you, Addy. I'm going to make love to you," I whisper hoarsely, sliding my lips over hers.

She sighs contently, her warm breath fanning across my face as I gently push forward, filling her completely. This. This right here. This moment. I've been moving through life, refusing to let anyone get close enough to care about, keeping those who try at arm's length. Why? Because without even knowing, my heart already belonged to this woman.

The woman I love.

The one who will always own my heart.

I know I'll never be the same.

I'm in a mood, and I know it. Anne is working the pharmacy counter with me and has been giving me a wide berth almost since she arrived. She may not know the reason why, but she senses my broodiness and has been keeping to herself for the better part of the day.

Why am I so sullen? Well, besides the obvious fact Addy is at her apartment right now getting it ready to move back into tomorrow? I woke alone.

Alone fucking sucks.

But I guess I better get used to it, right? Tonight's my last evening with them in my house, and the thought of her not being there, falling asleep in my arms or waking to her smiling face, is definitely weighing heavily on my mind.

And my heart.

"I'm going to take my break," Anne announces, a look of uncertainty on her face, which makes me feel guilty. It's not her fault I'm a grump.

"Absolutely," I reply, and as she turns to head toward the break room, I add, "Sorry about my attitude today, Anne. I've been a little off, but I'll do better."

She gives me a small smile. "That's okay. We all have those days, but I think you have them less than everyone else. That's why it throws us off when they happen."

I nod, appreciating her quick forgiveness and vowing to make sure I'm in better spirits for the remainder of the day, even if only through appearances.

The bell on the counter sounds, so I turn to help the waiting customer. As soon as I round the divider wall, my feet practically stumble when I see who's there. Brianne. Guilt hits me hard in the chest as I look at the woman I once dated.

"Hey," I say, stepping up to the counter.

Her eyes hold a hesitancy, as if she's quickly putting her guard up. "Hi."

"One, right?" I ask, referring to the prescription I know she's here to pick up, considering I filled it just an hour ago.

"Yes, please."

I type on the computer, bringing up her name and insurance information. "Listen, Brianne, I wanted to apologize."

Clearly, that catches her off guard, and she looks up with startled eyes. "What?"

I take a deep breath and give her my full attention. "Thursday night, at the art fair. You didn't deserve my curtness, and I apologize. I just..." I stop and sigh. "I was with Noah and Addy, and didn't want to divert my attention from them. I realize now I was short and rude to you, and I apologize."

Brianne stares back at me, as if struggling to believe what she's hearing. She subtly shakes her head. "Actually, that's why I was trying to have a word with you. I wanted to apologize."

Now it's my turn to be a little surprised. "You? Why?"

She exhales loudly and leans her hip against the counter. "Graham, you were very clear in your stance on relationships when we first started seeing each other. I knew you wanted casual, and I'm the one who wanted to change it. Even though I was upset you didn't want to take our relationship further, I get it. It isn't your thing, or at least I *thought* it wasn't your thing, but now I'm not so sure," she quips, her lips forming a sly smile. "I admit I was shocked to see you with Addyson, but I get it. My nephew loved her as his teacher last year."

My heart skips a beat at the mention of Addy. "She's great." I feel a slight blush creep up my neck. "I wasn't... uh, I wasn't expecting her."

Or the feelings she drummed up.

Brianne smiles widely now. "I bet you weren't. I'm sure it was amazing to watch the mighty Graham Morgan fall."

I snort a laugh, turning and grabbing her prescription from the bin. "I don't know about mighty, but it was a fast, hard fall."

"Good," she replies, drawing my eyes back up to hers. "I'm glad you're giving love a chance, Graham. You are a good guy, despite closing yourself off to those around you."

My chest feels lighter after having this conversation. "Thanks," I state with a small smile. I ring up her prescription and tap on the screen. "Ten dollars."

Brianne swipes her card, and I can't help but watch her with new eyes. She's always been a gorgeous woman, with dirty-blonde hair and striking hazel eyes, and even though she wasn't right for me, I know she'll make a great wife and mom someday.

Just as she's slipping her debit card back into her purse, someone behind her says, "Hey, everything good?"

Brianne immediately smiles. "Yes, sorry. I got to talking to a friend," she tells the newcomer, offering him a grin. Quickly, she turns back to me and says, "Graham Morgan, I'm sure you know Jared Johnston."

"Yes, of course. How are you?" I ask, extending my hand for him to shake.

"Well, thanks," he confirms, offering me a firm handshake. "You?"

"Good."

When Jared places his hand on Brianne's lower back, realization sets in. Jared was a year older than me in school, but I always liked him. Apparently, I'm not the only one. By the excited glimmer in Brianne's eyes, I think she's a little smitten with the local farmer. His family owns a large cattle farm outside town, and I heard he's recently making the transition to take it over.

"Well, we better get going. We're going to have a late lunch at the café before he has to get back out to the farm. It was good seeing you, Graham," she says, slipping her purse over her shoulder and grabbing the prescription bag.

"It was good seeing you too," I repeat, realizing I mean it. "Enjoy your lunch."

I watch as they walk off, Jared's hand never wavering from her lower back, and I'm happy for them. They're as night and day different with her designer clothes and his cow-shit covered boots, but maybe that's just what they both need.

With a smile on my face, I glance at the clock, knowing I have just a few more hours before I get to see Addy and Noah. While I head back to start the next prescription, I make a mental note to call the Italian restaurant for some to-go dinners. Then, I'll get to see my girl and her son—my boy—even if it's for the last time at my house.

This may not be my ideal situation, but I'll make the best of it.

I have to.

It'd be a crying shame if I didn't fight to hang on to what I want.

And I want them.

Twenty

ddyson

"Thank you for your help. I couldn't have gotten this far without you," I tell Joy. She was waiting for me outside my apartment when I got here this morning. I put Noah on the bus and drove straight here.

"The place looks great. You can't even tell there was damage."

"Oh, you know, except for the fact that I'm missing some furniture." I laugh, because what else can I do? At least the insurance paid for everything, and I'm not scrambling to replace what we lost out of pocket.

"This is true. What's next?" she asks.

"We're done in here," I tell her as I survey the kitchen. We took everything out of the cabinets and washed them. My landlord had a cleaning company come in and clean, so the place was already spotless. No signs of construction or pieces of the ceiling from the neighbors on top of us in sight.

"Other than washing the clothes that have been packed away, all that's left is picking out new furniture. I'm just relieved that most of Noah's room was okay. His bed is good. I need a bed, and we need a couch, and the tablecloth protected the wood of this old thing," I say, rapping my knuckles against the small kitchen table.

"How about we grab some lunch and head to the furniture store?"

"Yes. I also need to stop and get groceries."

"Are you staying here tonight?" she asks.

My heart sinks when I think about sleeping in a house that Graham isn't in. "No. We'll stay one more night with Graham."

"What if you don't have a bed by then?" she asks.

I shrug. "I'll bunk with Noah."

"What are you not telling me?" she asks.

"Nothing." I give her what I hope is an easy smile.

"Come on, Addyson. What's going on?"

"Noah asked him to be his daddy last night. Graham. He asked Graham to be his daddy."

Her mouth falls open. "How did he handle it?"

"Perfectly. He's so good with him, Joy. Then he held me and told me that he didn't want us to leave. That our place was with him. He then told me he knew why I needed to go but that we weren't over."

"Why are you moving out?"

"Because," I groan. "He's Graham, and I've crushed on him for years and this thing between us... It was fast and electric, and how do I know it was real? How do I know that he's not just feeling these things because he's been forced to live with us for the last couple of months?"

"First of all, he wasn't forced into anything. The way I heard it, Graham practically insisted that you and Noah stay with him."

"He did. But he's a nice guy. A good guy, and he's been in my life since I was a kid. It was the right thing to do, and Graham is that type of person. He does the right thing."

"Let's dissect that, shall we? First, he is one of the good ones, but he's also a grown man, and he has never been someone to do what he doesn't want to do. Look at everyone before you. He's never made a commitment to any of them. He's never asked them to stay."

"I'm a mom. He's only been with us in his home for a short time.

It's a lot of work and responsibility to raise a child, and Noah, he's not his, and I would never forgive myself if he changed how he treated him."

"Stop. Just stop. You're making excuses now. You and I both know that he would never. Graham is not that guy, and you're being unfair. Sure, Noah might not have his blood running through his veins, but we can all see how he is with him. The night of his birthday party, he didn't seem to care that Noah wasn't his son. He damn sure acted like he was. He was firm with him, yet kind, and speaking of his party, if he wasn't watching you, he was watching Noah. Take it from someone who is on the outside looking in. Graham loves you, Addyson. Both of you."

"He likes us."

"He might not have said the words, but he can't hide how he feels, and neither can you. If you're worried about the time frame, don't. It's not like you just met the guy, and you're moving in with him. You said it yourself. You've known him almost your entire life."

"I have Noah to think about."

Joy shakes her head. "If you for one second think that Graham doesn't know that—that he doesn't respect the fact you are a mother and Noah needs to come first—then you're living in an alternate universe."

I know she's right. I hate that she is, but I know she is. I've been dreading leaving since the day we moved in. Being with Graham, in his house, well, it felt like home. We felt like a family. "I'm scared," I confess. "I love him." My confession is whispered, but my sister-in-law hears me as if I shouted it.

"I wasn't around when you got pregnant. However, Adam has told me on several occasions that Noah's dad leaving turned you into a different person. You keep yourself guarded, and on the one hand, I understand. You don't want Noah to get hurt, but on the other hand, Addyson, you have to take a chance. You have to put your heart out there and trust he handles it with care. Does he make you happy?"

"Yes."

"Does he make Noah happy?"

I smile when I think about the two of them. "Yes. They're thick as thieves."

"You have your answer, Addyson. You just need to be brave enough to accept it."

"Ugh," I groan. "Why does this have to be so hard?"

"I'm pretty sure you're making it harder than it needs to be." She chuckles.

"You can't tell me you and Adam didn't have any hiccups."

"No, we did, which is why I can tell you you're letting your fear overrule your heart. I was cautious too, and it was my mom who helped me see the light. She was always your brother's biggest cheerleader. She still is." Joy playfully rolls her eyes, but the smile on her face tells me she's not the least bit bothered that my brother and her mom are so close.

"I thought you were hungry?" I say, sticking my tongue out at her.

"Fine. Deflect." She steps in close and hugs me. "I'm here if and when you need to talk, but really, Addyson, think about what I said. I've been there, and if I let my fear control me, I wouldn't be happily married and trying to start a family."

"No! You're trying? I'm so happy for you. I knew that you were talking about it. I can't wait to be an aunt."

"We're trying." She nods. "Now feed me, woman. I need my energy."

"Ew, that's my brother."

Her laughter leads us out of my apartment.

"Thanks for lunch," I tell Joy as I push open the door to the small café here in town. I'm looking over my shoulder at her, which is why I don't notice the man entering until I bump right into him. His hands land on my hips to steady me.

"I'm so sorry." I look up and freeze.

"Hello, Addyson." The man who I never wanted to lay eyes on again greets me.

"Addyson?" Joy asks.

She places her hand on my shoulder, and that spurs me into action. I shake out of his hold and step out onto the sidewalk. I don't need a café full of busybodies to hear this conversation.

"What are you doing here, Tommy?"

He places his hand over his chest as if I've wounded him. "Not happy to see me?" he asks, letting his eyes rake over my body.

"Not even a little bit."

"You look good, Addyson." He nods, running his tongue over his bottom lip.

"Hi, I'm Joy. I don't think we've met."

"Damn, where have you been hiding?"

Joy looks at me, and I roll my eyes. "She's married, asswipe."

"I won't tell if you won't." He winks at Joy, and I cringe.

"Where is your wife?"

His eyes darken. "She's not here."

"Well, as fun as this has been, we have to go."

"We should meet up later. Have a drink for old times' sake," he suggests.

Bile rises in my throat. "Not a chance in hell."

"Aw, come on, doll, are you still mad at me? That was years ago." He waves his hand in the air. "Water under the bridge."

Something inside me snaps. I'm not that same person I was the last time I saw Tommy, and he's about to witness that. "Water under the bridge?" I seethe. "Is that what we're calling it these days? You knock me up and tell me after the fact you're married and to get rid of it." Joy gasps from her spot beside me, but I keep going. "You call that water under the bridge? How about asking about your child? No, you know what, scratch that. He's not yours. He's mine. You might have donated sperm, but there is nothing about him that is you." I spit the words. My hands are shaking, my heart hammering in my chest, and I feel light-headed. He moved away, and I had hoped to never see him again.

"I think you should go," Joy tells him.

"Whatever. You were supposed to get rid of it." He shoulders past me and into the café.

"Get me out of here," I tell Joy. My voice cracks, and even I can hear the desperation with my own ears.

Joy leads me to her car and opens the door for me. She waits for me to slip inside before closing it behind me and rushing to the driver's side. As soon as her door is shut, she starts the car and pulls away. She drives and doesn't say a word, and I'm grateful. I just need a minute to process this. To process the fact that he's back. I truly thought he was gone for good. He's never been close to his parents, but that could be another lie he told me.

It's not until Joy reaches over and places her hands on mine, which are fisted tightly in my lap, that I realize that the car has stopped moving. Lifting my head, I blink a few times to bat away the tears and see that we're sitting in the parking lot of the furniture store.

"Talk to me."

"That was Noah's dad."

"I gathered that."

She doesn't ask for details, but I want to give them to her anyway. I've kept them to myself all these years. The only person who knows the truth is Tosha, my best friend.

"Tosha and I went out one night. I'd been at my parents' for a barbeque, and she came with me. We decided to hit a local bar before going home. That's where I met Tommy. Well, I knew him. He was older than me in school, the same age as Adam and Graham. Anyway, I didn't know anything about him. Just that he grew up in Oak Valley like we did." I pause. "We hit it off that night. He asked for my number, and over the next couple of weeks, we kept in touch. He was sweet with his words, and when he asked me on a date, I said yes. One date led to two, and before I knew it, we'd been dating for a month."

I inhale a deep breath and keep going. "He invited me to his place, which was an apartment over his parents' garage. He said that he was saving for his dream home for when he found the right woman, and I fell for his lies hook, line, and sinker. We hooked up that night, and things started to change. He didn't call as much, and our dates were less frequent."

I close my eyes and think back to the day that I took the pregnancy test. Tosha was sitting on my bed, and on the other side of the bathroom door, I watched as two pink lines appeared, changing my life forever. "Not once..." I start and clear my throat. "Not once did I ever think of terminating my pregnancy. I was scared, nervous, and worried about what Tommy would say, but never did I ever consider the fact that I wasn't going to be a mom. The moment I saw those two pink lines, I loved him."

"Of course you did. He was a part of you."

I nod. "I called Tommy and asked him to come over. I was shocked when he said he would without the usual drama of logistics that he usually gave me. Looking back, that should have been my first clue. Anyway, he arrived and started kissing me and tearing off his clothes. I pushed him back and told him to sit, that we had to talk. I just let the words spill out of me, and the first thing he said was... are you ready for this?" I look up at Joy. "He said 'I'm married.'"

"What a piece of shit."

"I'll spare you the details of the conversation, but the CliffsNotes is that he told me that I was just something fun, but he loved his wife and that I needed to handle the situation. He then stood from my couch and walked out the door. I haven't seen or heard from him again until today."

"Wow," she breathes. "I'm not sure I know what to say."

"I hate him. He used me."

"Why have you protected him all this time? Adam said you wouldn't tell anyone who the father is. He said the only information you would give was that it was a temporary relationship and that the father was no longer in your life, and you were doing this all on your own. And you've done a spectacular job, by the way. Noah is a great kid."

My heart warms. "Thank you. He really is."

"So, why protect him? His wife should know."

"She knows."

"What?" Joy raises her brows, confused.

"Two weeks later, I talked myself into coming clean with my brother. I wanted him to be there with me when I told our parents. I drove to his place, and Graham was there. They invited me in just like any other normal Saturday afternoon. I was working up the nerve to tell them my news when Adam told Graham that Tommy's parents found out he was using their house as a fuck pad, Adam's words, and that his wife found out."

"Like I said, piece of shit. That still doesn't explain why you protected him."

"I wasn't protecting him. I was protecting myself. I was protecting Noah. I heard the way they were talking about him. They hated him. Said he used women, and here I was sitting there, and I was one of them. Tommy had told me he and Adam were acquaintances, and that's why I hid that we were even dating. He's always been a little protective, and I didn't want him to interfere."

"Damn."

"Yeah. So I changed course in my mind. I didn't tell my family that day. I waited two more weeks before I confessed that I was pregnant and that the father was no longer in town or in my life. It wasn't a lie. The only lie I told was when I told them all that they didn't know him. I was so ashamed that I fell for his tricks and got pregnant. What's worse? I was on the pill, and we used protection. We doubled up, and I still got pregnant."

"Noah was always meant to be." She smiles softly.

"He was."

"Something you said stands out."

"What's that?" I ask, wiping the tears from my cheeks.

"You said that Adam has always been protective."

"He has."

"He seemed fine when he found out about you and Graham."

"Yeah, I was just as surprised as you are, actually."

"That's because Adam knows his best friend. He knows he's a good guy, and he knows that Graham is serious about you. He wouldn't risk a life-long friendship otherwise."

"You're right," I confess. "I know all of that, and you're right; I've been letting my fear hold me back. I've already made a huge deal about moving back to my place, and I think that I need to follow that through. I need to give us some time apart and then go from there."

"Be open to the idea, Addyson. Don't let the wrongdoings of one man keep you from giving yourself completely to another."

"That's just it. I've already done that. Graham owns me, Joy. I love him with all that I am."

"Then maybe you should tell him that."

I nod. "You're right. I will. I just need to be settled back into my place and see how it goes. I do think it's important for us to see what life is like dating without living together. We went about things backward, and it's important to make sure."

"I understand. Just keep your mind and your heart open. Now, are we ready to put the past behind us and buy you some new furniture?"

"Yes. Let's do it."

Doing just as she says, I push Tommy out of my mind and spend the next couple of hours picking new furniture. However, now that he's back, I know I need to be honest. I need to tell my parents, my brother, and most of all, I need to tell Graham. He needs to know all my truths before he decides that Noah and I are his future.

Once we get settled in our new place, I'll have my parents or Tosha watch Noah for a night and invite him over. I'll tell him everything and let the cards fall where they may.

Twenty-One

Graham

The moment I pull into my driveway, I want to leave. I want to go back to her apartment—no, I *need* to go back—but I won't. This step is important to her, to us.

I sit in my truck and replay the look on Noah's face when I told him I was leaving. He convinced me, which really took no convincing at all, to read him an early bedtime story before I left. I helped him set up his room, and while I could see he was happy to rediscover some of his forgotten toys, there was a heaviness and sadness about him.

Same as me.

When it was time for me to walk out the door, I gave my little man a big hug, promising I'd see him soon before sending him to his bedroom to get ready for his bath. Then, I took his mother in my arms and kissed her with every ounce of passion I possessed. I needed her to know, to feel, that we aren't over. Just because she's back in her apartment doesn't mean anything. If anything, it deepened my desire for her.

Now, I've been sitting in my truck and wishing I didn't have to go into my cold, empty house. I know that's how it's going to feel. No running feet on the hardwood. No scent of vanilla lotion clinging to my sheets and the air. No laughter. No life at all, because my life has moved back to her place without me.

"Jesus, get it together," I mutter, practically ripping my keys from the ignition and jumping from the cab. "Quit being a pussy."

But the moment I step inside the mudroom, the sullen mood I felt weighing down on me in the truck only grows heavier, until I swear I'm going to suffocate from the pressure.

"You can do this. Just like before Addy and Noah lived here. You preferred your own space. You preferred the quiet."

These are just a few of the lies I tell myself to keep from jumping back in my truck and going back over there.

I don't need them here.

This will be fine.

With leaden feet, I move to my bedroom, instantly assaulted by all things Addy. I can still see the indention from her head on the pillow she slept on last night. I can feel the way her naked body molded to mine, as if she were made perfectly for me. I can hear her whimpers and the noises she made as I filled her, slowly making love to her until we were both sated. Then I did it all over again, fearful it would be for the last time.

"Jesus, man. You're still dating her. She's just not living here anymore."

Which is fucking stupid.

Needing out of the room, I head to my closet and throw my clothes into the hamper before slipping on a sleeveless tee and a pair of athletic shorts. I throw on the first pair of socks I dig from my dresser, not even caring they're black trouser socks, and grab my running shoes. Ignoring all signs of Addy, I leave my room and head straight for the basement steps.

I crank up the music, not needing to worry about waking up anyone in the house anymore. Metallica pumps through the speakers, vibrating off the soundproof walls like a sledgehammer. I do a few stretches, but not as many as I'd usually do. Instead, I jump on the treadmill and start pounding out the miles. Two turns to four, which turns into five and six. I've never been a distance runner, but tonight, no matter how far I go, I can't outrun my thoughts.

She's with me still, despite trying to push her from my mind.

Something tells me, she'll always be there, burrowed in so deep, she's just a part of who I am. And even though I never wanted this to happen, never pictured myself falling in love, especially with my best friend's sister, I wouldn't change one second.

No, I'd rather spend the rest of my life loving her than a single moment not.

This is my new reality, and I accept it.

I just have to take my time and convince Addy I'm worth the risk.

Tuesday night.

How I've made it three nights without them is beyond me. Actually, I know exactly how. Brutal workouts until I'm so fucking tired I can't even stand to shower, followed by dreams filled with both Addy and Noah.

I have yet to physically see them, even though I've talked to them through text and video chat a few times. Sunday, I wanted nothing more than to take them to lunch or dinner, but she was busy finishing setting up the apartment, and then prepping for her workweek.

Monday, I sent her flowers, because that's what boyfriends do when they're thinking about the one they love. Well, at least I think that's what they do, considering I've never actually sent anyone flowers before, besides my mom on her birthday every year. But I remember Adam sending them to Joy often. I'd make fun of him, calling him pussy-whipped, but I get it now.

I understand.

Last night, she called to tell me thank you for the gorgeous wildflowers, and Noah insisted he get a few minutes of my time. A few minutes turned into twenty, complete with him sharing every detail of his bus ride from his new location, his day at school, and what his mom made him for dinner. It was the best, yet the hardest twenty minutes of my life, because he should have been here, telling me all about it in person.

I head over to the fridge, my eyes automatically going to the picture still carefully positioned in the middle of the space. It's one of the only things there, the art piece Noah made of his family. Of Addy, him, and me.

Together.

Running my hand over my face, I just stand here and stare at the crayon image. It's actually quite comical, considering Noah's body is nearly as big as Addy's, her nose is a bit reminiscent of a puppy's, and my feet look like something Bozo would have. But what the drawing represents means more to me than I ever expected some crayon scribbles to represent.

"Fuck," I growl, ripping open the door and grabbing a bottle of water. I quickly chug half the contents while pacing the kitchen floor. My fidgetiness has been almost unbearable since Saturday night. I can't seem to stop myself from moving, and everything I try to slow my brain is only temporary.

My phone chimes, and I've never been so grateful in my life.

Adam: What are ya doin?

Me: Not much. Going crazy here.

Adam: I figured. *insert smirk*

Me: Is there a reason you're bothering me?

Adam: Wanted to see if you wanted to grab a beer. Joy is working tonight.

. . .

I feel a deep sense of relief at the prospect of getting out of the house. I almost can't send my reply fast enough.

Me: Yep. Meet you there in twenty.

Adam: K.

I run to my room and strip out of my work clothes, throwing on a pair of dark gray shorts and a blue T-shirt. I don't even care they don't really match. I'm not going to impress anyone. A few minutes later, I have my keys and my wallet, and I'm heading to my truck for the short drive to Hank's.

I'm the first one there, so I grab a seat at the bar and order a beer. It only takes a few minutes for my friend to arrive, and I can't help but recall how similar this scenario was to the one that ultimately sent Addy and Noah to my house.

"Hey, man," Adam says, sliding onto the stool beside me and flagging down Hank.

When his beer is set in front of him, I finally reply, "How's married life?"

"Great." I can hear the happiness in that one simple word.

"And the baby part?" I ask between sips of beer.

He turns a wide grin my way. "Practicing every chance we get."

I hold up my bottle for him to tap, which he does. "I'm sure it'll happen soon."

He sighs. "I hope so, but Joy is trying to be realistic. She says it can take months before it happens, but I'm pretty confident in my swimmers."

I snort a laugh.

"So, how ya holding up?" he asks after a few moments of silence.

"Not well."

Adam turns in his seat and faces me. "Wanna know what I think?"

"Do I have a choice?" I quip.

"No," he replies with a hearty laugh. "You don't. You're my best friend, so you're gonna listen to what I have to say. My sister is one of the best women I know. She's strong and independent because she had no other choice but to be, but do you know what? When she's with you, she doesn't have to be Wonder Woman single mom anymore. Do you know why?"

I have my guesses, but since my throat is thick and it's hard to swallow, I just shake my head.

"Because of you. Because you're strong *with* her, not *for* her. You're not trying to take over or show her how much she needs a man in her life. Honestly, I can't believe I never saw it before she moved in with you, man. It's like... it's like you see Addy in the exact same light I see Joy. At your birthday party... Jesus, Graham. You had this look in your eyes every time you saw her. It was a mixture of happiness and pure shock, as if you couldn't believe she was with you. I know that feeling, because I still feel it. Every damn day. It probably never goes away, and that's okay. I don't ever want it to."

I think about his words and know he's right.

I want to walk beside her, holding her hand every step of the way. I want to help her raise her amazing son. "I just want to be a part of their life. She doesn't need me, Adam, but do you know what? I fucking need her."

He grins. "I know."

"Leaving them at the apartment Saturday killed me, and even though every instinct inside me said to stay, to fight, I knew I couldn't." I take a deep breath. "She doesn't quite trust me. Not with their hearts. She's been hurt, even if we don't know the circumstances of it. She's never talked about Noah's biological father, and I think the reason why is because he hurt her. Not just that he left town and didn't want anything to do with them. She's been hurt, and she's scared.

"I'm miserable at home. Hell, it doesn't feel like a home. Not without them. But I won't rush this. I won't risk hurting her by pushing when she's not ready to take this next step with me. We've already decided we're going to continue to date. She needs to see I'm in this without the proximity of convenience. I am, so if that's what it takes,

I'm all in. So if that means biding my time and being a complete miserable fuck, then that's what I'll do."

Adam leans forward and smiles, holding my gaze. "I never thought I'd see it. The mighty Graham Morgan has fallen." He lifts his beer in the air in salute. "This is a beautiful day."

A deep chuckle erupts from my gut, the ball of tension I seem to carry in my chest easing just a bit. "Actually, that's basically what Brianne said."

"Brianne?"

I tell him about running into her at the art fair last week, as well as at the pharmacy on Friday, and by the end of the story, I feel even lighter yet. Talking to my best friend, Addy's brother, and having him not only approve of our relationship, but give his blessing is a heady feeling. It makes all this heartache I feel in my chest worth it.

She's worth it.

Just as I'm about to pay my tab, my phone rings. Glancing down, I see her name and smile. "Hello?"

"Graham?"

"Noah? What's up, buddy?" I ask, leaning my elbow on the bar, my face turned toward Adam.

"G, can you read me a story?"

My heart aches in this moment and I have to close my eyes, fighting the onslaught of emotion bubbling to the surface. Instead of answering his question, I ask, "Where's your mom?"

"She's in the hallway with the man. She got mad he was here and told me to go get ready for bed, but I haven't had a bath yet. She always makes me take a bath before bed."

I chuckle, practically picturing the image he paints in my mind. "Is she still in the hallway?"

"Yep. I think she's mad too. She yelled at him."

I sit up straight, my eyes holding Adam's. "She did?"

"Yep, but I can't hear them now. Can you come read me a story, G? Mommy does it at bedtime, but she doesn't do it right." He complains, bringing yet another smile to my face.

"I don't know, Noah," I start, but he interrupts me.

"Please," he begs, drawing out the word for several seconds. "I've been super good. I ate my broccoli at dinner, even though broccoli smells like sweaty feet."

A bubble of laughter spills from my lips. I catch Adam's eye once more as I reply, "I guess I can stop by for *one* story."

"Yes!" Noah bellows into the phone. "But hurry because I don't like sitting in here by myself."

The hairs on the back of my neck stand up. "Mom's still out in the hall, huh?"

"I think so."

"Okay," I start, pulling money from my wallet, "I'm on my way, but promise me you'll stay in your room until I get there or until your mom comes back in, okay?"

"I'm going to find which book I want you to read. I brunged two new ones home from school."

"Tell you what, No. If you stay in your room until your mom or I tell you to come out, I'll read both of them."

"Deal!"

"All right, I'll be there in just a bit."

"Bye, G! Love you!"

I swear the entire bar can hear the pounding of my heart as I throw money on the bar and turn to Adam. "I gotta go."

"Everything okay?" he asks, a worried expression on his face.

"I think so. Someone stopped over and Addy's talking to him in the hallway. She made Noah go to his room until she was done, and that's when he called me. I'm going over there to make sure everything's okay, but also to read him a bedtime story."

Adam nods. "Call me if you need help. I don't know who could be over there."

"Me either, especially if she made Noah go to his room."

My friend smiles. "You're good for them, Graham. They're both lucky to have you."

"No, I'm lucky to have them," I counter.

With a serious gaze, he says, "Don't give up on her. You don't want to push her, but maybe she just needs to know you'll catch her when she falls."

I nod, practically running out the door to my truck.

It doesn't take me long to get over to where Addy's apartment is. When I climb from my truck cab, I don't notice anything amiss. Not that I'm expecting trouble, but I can't help but be a little worried about who dropped by and upset her. I take the steps two at a time to her floor, not bothering to wait on the elevator.

Just as I pull the stairwell door open, I stop and listen.

"You need to leave. Now. Don't come back," Addy says to whoever is at her door.

A decisive click echoes down the hall, followed by the sound of a lock engaging, letting me know she's probably back inside her apartment, leaving her visitor on the opposite side of the door.

That's when I make my move. I step through the entrance and turn the corner, almost stumbling when I see a familiar face starting to walk my way. "Tommy?"

Tommy Schroeder was a classmate of mine and Adam's, but I didn't care for him much. Fine. I fucking hated the guy. He was a cocky, arrogant jerk, who thought he was better than everyone else. He slept with girls just to add to his tally, including a girl I was seeing senior year. Hell, not even just the girl I was seeing, but Adam's girlfriend of three years too. It took everything I had not to beat the shit out of this guy in high school, and I can't help the same feelings resurfacing now.

"Graham Morgan, how are you?" he asks, coming to a stop in front of me.

"Not bad," I reply, shoving my hands in my pockets. "Whatcha doing here?" I ask casually.

"Stopped by to see an old friend. Addyson Sinclair and I have history," he informs me, waggling his eyebrows suggestively. Good thing I shoved my hands in my pockets, or my fist is liable to meet his smug face.

"Really?" I ask. "I wasn't aware you knew Adam's little sister."

"We had a thing a few years ago, and now that I'm back in town, she's trying to start things back up again." He flashes me a wide grin, and I swear, I feel my eye tick.

"Really? Because it sounded like she was telling you to get lost and never come back."

His casual, smug face sobers.

"I don't know why you're really here, but I have a piece of advice for you. Stay the fuck away from my family, Schroeder."

"*Your* family?" he asks, his voice raised.

"*My* family. Addy and Noah."

After a brief stare down, he laughs. "Oh, I see how it is. You take my place after I left, Graham? You like my sloppy seconds?"

My feet move before I can even register the insult. "Stay. The Fuck. Away. She doesn't need or want you. I heard it with my own two ears. Now is the time for you to catch up." We're practically toe to toe, but I don't care. I've got several inches on Tommy, not to mention a ton of muscle. If he decides to make a move, I'm ready.

He backs down, just like he used to in school. "Whatever, man. I just came by to tell her to stay away from me. I'm not interested in her anyway. You can have her. Her and the kid. I didn't want him then, and I don't want him now."

My entire body practically seizes from his statement. I'm so shocked, it's the only reason I don't throw my fist through his fucking face or stop him when he turns and jumps on the elevator. I'm so surprised by his words I don't even realize Addy's standing there, not until the silence in the hallway breaks through the war in my head.

I look at her stricken face. It's part anguish, part humiliation, and I hate what I see.

Tommy is Noah's dad.

How the hell did we not know that?

Twenty-Two

A sob breaks free from my chest as I close my eyes. I can't look at Graham. I'm humiliated by what he just witnessed, and my heart is cracking wide open that he had to find out about Tommy like this. I'd planned to tell him tonight. After running into Tommy last Friday, I knew it was time. I was going to call him once I got Noah in bed and explain my history and reveal the identity of Noah's father, but fate had other plans.

My hands are shaking, and there is a slight tremble in my knees. Falling back, I rest against the wall in the hallway. I didn't want him to find out this way. Why is Tommy back and barging into my life? He doesn't want Noah. He doesn't even want to meet him, not that I would let him anywhere near my son. Why did he have to come here?

Tears race down my cheeks as I wait for Graham to tell me he's done. I know how he and Adam feel about Tommy. He hates him, but whether I like it or not, he is Noah's sperm donor, and that will never change.

"Addy?" Graham's voice is thick with emotion. "Addyson," he tries again. This time his voice cracks.

I don't open my eyes. I can't. I can't bear the thought of seeing him look at me with disgust and disappointment. I just can't do it. I was wrecked when Tommy told me he wanted nothing to do with me and our baby. This feeling, the feeling of losing Graham, is a million times worse than that moment.

Graham Morgan is the love of my life, and my past is going to push him away. I should have been honest with him. I should have told him as soon as he became more than just my brother's best friend.

"Arms around my neck. Legs around my waist," he says, his voice gruff.

The next thing I know, his hands grip the back of my thighs, and he's lifting me. I do as he says and wrap my arms and legs around him, burying my face in his neck. My sobs become uncontrollable as he holds me tight against him.

"Addy, baby, did he hurt you?"

I shake my head, but I know Graham well enough to know he's going to need me to spell it out for him. "No. He didn't hurt me." His being here, that hurts me. Graham finding out about him the way that he did? That hurts me.

"Thank fuck," he whispers. His grip on the back of my thighs tightens. He doesn't say anything else. He holds me while I get my emotions under control.

"I'm sorry," I tell him.

"You have nothing to be sorry for. Where is Noah?"

"Inside. I told him to grab a book and get ready for bed."

"Mommy, are you coming?" Noah calls through the door.

"Just one second," I call back, trying to hide the tears from my voice.

"We're going to go in there, and we're going to read our boy a story, then you and I are going to talk."

"You're staying?" I ask. I can hear the pain and shock in my words.

"Nowhere else I'd rather be." He kisses me. It's brief as far as kisses go, but it is fierce all the same. He releases his hold on me and slowly allows me to plant my feet on the floor. He wipes at my cheeks with his thumbs before kissing my forehead. Sliding his hand into mine, he pushes open the door.

"Graham! You came!"

"Of course I did." Graham smiles down at Noah.

"Mommy, he did it. I called him, and he came." There's awe in my son's voice.

"What do you mean you called him?" I ask Noah, looking between the two of them.

"I wanted G to read me a story, so when you were yelling at the man in the hall, I called him. He said so, right, G? You said I can use Mommy's phone to call whenever I want."

"I did. I also said, with Mom's permission, but you're not in trouble for calling me," Graham is quick to assure him. I don't chime in and say that whether or not he's punished is ultimately my decision because it's in the moment I realize it's not just me. Graham is not only someone Noah looks up to, but he too is an authority figure, much like a father in Noah's life.

"Can we read a story now? Is the man gone?" he asks.

"The man is gone, and we can read you a story, but your mom and I need to talk to you about something first." Graham's eyes find mine, and he must see my panic. Surely, he's not going to tell Noah about his dad. Right? He wouldn't do that. "No, did you brush your teeth?" Graham asks him.

"Umm... be right back!" Noah shoots off down the hall and into the bathroom.

"Graham, you can't tell him. Please don't tell him about Tommy," I whisper his name.

Graham's eyes turn molten. "I'm not telling him about Tommy."

"Then what are you going to tell him? What do *we* have to talk to him about?" I emphasize the word we because he told Noah it was both of us.

"You heard what I told Tommy, right?" he asks.

I swallow hard and nod. "I heard."

"That's what we're going to tell him. That we're a family, and even though the two of you are living here, I still love you both with all that I am, and nothing is going to change that."

"What?" I whisper.

His eyes, which were just moments before full of anger, soften, and his lips tilt into a smile. "You heard me, Addy."

"Say it again."

His hands rest against my cheeks. "I'm in love with you. In love with Noah. The two of you are my family. It doesn't matter if you live here or with me. You both still own my heart."

"You love us?"

"Addy," he whispers as he leans in and kisses me. "You fucking own me. You and our boy."

Our boy.

He still wants us.

Tears well in my eyes, but he shakes his head. "No tears, baby. We're going to talk, and I'll take care of Tommy."

"What...? Did you kiss my mommy?" Noah asks.

"Shit," I mutter.

Graham isn't the least bit flustered. "I did kiss your mommy. How do you feel about that?"

Noah taps his chin as if he's thinking. "Do we get to move back with you?"

"When you and your mom are ready for that move, then yes. Your room will be ready and waiting for you."

"Mommy?"

"Y-Yes?"

"Do you want Graham kissing you? No, wait, G, girls have cooties." Noah wrinkles his little nose.

"Not the ones you love."

Noah's mouth falls open. "You love my mommy?"

"I do. I love both of you very much."

"Mommy, did you hear that? G loves you too." Noah pumps his fist in the air.

"Come here, Noah." I bend down and open my arms for him. I hug him tight. "I love you."

"Do you love G too?" he asks.

I glance up at Graham only to find that he's kneeling next to us. "Yeah, bud. I love G too."

"Thank fuck," Graham whispers.

"Uh-oh, G said a bad word." Noah giggles.

"Come here." Graham takes Noah into his arms and stands, swirling him around. His laughter fills our small apartment and lightens the load on my heart.

When he finally stops spinning and settles him on his hip, he reaches for me. "No, you know what this means, right?" Graham asks him.

"What?"

"That your mom is my girlfriend."

Noah furrows his brow. "Does that mean you can be my daddy now?"

Graham's eyes find mine, and they're pleading. "It's bedtime," I tell my son. In fact, it's well past. "Go get in bed and get your book ready. It's okay to skip your bath tonight. Graham and I will be right there."

"Okay." He presses a kiss on Graham's cheek. "Love you, G." He leans over, still in Graham's arms, and does the same to me. "Love you, Mommy." The words are barely out of his mouth before he's wiggling to be placed back on his feet. As soon as Graham sets him down, he's off like a rocket, racing toward his bedroom.

"I'm sorry," I tell Graham.

"Don't be. I'd be honored for him to call me Dad, Addy."

"Wh-What?"

"You heard me. When you're ready for us to take that step, you let me know, and I'll tell Noah. Can you do that for me? Can I be the one to tell him that I get to be his dad?"

"Graham…" Words fail me.

"You and Noah are my family, Addyson."

"But I didn't tell you—" I start, but his kiss keeps me from saying more.

"I don't care. You had your reasons, and once we get our boy to bed, you can tell me all about them. Whatever the reason, it doesn't change the fact that I love you both. So much, Addy. I love you both so much."

"I love you too."

His eyes sparkle as he bends for another kiss.

"Let's go read a story." Together, hand in hand, we walk to Noah's room. He's already under the covers in the middle of his twin-size bed.

"This bed is smaller. I don't know if all three of us will fit," he says, with sadness in his voice.

"We might not fit as we did in your bed at my house, but with some maneuvering, we'll make it work. Slide over all the way," Graham tells him. Noah does as he says and wiggles to the other side of the bed. "Mommy, your turn," Graham says. There is something about the way he calls me mommy. He's never called me that directly until now, and it feels... intimate. It feels right.

I don't question him. Instead, just as Noah did moments before, I climb into bed. I wrap my arms around Noah and squeeze him tight, making him laugh. The bed dips, and Graham wraps his arms around both of us.

"Our family." Noah grins, and my heart cracks wide open.

"Always, No. Always," Graham says before he grabs the book from Noah's hand and begins to read.

―――

"I'm surprised he fell asleep as fast as he did," I say once we're in the hallway after slipping out of bed with Noah.

"It was a big night. I thought it would take some time too."

"Must be you." I smile up at him. "It's hard not to drift feeling safe in your arms."

"I always want the two of you to feel safe and protected with me."

"We do."

He nods. "Where do you want to sit? Living room? Kitchen?" he asks.

"My room."

The look on his face tells me he's surprised.

"Can you stay? Tonight? Will you stay?"

"Yes." He doesn't even think about his answer. "If you're inviting me to stay, I'm going to stay."

"Well, I mean, Noah knows about us now, and so does everyone else. I don't want to hide how I feel about you. In fact, I know I can't."

"Good." He kisses my temple. "I'll lock up and meet you there." He takes off toward the living room while I rush to my room and change into one of his shirts that I stole when we were moving.

"I like this." He waves his finger around.

"I guess that's another confession, an easy one. I stole it."

"Nah, what's mine is yours, babe." He undresses and climbs into the opposite side of the bed and slides under the covers. I turn out the small bedside lamp and climb beneath the covers snuggling up to his chest. He wraps his arms around me tightly. So tight, in fact, it's as if he fears I might disappear.

"Nothing you tell me is going to change how I feel about you or Noah."

"Tosha and I went out one night," I start. I don't stop until I've told him every detail of what happened between Tommy and me, minus the intimate parts. I tell him about falling for Tommy and his lies and finding out I was pregnant, how he told me to end it, and walked away. I tell him how I had planned to tell Adam until the two of them mentioned how much they hated Tommy, and I realized I'd been played for a fool.

"I was going to tell you tonight. I ran into Tommy last Friday at lunch with Joy, and I confessed everything to her. I told her I was going to tell you and Adam. I was going to call, but he just beat me to it."

"You're incredible. So fucking strong, Addyson. You dealt with his rejection, and you did it with your head held high. You are an amazing mom to that little boy. He knows he's loved beyond words. He's smart, funny, and well-adjusted. That's all you, Addy. I wish I would have known."

"The tone of your voice tells me things wouldn't have ended well for Tommy, especially not with you and Adam on the giving end of whatever beat down the two of you would have served him."

"He deserves it."

"It's in the past, Graham."

"He upset you. He came to your place, harassing you."

"He was drinking, and he wasn't here for Noah. He was here for sex."

His arms stiffen. "What?"

"He was asking for a repeat and said he needed some relief. I turned him down, and he got pissed off and told me it would have been a pity fuck anyway."

"Motherfucker," he rumbles. His voice is low, deep, and deadly. I know that if Tommy were anywhere close, he'd be sporting a busted face.

"He won't come back, not now that you know. He's a coward."

"He's a worthless piece of shit. He should have been supporting you and Noah. He still should be."

"No. I don't want that. I don't want anything from him. I have Noah, and he's my son. He's not his. He's... ours," I say softly.

"Fuck yes, he is." Graham moves with precision. My back is flat on the bed, and he's hovering over me. "I want that, Addy. I want that more than anything."

"Can you give me some time? It's not that I don't love you or that I don't trust you. Let's just give Noah some time to adjust to us being an item, and we can reassess from there."

"Deal." He kisses me with urgency. His tongue demands entrance into my mouth.

"I need to lock the door," I mumble against his mouth.

"Already done."

Two words and I surrender. I open for him and take everything he's offering. His kiss is deep and frantic, sloppy as if he's worried this could be our last.

It won't be.

"I need you," I pant as his lips trail down my neck.

"Fuck," he rasps. "Baby, I can't be gentle." He goes to move away, but I wrap my legs around his waist, holding him to me.

"I love all of you, Graham. You've made love to me more times than I can count. You don't always have to be gentle. I'm not made of glass."

"No, but you come before me. Always."

In a flash, he's off the bed. "What are you doing?"

"Need you naked, Addy. Now." His tone is not only demanding, it's full of need, and it's sexy as hell.

Jumping into action, I pull his T-shirt over my head and slip out of my panties. The bed dips, and he's back nestled between my thighs where he belongs. "Fuck. There is nothing better than being bare inside you," he rasps.

"It's a risk."

His deep rich laughter fills the room. "Baby, there is no risk."

"I was on the pill, and we used protection. Were you not listening earlier?" I ask him.

"First of all, we don't talk about you with him or anyone else in our bed. Second, do you really think the thought of you carrying my baby is something that scares me? No, sweet Addy. It makes me want to toss your fucking pills in the trash, so we can make Noah an older brother."

Why is that so hot? "That's... okay." I don't know what else to say other than yes, please, and as much as the thought of having his baby thrills me, we're not there yet.

"You sure? It's not just me in this relationship."

"I'm sure. You're not a man of empty promises." I wrap my legs around his waist and reach between us, gripping his cock, guiding him to where I need him to be. "You're the man I love. The man who loves my son as if it were your blood running through his veins. You're our forever, Graham."

"Damn right," he says as he pushes inside. He doesn't stop until I've taken all of him. "Fuck, I've never felt anything like this. Like you. You were made for me, Addyson."

I wiggle my hips. "Nothing between us but love." I'm smiling even though he can't see me.

Holding his weight with one arm, he slides his hand between us and begins to massage my clit with his thumb. "I need you there. I'm not going to last. Not with your wet, tight, raw heat wrapped around my cock, and no fucking way am I coming before you do."

Reaching between us, I knock his hand out of the way and take over. "Fuck me, Graham. I need you to move."

Not needing to be told twice, he rocks into me at a punishing pace, and it turns out I need my hands more to hold on than to massage my clit. Fire rises in my core, and with one more thrust, I'm falling over the edge.

"Oh, fuck, that feels... Fuck. Fuck. Fuck," he whisper shouts as he stills, and I feel him release inside me. His head dips to rest against mine as we both catch our breath to come down from our high. "No more condoms. Ever. I don't care if we end up with a fucking baseball team. That's... damn, I never want to live another day without feeling you like this."

"Always a boy scout."

He laughs. "Nah, baby. I was just waiting for you. The love of my life." He kisses me slowly for what feels like hours until he pulls out and carries me to the shower before we both fall into bed, letting exhaustion take us.

Epilogue Graham

Graham

Two Months Later

"Let's go!" Noah bellows from the back seat of my truck, practically jumping out before the ignition is shut off.

"Buddy, settle down. The fall festival is just getting underway, and we have three hours to enjoy all the games and activities," Addyson says politely, turning to face her son in the back.

"I know, but I told Jackson I could throw the ball in the barrel more times than he can," Noah informs us, referring to one of his classmate friends as he unfastens his buckle and leaps out of his booster seat. "Can we go in now?"

Addy glances my way, a smile on her gorgeous face. "Yes, Noah."

"Finally!" he proclaims, reaching for the door handle.

I move fast to release my own seat belt and open my door. "Wait for me, No. There's a lot of extra traffic in the school parking lot." Plus, I don't want him to ding the car next door by eagerly letting the door fly open.

"'Kay. But hurry, G."

Chuckling, I open his door and step back, waiting for Tornado Noah to touch down and take my offered hand. He practically drags me across the lot, straight for the front entrance. "I don't think you're this excited to come to school any other time," I tease.

"Yes, huh! I love riding the bus and picking new books to read every day."

I glance over to Addy, who's having to practically jog to keep up with Noah's pace. "This is true. It's the first thing he tells me when he gets to my classroom after school."

"See?" Noah asks, pulling me through the already open front doors of the school.

We step inside the gym, and I have to admit, I'm impressed. It's decorated in pumpkins, cornstalks, apples, and mums. There are scarecrows and hay bales and every kid's carnival game you can imagine. Milk can hula hoop toss, disk drop, beanbag toss, balloon pop, football toss, mini golf, and even bowling. Not to mention face painting, different craft tables, and plenty of fall foods to snack on.

"Wow," I say, stopping at the entrance and taking it all in.

"Didn't they do a great job?" Addy asks, her hand slipping into my right, while Noah is still firmly holding my left. "The committee worked all day yesterday to set it up."

I glance down at our eager boy, the excitement radiating from his small body. "Where to first?"

"The beanbag toss!" he announces.

"How about we start at the beginning and work our way around to the beanbag toss, Noah? We'll take a little break and eat before I have to help at the face painting booth the second half of the festival," Addy reasons.

"And then me and G can play more games?"

"We can, No. We can play until they close it down," I confirm.

He throws his arms, which includes my left one, since we're still linked together, in the air. "Sweet!"

Chuckling, we start down the line, and over the next hour, we watch Noah play any and every game he wants. He chats easily with classmates, and Addy engages with every parent she meets. She introduces me as her boyfriend to those fellow teachers I haven't met yet, as well as her principal, Mrs. Gerth.

We slip into the cafeteria for pork burgers, chips, and caramel apples, which is available for a donation only, with all proceeds benefiting their Parent Teacher Association. I make sure to throw extra money in the jar.

"Hey, what did you find out about that chain pharmacy?" Addy asks as we take a seat at an open table.

"They pulled out. Apparently, we didn't meet all of their demographic needs," I tell her, still feeling the relief I felt earlier in the day when my dad told me the news. "That doesn't mean they won't take a look at this town, or any other chain for that matter, in the future, but at least they're not coming in right now."

She gives me an easy grin. "I'm glad."

Finally, it's time to start the second half of the festival.

"I need to head to the face painting booth," Addy informs us as we work our way back to the gym.

"Can I get my face painted?" Noah asks, his small body tucked between us.

"You can be my first customer. What would you like? A flower? A princess crown?" Addy teases, trying not to smile.

Noah pulls a horrified face. "I want a dinosaur!" he proclaims.

She meets my gaze and laughs. "I should have known."

"And G wants a dinosaur too, right, G?"

"Of course I do," I agree, shaking my head at the thought of getting my face painted.

But do you know what? The moment we get to the booth and Addy receives her instructions from the teacher she's replacing, I sit down and get a dinosaur painted on my cheek. Why? Because Noah was so excited to get matching dinosaurs, there was no way I could tell him no.

"Hi, Noah!" a young boy greets as he gets in line to get his face painted.

"Jackson! Do you see my dinosaur?" Noah says, turning to show the newcomer his now-dry paint.

"That's what I want. Dad, can I get a dinosaur too?" Jackson asks his father, who's standing behind him.

"You can get whatever you want," the man confirms. "I'm going to step across the aisle and watch your sister play the hula hoop game, okay?"

"Okay," he replies to his dad before turning back to Addy. "I want one just like Noah's," Jackson declares with a decisive nod.

"G is getting one too," Noah informs him, pointing to where Addy finishes my face paint. "He's my dad now."

Addy's hand pauses, her wide eyes meeting mine, and it takes everything I have not to turn to the boys.

"My mommy said you don't have a dad," Jackson states innocently, but the look on Addy's face breaks my heart.

"I didn't, but I do now. My mommy says G can be my dad if G wants to, and he said yes," Noah replies, matter-of-factly. "Right, G?"

I reach up and take Addy's shaky hand in mine before turning to face the boys. "You're right, No. I'd be honored to be called your dad. Sometimes families aren't blood, but they love and protect you just the same."

"And we're family," Noah agrees quickly, as if it's the easiest, most natural statement in the world.

And it is.

Because we *are* family.

The boys jump into conversation about what games they're going to play when they finish with the face painting, so I turn back around to Addy.

"What are we doing?"

Her question catches me completely off guard and panic sets in. What is she saying? Does she not want to date anymore? Does she not see me as a positive father figure for Noah?

My eyes must show my fear, because she quickly reaches up and cups my cheek not currently being painted with a green dinosaur. "We live in separate houses. Why?"

I don't think she's actually asking me this question. The way she says it and looks away, it's as if she's asking herself. Clearing my throat, I mutter, "Because that's what is best for you and Noah."

She finally meets my gaze, confusion written all over her face. "But is it?"

I want to tell her no, but I won't. This isn't my decision to make. It's always been hers. Ever since the day she moved into my house, and especially since she moved out, I've followed her lead.

Before I can even reply, she squares her shoulders and lifts her chin. "This is stupid. I don't want to live apart anymore." I open my mouth, but she continues, "If the offer is still on the table, then, yes. Yes, we'll move in with you."

A wide smile spreads across my face. "When? We can leave right now and pack you both up, Addy."

She snickers at my comment, probably assuming it's a joke. It's not. I'd leave right now and load their stuff up in my truck. Both of them would be in my house—where they belong—by the end of the night.

"Not right now, Graham, but soon? Maybe this weekend?"

It's Wednesday now, the night before Thanksgiving. We have lunch plans with her family tomorrow, followed by dinner at my parents' house.

"I have to work Friday, but I'm off this weekend," I confirm.

She smiles. "I know. Noah and I can spend the day sorting through stuff. I still have my lease to contend with, but that's okay. It's up next month anyway, so that gives me time to slowly move."

"No, fuck that." I didn't even realize I said it until her eyes widen. I quickly look around; grateful little ears didn't hear my profanity. "You guys are coming home with me tonight," I add, taking her hands in mine and moving to the edge of my seat so we're closer. "You can pack up necessities Friday, and I'll help move anything else you need on Saturday. I want you in my bed tonight and every night after. There will be no slow move, Addy. I've been waiting for this moment since that awful night I left you at your apartment and went home alone."

Her brown eyes sparkle with excitement. "So we're doing this? We're moving in together officially?"

"We are," I agree, leaning forward and swiping my lips across hers as I entwine our fingers. "This is just the start. I want to adopt Noah. I want to make it official. Even though I'm already his father in my heart, I would be honored to stand before a judge and see it in black and white on paper. I know that's your decision, but just know I'm ready."

It's her turn to move, pressing her lips to mine hard. "Yes. I want that."

"Good," I whisper, placing my mouth to hers one more time, as if sealing the deal.

"See? That's what mommies and daddies do, Jackson. Even though girls got cooties, they still kiss." Noah's words break through the fog, and realization sets in. We're sitting in the middle of a school gym, surrounded by kids. Thank God, I hadn't started mauling her the way I want to.

"Yep. My mommy and daddy kiss lots too. It's gross."

"Yep. But G says it's because they're in love," he sings, followed quickly by a gagging noise that makes both boys laugh.

Laughing, we break apart, and there's no missing the pink blush creeping up Addy's neck. It's cute as fuck and does things in my groin area. Things I need to put an end to right away, considering my present company and location.

I look over at Noah, who's grinning from ear to ear. "See, Jackson? He's my dad."

Lifting him up, I set my son on my lap and kiss his head. "Yes, yes I am." Then I meet his mother's eyes and mouth a quick "Love you." She returns the sentiment, making my heart sing. "We're a family."

He looks up at me and grins a toothy smile. "We're a family."

Then Addy confirms, "We're a family."

And we are. The family I never knew I wanted. The one I never want to live without.

Mine.

Forever.

Epilogue Addyson

ddyson

Two Years Later

"Dad, can I carry Callie so I can show her to all of my friends?" Noah asks from the back seat of my SUV.

I glance over at my husband and smile. Noah has been calling him dad since our first fall festival. We made it official a few months later as we stood before a judge, and in the eyes of the law, not just his heart, Graham became his father. Since I hadn't put Tommy on the birth certificate, there was no need to include him. Not that he'd object. He made is stance where Noah is concerned very clear.

We had a lot of changes after that first festival. Graham and I had a destination wedding in Florida. Noah, our parents, Tosha, Adam and Joy all joined us for a New Year's Eve wedding on the beach. Graham said he wasn't going to live another year without my last name being Morgan.

He got his wish.

"Dad? Can I?" Noah asks again.

Graham's face lights up just like it does every single time Noah calls him Dad. It's impossible to miss the love he has for our son.

"Son, she's still pretty tiny. How about we let you push her in her stroller?" Graham suggests as he pulls into the already packed school parking lot.

"But what if she wants to play games?" Noah counters.

"No, she's only four weeks old. She's still too little to play games."

"All she does is sleep and poop. You said being a big brother was going to be fun," Noah huffs.

I have to cover my mouth to stifle my laugh. My husband grins as he turns in his seat to look at our son. "She's still a baby, Noah. It's your job as her big brother to love and protect her. As she gets older, you'll get to teach her everything you know."

"How long does that take?" he asks with a huff.

"Trust me, kiddo," I chime in, "it will be here before you know it."

"We need a brother," he says. "I can't handle all of that pressure on my own."

This time we both can't hold on to our laughter. "We will definitely take that into consideration, but you know we don't get to choose, right? When you have a baby, you don't get to choose. It's uh, up to nature." Graham fumbles over his words.

"Fine. Can we go now? Jackson is waiting on me."

"How do you know?" I ask him.

"Because that's his mom's car." He points to the blue minivan we parked behind, and it does indeed look like Jackson's mom's car. "Wait for Dad to help you out."

"I'm not a baby," he huffs.

"Noah." Graham's voice holds warning.

"Sorry," Noah grumbles.

Graham opens his door before taking him by the hand, moving to the back of the SUV, and grabbing the stroller. Within no time, the stroller is set up, and Callie's car seat is attached. Graham grabs the diaper bag and shoves it underneath.

"No, you want to help me push?" he asks.

"I can do it," Noah tells him.

"Not by yourself in the parking lot. There are too many cars."

Noah places his hands on the stroller as he stands in front of Graham. My husband guides our son with one hand while holding my hand with the other. "Let's start at the beginning," I tell Noah.

He nods and continues to push the stroller. We've made it halfway around the gym when we stop next to the second-grade exhibit. Noah shows us his drawing, and we ooh and ahh over his work.

"Hi, Paxton." Noah waves to his friend.

"Is that your sister?" Paxton asks.

"Yep. She sleeps a lot," he tells him, making Graham and me smile.

"Graham. Addyson. Hi." Brianne waves. "It's good to see you."

"Brianne," Graham greets her.

"Hi." I wave awkwardly.

"Who is this?" She peeks into the stroller.

Graham wastes no time unbuckling our baby girl and lifting her into his arms. She's still sleeping as she rests peacefully against his chest. "This is Callie," he tells Brianne.

"She's adorable."

"Thank you," I reply.

"We think so." Graham smiles at me.

"Dad, can I go play ring toss with Paxton?" Noah asks.

Brianne's eyes widen at Noah calling Graham dad. "Stay where I can see you," Graham tells him in his best dad voice.

"Okay."

The boys move to the next station where the ring toss is taking place. "So full of energy," I say, trying to break the awkward silence.

"Right? To be young again." Brianne laughs. "You have a beautiful family," she tells us.

"Thank you," Graham and I say at the same time.

"I'm going to go make sure they don't get into any mischief. My sister is running late, so it's Aunt Bri to the rescue." She laughs and turns to walk away.

"That was—" I start, but Graham stops me.

"That was exactly how it was supposed to be. You and me, Addy."

"I mean, at this point, you're stuck with me. A marriage certificate and two kids later," I tease. We don't talk about him adopting Noah. In his eyes, Noah is his, and that's all there is to say about the topic.

"When you're ready for number three, you let me know." He winks.

I push the stroller while he carries Callie. "Let me heal from this one."

"Last year, we were here as a family of three, hoping to be four, and now this year, we are a family of four."

My sweet sexy man.

"Well, don't get your hopes up for a family of five next year," I warn him. "I want at least a couple of years before the next one."

"Two years, I can do that. Besides, we're really good at practicing." He wags his eyebrows.

Callie is four weeks old, and it's been a long four weeks. I miss sex. Not just the act but the intimacy that it brings. Graham is such a boy scout. He refuses to touch me until I'm cleared by my physician. I guess witnessing your wife push a baby girl the size of a watermelon out of her vagina will do that to a man.

Over the next couple of hours, most of my coworkers have stopped us to say hello and to meet Callie. I promise them I'll bring her to school one day before I come back to work. I'm taking three months off. I didn't get that luxury when I had Noah, and Graham was insistent that I take the time with Callie.

He's tried a few times to get me to just stay home with the kids, and one day I might decide that's what's best for our family. Right now, I'm not ready to give it up. I love my job and my students. We'll just have to see how things play out. Callie could be our last, but somehow, I doubt it. Not when my sexy-as-hell husband can't stop talking about more. The sleepless nights and constant diaper changes don't deter him. He's a man on a mission.

By the time we get home, both kids are conked out. "Stay here with Callie. I'll take No to the bed and come back to get her."

"I can carry the car seat. I'm fine."

"Addy, just humor me, yeah?" He climbs out of the SUV that's parked in our garage and gently unbuckles Noah, carrying him inside.

I do as I'm told and don't bother with the car seat. Instead, I unbuckle our baby girl and lift her into my arms, making my way into the house. I'm not breaking the rules. Walking down the hall, I pass Noah's room just in time to hear Noah say, "Love you, Daddy."

"I love you too, son," Graham's soft, gruff voice replies.

He steps into the hallway and pulls Noah's door closed, leaving a small gap in case he needs us in the night. He's seven now and rarely needs us, but Graham still leaves a small gap just in case.

"Hey." I smile at my husband.

"Baby, I told you not to carry the seat."

"I didn't. I left it in the car." I smile up at him.

"Stubborn woman."

"You love me."

"You and our kids. More than anything."

"I'm going to put her to bed. She's going to be up soon to eat."

"I'll take the feedings tonight."

"You took them last night."

He shrugs.

"Callie girl, a month on this earth, and you have your daddy wrapped around your little finger," I whisper to our sleeping daughter.

"Baby girl, her momma, and her brother. There isn't anything I wouldn't do for my family."

And we are. The family I always wanted. The one I never want to live without.

Mine.

Forever.

Epilogue Noah

Epilogue – Noah

Ten years later

I'm terrified as I step onto the stage, feeling the pressure of every set of eyes on me. I don't let it show, though. I hold my head up high as I make my way to the podium. I look down, finding my prepared speech already there. I quickly scan the opening line, but I know in my heart, I don't need to. I know the entire piece by heart. I agonized over what to say for days—weeks, really. Ever since I received word that I was officially selected as Valedictorian.

Taking a deep, calming breath, I finally look up, surprised to see the high school gymnasium so full for today's graduation ceremony. Besides the occasional cough or the scraping of a chair on the floor by one of my classmates, you could hear a pin drop as everyone waits for me to begin, and that's when the familiar rush of worries sweeps in once more.

Until I look out in the crowd and see his face.

He looks equal parts eager and nervous, and I know it's on my behalf. Dad knows I'm not a fan of public speaking, and the thought of having to stand up here today has been weighing heavily on my mind.

He was the driving force behind today's speech, even though he hasn't heard it. He lent me his support, offered suggestions, and sat with me several nights while I discussed ideas I had, but when it came down to finally putting pen to paper—or typing it on my computer—he has no idea what I'm about to say.

Mom does. I tried to keep it from her, but late one night, I desperately needed her thoughts on the final version. I'll never forget the moment I finished and looked up. She was crying. It took her several minutes to compose herself enough to finally whisper, "You are an amazing young man, Noah Morgan, and we are so very lucky to be your parents."

My family.

Closing my eyes, I picture that very first drawing. The one I made in kindergarten and displayed in the art fair featuring the three of us. Of course, that was before we were officially a family, but that didn't matter to me. My young, five-year-old mind couldn't comprehend the fact we weren't *actually* family. Not in the traditional sense. Because I knew, even then, from the very beginning, that Graham Morgan was different. I knew he was someone I could trust, look up to, and learn from.

I knew he was my father.

So when I open my eyes, I offer a small smile to the man who loves me more than any other man alive and say, "A very wise man once said, sometimes families aren't blood, but they love and protect you just the same."

A flash of surprise fills his blue eyes as he returns my smile, relaxing in his seat and taking my mother's hand in his. My grandparents, Uncle Adam and Aunt Joy, as well as my three cousins, sit directly behind my parents, all hanging on my every word.

"Ever since we stepped into the school as eager, energetic kindergarteners, we formed a family. No, not a traditional one, but a big, messy, supportive family, nonetheless. Many of us have been together for thirteen years. We've laughed. We've cried. Sometimes, we've even fought," I say, drawing a few chuckles from my classmates. "But at the end of the day, we've always been family.

"I learned the meaning of family that same year. The same day, as a matter of fact. The morning I got on the school bus with my brand-new dinosaur backpack," I say, again, earning some laughter. "It wasn't just me who was excited and nervous, much like we are now in this moment. I saw it in the eyes of the kids around me and in the eyes of my mom... and my dad. I saw something I didn't truly understand until years later. The value of that one single word. Family.

"I think you can all agree, we didn't make it easy on our parents. They set boundaries, we pushed them. They said no, we argued. They asked for help, and we said, bruh, I'm too busy." The entire gym laughs. "But when we needed them, they were there. Just like those sitting right next to you."

I look up and scan the faces of those I've known most of my life. Their blue and white caps and gowns are pressed, their smiles wide, their futures before them. "This is our family. Friends will always come and go, but your family is forever. When you leave this gym today, there is a great big world before you. Every step you take leads you to endless possibilities. Along the way, you'll misstep. You'll trip. Maybe you'll even fall. But we're all there for you, helping you up. We're all there *with* you as you take that next step.

"We are family."

I take a deep breath. "Cedar Hills graduating class, please rise. Look to your left. Look to your right. These are the faces of your friends. Your classmates. Your family. And I have no doubt that every one of them has your back, just like Mom. And Dad. Brothers and sisters. Your grandparents. Aunts and uncles."

I meet my dad's tearful gaze over the heads of those who separate us. "Wherever the road takes you in this life, do it with style, grace, and dignity, but know all roads will also lead you home."

My throat is thick as I step around the podium and grab my tassel. "Classmates, welcome to my forever family."

The entire gym erupts into applause as my classmates all move their tassels from left to right, signifying the moment we've all been anxiously waiting for since we first stepped foot in high school, and while I'm overwhelmed by the magnitude of this moment, I'm just happy to share it with those I love most in this world.

My parents.

My sisters Callie and Grace.

My brother Dane.

My family.

Thirteen years ago, my life changed. My mom and I found an amazing man who brought us into his home. Who cared for us. Who loved us. Who loves me still, as if I were his own. That's why I'm honored to start college this fall, preparing to step into the family business. Grandpa wants to retire, and it would be a dream to work alongside my dad every day, learning from the best of the best.

I can't imagine what my life would be like without him.

He's my family.

My dad.

It'd be a crying shame not to carry on the family tradition.

The End

Thank you

Thank you for taking the time to read Crying Shame.

Be sure to sign-up for my newsletter and never miss a new release!

Never miss a new release:
https://tinyurl.com/4pznzd97

Contact Rebel Shaw:
www.rebelshaw.com

Rebel Shaw is the alter ego of the romance writing duo Lacey Black and Kaylee Ryan.

To learn more about these two authors visit their websites here:

www.laceyblackbooks.com

www.kayleeryan.com

Acknowledgements

There are so many people who are involved in the publishing process. We write the words, but we rely on our editors, proofreaders, and beta readers to help us make them the best that they can be.

Those mentioned above at not the only members of our team. We have photographers, models, cover designers, beta readers, formatters, bloggers, graphic designers, author friends, our PA, and so many more. We could not do this without these people.

And then we have our readers. If you're reading this that means you took a chance on a new to you author, and we cannot tell you what that means. Thank you for spending your hard-earned money on our words, and taking the time to read them. We appreciate you more than you know.

Special Thanks: Becky Johnson, Hot Tree Editing.

Deaton Author Services and Kara Hildebrand, Proofreading
Book Cover Boutique – Cover Design
Chasidy Renee – Personal Assistant
Jo, Sandra, Jamie, Stacy, Lauren, and Erica
Bloggers, Bookstagrammers, and TikTokers
Tempting Illustrations, and Graphics by Stacy
The entire Give Me Books Team
And our amazing Readers